ADVANCE PRAISE FOR WORST. DATE. EVER.

"Kopcow's stories ring weird and true, as they chart a tough trajectory through the heart-infested waters of human attraction."

- "Ask Amy" advice columnist, Amy Dickinson

"Romance is weird under the best of circumstances, and Kopcow's collection takes us far afield from the best of circumstances. Ghosts haunt, the end of the world looms, and Kopcow's narrators strive to find love in ways that are by turns funny and sad, but always deeply human."

- Bob Proehl, author of *A Hundred Thousand Worlds* and *The Nobody People*

WORST. DATE. EVER.

Dan Kopcow

Regal House Publishing

Published by
Regal House Publishing, LLC
Raleigh, NC 27612
All rights reserved

ISBN -13 (paperback): 9781947548169
ISBN -13 (epub): 9781646030217
Library of Congress Control Number: 2019941543

Interior and cover design by Lafayette & Greene
lafayetteandgreene.com
Cover images © by alaver / Shutterstock

Regal House Publishing, LLC
https://regalhousepublishing.com

Printed in the United States of America

To my beautiful and amazing wife, Angela.
All the flattering bits are about you.

"We have only this moment, sparkling like a star in our hand—and melting like a snowflake."

- Francis Bacon

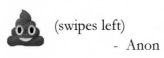 (swipes left)

- Anon

CONTENTS

INTRODUCTION

When it comes to engaging in romance, people walk around with their defenses up all the time. In World War II, you could enter a danger zone or other country only if you passed a series of gates and armed guards. These passageways were called Checkpoint Charlies. Make the wrong move, show the wrong credential, and you found yourself spending time in a prison that looked nothing like *Hogan's Heroes*. Or maybe you ended up succumbing to sniper fire or barbed-wire-induced injuries.

My own Checkpoint Charlie makes me very elliptical when it comes to women. I could never just tell a woman I liked her and wanted to go out with her. I insinuated. I intimated. I suggested. In business jargon, I'm not exactly what you would call a closer.

I'll give you an example.

There was this woman I was crazy about in college. Let's call her Angee. Angee and I were both Resident Advisors in a co-ed dorm. Rather than asking her out, I devised a foolproof two-phased Master Plan that would win her over.

PHASE I

As RAs, we each had to lead some type of extracurricular group. Some RAs were on the Dorm Party Committee, some led the Study Group Committee. Not me. I started a whole new group: the Special Recognition Committee. The mission of the Special Recognition Committee was ostensibly to provide an opportunity for students to give recognition to their roommates for acing tests, or to help people who were homesick, or generally to make people feel better. Which we

1

actually did. However, the real mission of the Special Recognition Committee was to act as a springboard for Phase II of my Master Plan.

PHASE II

When Valentine's Day rolled around, the Special Recognition Committee, still ably led by me and still operating under incredibly false pretenses, organized a massive kissing booth in the lobby of our dorm. Massive may be an overreach. A female RA and I stood behind a table under a sign that read, "Kissing Booth - $1 for a Kiss. All Proceeds Go to Charity." The female RA, who was very attractive but no Angee, was doing a brisk business and our selected charities ultimately benefited tremendously from her generous lips. I, on the other hand, was having a going-out-of-business sale. I was the Willy Loman of canoodling. Then, the big moment came. I saw Angee walking out of the elevator and toward our kissing booth. Finally, all my hard work would pay off. The months of planning and philanthropic works would come to full fruition. Instead, she walked right by me with her friend without even acknowledging I was there. She was on her way to the dining hall, so I thought she was hungry and I would catch her on the way back. I waited long after the kissing booth should have closed up shop. My female co-RA had already left. On a date, no doubt. Angee never walked back my way. I clearly needed a Phase III to my Master Plan.

PHASE III

After weeks of heartache and pep talks in the mirror, I finally asked Angee out directly. I somehow thought it would be romantic to take her to *Sweeney Todd, The Demon Barber of Fleet Street*. For some reason, she didn't go out with me again for twenty-five years.

Clearly, a reformulation of my Master Plan was needed. I appended two subsections to Phase III:

PHASE III.A

I figured twenty-five years was enough time to have passed. She would have had plenty of opportunity to shake off our first date. I reconnected with Angee, now going by Angela. She agreed to get together. This mini-triumph led to the final phase in my Master Plan. It was all coming together.

PHASE III.B

Angela and I met at a county park in the middle of the day during the week. There was no one else around, and we would have the whole park to ourselves. It was wonderful to see her again, and it felt like no time had passed since we had watched people's throats being slit before they were turned into meat pies.

We sat at an old wooden picnic table and caught up on what we'd been up to for the past quarter-century. While I was providing my update, I noticed she was wriggling uncomfortably. All my insecurities came to bear. I pictured her bolting up and driving away, and I started sweating. It was the kissing booth all over again. I wondered if I would have to wait another twenty-five years before we could actually finish a date. I asked her what was wrong. She said she needed a moment and looked around for a bathroom.

The women's bathroom in the park was in a small, cinderblock building near the parking lot that probably only let in thin daggers of sunlight. She had been in there for about ten minutes when I yelled through the door, asking if she was all right. She hesitated and then asked if I could go to her car and grab her first aid kit. I inquired again what was wrong, but she seemed uninterested in pursuing my line of questioning at the moment. Instead, her disembodied voice echoed out of the cinderblock chamber with pleas for her first aid kit. To punctuate her point, she tossed her car keys through the tiny bathroom window opening.

I got her keys, went to her car, and returned with the first aid kit. She asked me to leave the kit and her keys at the door. I walked away to give her some privacy and heard the door quickly open and close. When I turned around, the kit and keys were gone, having been swallowed up by my date inside.

After a respectful ten minutes had gone by, I asked again if there was anything I could do to help. She finally told me what was going on. While we were talking at the wooden picnic table earlier, she had sat on some broken glass. A small shard had penetrated her jeans and into her right buttocks. Between the odd angle and low lighting, she couldn't get out the shard. She had managed to stop the bleeding. I asked if I could help, and she immediately said no, perhaps more forcefully than she intended.

She told me later she did not want me to see her butt after twenty-five years, thinking it would scare me away. Also, knowing we were going on a hike, she had chosen to wear beige granny panties and she added this to the list of visuals from which she wished to spare me. I assured her I just wanted to help. She finally acquiesced and allowed me into the bathroom. She handed me tweezers from her first-aid kit and told me to pull out the shard with one condition: I had to keep my eyes closed. She didn't want me to see her like this. Effectively, she was asking me to play the game Operation blindfolded. If I had started singing, this wasn't a million miles away from *Sweeney Todd*.

I removed the shard with my eyes closed in one of the few heroic moments of my life. She was fine, and we proceeded with our hike. A few years later, we were married. I still have the glass shard as a souvenir from our second date.

Ultimately, my Master Plan worked, but I attribute it wholly to her letting down her Checkpoint Charlies rather than any strategy on my part.

I hope you enjoy these stories and that you never get glass shards in your bottom.

WHEN JILTED ALICE SPOKE

At forty-three, Jilted Alice had finally decided to find her voice. She drove along the two-lane ribbon of road near Butte, Montana, toward Basil's house. Although it was her sixth Thursday date night at Basil's, Alice was honored to have Stagecoach Mary riding shotgun this time. Alice knew she'd have to be on her best behavior tonight.

Alice flirted with the possibility that she might be Basil's first true love. Her mind and body were nimble enough to carry out this new relationship. In an act of puppy love trust, Basil had given her a copy of his house key after their third date so she could let herself in before he got home from work. Alice would arrive early, surrender to the house's majestic calm, and wish she had her own peace.

Her routine consisted of two tasks: 1) she would gracefully prepare dinner with her nine fingers, and 2) she'd mix Basil's special drink with her long toothpick. In addition, tonight, after letting herself and Mary in, she went into his bathroom, slipped off her jeans, and sliced a small gash into her left thigh with her chef's knife. The gash stood at attention like a little red soldier.

Alice hadn't spoken a word since she was eighteen, after her bitter mother died. Alice's father had run out on them years before and quickly remarried. Alice portrayed herself as mute to all she met. It's what attracted Basil to her. It's what attracted all the men to her. But these men, without fail, also assumed she was deaf. They never bothered to ask.

They just calculated that her signing and smiling equaled deaf-mute. Her expressive hands waved in the air, compelling her sign language to float across to her intended's eyes. *What a funny way to speak*, she'd thought when she first started signing. *From my hands to their eyes. No lips, no ears.* Also missing was the heart of her conversation, the distinct inflections, sighs, and tones that she was unable to declare. That was okay with Alice, especially when she had to speak with men.

The men she dated were full of assumptions. They made the mistaken leap that a deaf-mute was also dumb. They all reasoned that she made up for her lack of hearing and speech by overdeveloping her sensual side, her tactile needs, and her risk in pleasure. In short, they presumed she was easy.

They would talk and talk to her as if she were a confessional with lipstick. They were all attracted to her silent, unquestioning sexuality and implied lack of judgment. Alice understood she exuded these qualities to the world even though she knew differently. It was like her old restaurant job. She had loved turning out dinners for others but she never ate her own food. Currently, Alice was not affiliated with any restaurant. Not since hers had burned down.

Her burning restaurant had set off flickering memories. Her life's thieves. They were all men. They all stole from her. Her father fled with her childhood. Caesar robbed her creativity. Stu ran off with her heart. And finally, Alfredo took her money.

Basil's kitchen was fairly well stocked for a civilian's. This pleased Alice. Mary, Alice's best friend, turned to Alice and said, "Girl, look at you in that kitchen." She knew all of Alice's secrets. "You best steel yourself."

Alice took a deep breath and snapped herself back to the present. A pang of guilt wafted in the air. She lit some candles and waited for Basil.

Alice had met Basil at his shoe store six weeks earlier. He was a skinny assistant manager who clutched his stomach occasionally from a developing ulcer. On their first date, he told Alice that it had been a long day until she walked into his store and made the air in the room stop moving.

Basil couldn't tell at first what she looked like. He had lost his thick glasses that day and was practically blind without them unless things were really close. Alice had walked right up to him and stared so fiercely, it made him drop his head toward her feet.

"What size are you?" he'd asked, in an attempt to regain his confidence. She'd begun signing to him but realized quickly that he wasn't looking at her. Basil had started sweating. She'd pointed his hands to a pair of loafers and held six of her fingers in his hands to indicate her foot size. Keeping his head bent toward the floor, Basil asked, "Do you know how beautiful you are?" Alice pretended not to hear as she scanned the shelves for strappy sandals. "I've always wanted someone like you," whispered Basil, to the worn carpet. Their breathing was in perfect unison as he slipped the new shoes on her feet. At the same time, she caressed his left ear with her index finger. They had their first date at Basil's that same night.

Alice peeked out of Basil's front window. An old Jeep pulled up, and Basil hopped out of the passenger side.

"So that's him," said Mary, unimpressed. "Child, that boy looks like he won the lottery. I mean, look at him, prancin' home to sexy, voluptuous you."

Alice let go of the thin curtain. Basil had a tender manner. He reminded Alice of her father. That's what had impressed her. He always handled her gently, as if he were fitting a whisper-thin leather sandal on a child's foot.

Basil opened the door, stepped into his house, and smelled the air. Alice knew the glorious mix of perfume and food would tantalize him. She watched him eat and drink. She'd push his black hair to the side; it had a wonderful tendency to fall over his eyes while he ate. He'd ask her to stop, but it was a ritual that endeared him to her even more. Basil's dark hair reminded her of her father's.

After dinner, they went to his bedroom without a word. He had a single bed so they lay on their sides, facing each other. Their bodies were only inches apart, their mouths, their lips, closer still. They almost never touched.

"That boy knows you'll cause a world of trouble if he breaks into your space," noted Mary. "Your rules entice him."

Alice stared into Basil's eyes. He would always talk about his passions, his dreams, and his fears; how his mother used to hit him; and how he had gone from feeling angry to lonely to lustful—things he had never told anyone else. It was like therapy but with the added promise of something more. Then, one day, it occurred to Alice what else was in his voice: release. She offered him release.

Alice listened carefully to Basil, but as the night wore on, his speeches turned her thoughts inward. She gave the illusion of listening by occasionally letting him caress her face while he spoke. Basil was saying, "You're like no other woman I've known. You are complete with or without me..."

Week after week, Alice found herself drifting back to her own past, like an anaconda swallowing its own tail. Back to how her mother convinced Alice that all their ills were due to "that man" walking out on them. Back to her mother dying, still cursing Alice's father, and Alice choosing silence for all her coming days. She'd replay how she ended up here in Montana, how she had lived and worked in New Orleans, San Francisco, and New York City—the three greatest culinary cities in the country—with the help of men; how these men had driven her out of these cities just as fast, why she hated men, why she loved them, why she had decided to do what she was doing, and why Stagecoach Mary was her best friend.

"It's this simple," Mary interrupted. "This boy, Basil, is still

made of tomorrows. You, child, are made of yesterdays."
Basil tried putting his hand on Alice's waist, but she winced.
His hands were rough and not at all symmetrical. It made her
think of Caesar's hands, and Alice began to shake her head.
"He knows to back off and keep gabbin'," said Mary. Alice
looked up and smiled at Mary.

After Alfredo had burned down her restaurant, Alice had
tried to start over in Montana. She had tried to buy an old
restaurant in Bannack. During her inspection of the restaurant, she discovered an old photograph of a large, severe
black woman holding a shotgun and a bottle of whiskey.
The inscription at the bottom, in thin black letters, read St.
Mary. Taped to the back of the picture was a long toothpick.
The picture enchanted Alice. An afternoon's research at the
library revealed to her that this was Stagecoach Mary.

A century earlier, Mary had been a forgiving woman, offering food for the hungry at her restaurant back in the gold
mining Wild West days. Her reputation for kindness gained
her the ultimate respect of the harsh men in the Montana
climate. Before it was abandoned, the restaurant had been a
hotel, pool hall, brothel, and museum.

After completing her library research, Alice went back
to Mary's old restaurant. Inside, it was dark except for the
streetlight pressing its face against the front window. Suddenly, Alice heard the drafty wind turn into a voice.

"I knew you'd come by," said Mary, momentarily startling
Alice as she emerged from the shadowed carcass of the old
bar. "Best huckleberry pie in these parts." Alice remained
calm. Somehow, she knew she was supposed to be here.
"Yeah, I know," said Mary. "You don't speak. All the better
'cause I talk too much. You see, Alice, we're partners here.
And we're gonna get along like beans and bacon."

Alice couldn't help but smile. That first magical night
together, Mary told her the story of the long toothpick.

Afterwards, still surrounded by the utter darkness of Mary's hundred-year-old restaurant, Mary delicately fed Alice a huckleberry with her fingers. And with that intimate communion, without uttering a word, Alice completely accepted Mary into her life.

"Men," said Mary. "They put the 'queasy' in cuisine."

Alice thought about what she was doing to Basil. She thought about forgiveness. Her childish thoughts came back to play in her head. Even her name, she mused, was forever one letter away from being Alive. Alice watched Basil's expression, but she was fixated on something else that night—Caesar's hands.

In the elevator of the Harkin Insurance Building, in Philadelphia, on her way to a sous chef interview at an exclusive restaurant, she first made contact with Caesar's hands. He had been standing next to her in the crowded elevator when three people got on at the eighteenth floor, and he had been forced to move so close to her that his hands brushed up against her hip. She'd looked down and fell apart at the sight of those muscular hands and the black curly hair between his wrist and knuckles. When she was able, she looked up into his green eyes but all she saw were his strong hands. She frantically scanned the rest of him. He was a bit of a pretty boy, primped and coiffed, but his hands were all she could see. It was a shame, she thought, that the rest of him hadn't matched up.

Caesar said something but she was too flustered to listen. He bid her goodbye and got off on the twenty-third floor. A few days later, she bumped into Caesar again. He couldn't quite recall where he'd met her first, but, of course, he rapidly became enthralled when he discovered her to be a deaf-mute. Caesar had asked her out and she nodded in agreement, her eyes swimming toward the shores of his hands.

Caesar rattled on about her beauty that night in her apartment, but all the while, Alice remained silent, entranced by his gorgeous hands, waving around like a symphony conductor. She knew the precise moment it occurred to him that he could say anything he wanted to her and she couldn't hear. They were on her couch. Caesar had described in great detail what he wanted her to do for him sexually. In response, Alice rose to her feet and began cooking. After Caesar had eaten dinner, it became clear that he expected Alice for dessert. Still, she shook her head. He leaned against the wall by the front door as if it had been constructed just for him, just for this moment, and looked at her with a well-rehearsed confidence. "Next time, I will have you," he said.

Alice opened the front door, resting her right hand on the door jamb, signifying that Caesar needed to go. He paused in the doorway, daring her to refuse him again. Alice, sighing deeply, shook her head quietly and purposefully. The menace rose in his eyes, and he stormed off, slamming the door behind him. The door crushed her right index finger, destroying her cooking potential and her beauty forever. Alice neither screamed nor cursed but simply walked the few blocks to the emergency room and lost her finger, never uttering a word.

Now, Stagecoach Mary reached out to Alice and told her to put away the angry memories, to move on with her life. The connection between those two women, bridged across a century, was immediate and visceral to Alice. Mary loved telling the story of her guitar toothpick, so when Alice finished thinking about Caesar, and as Basil droned on about his job, she thought, "Can I hear it again? One more time?"

"You bet, child," said Mary.

In 1863, Julian Santos traveled from Spain to Massachusetts to better his singing opportunities. When the Civil War broke out, he followed the path of many a young foreigner—he went West. Ultimately, he landed a job as a bartender in Cyrus's Saloon, a shady and disreputable bar in Bannack,

11

Montana. His only possessions were a comb, a grainy picture of his mother, and his guitar. He took that gleaming wooden instrument everywhere he went. Julian's grandfather had made the guitar for him when Julian turned fifteen. The strings, the shape of it, the weight of it, were as familiar to Julian as his own hands.

One night, as Julian was performing for some drunken miners with gold dust to spend, the usually noisy saloon went quiet with a palpable shudder. In walked a black stagecoach driver—two hundred pounds, a rifle in one hand, a pistol and a Bowie knife tucked away in her belt, puffing a cigar and wearing a scowl.

Everyone knew not to cross her. Even from five counties away, people had heard of Stagecoach Mary. She was the only woman in town who was allowed to drink or even enter the saloon. She would sit by herself, which was typically her inclination, open a bottle of whiskey, and begin a deep and personal relationship with it. It took two and a half songs for Mary to notice the foreign singer, being unaccustomed as she was to noticing men.

"So Julian comes up to Ol' Mary and asks me to take a drink with him. I holds up my half-empty bottle of snake juice and tells him I's plannin' on killin' the rest of the night by myself. But he jest looks at me, all serious. Leans over and tells me, all soft in my dusty ear, that he could drink my eyes in. Well, darlin', Ol' Mary nearly lost herself a lung in that saloon from laughin' so hard. What the hell this crazy Spaniard be talkin' 'bout? Drinkin' in my eyes, like my face is a damn prairie and my eyes are gulches. So this Julian's pretty embarrassed right about now, especially since they's all lookin' at me laughin' at him. Pretty soon, they starts to laughin' themselves. Girl, it spread like wildfire on dry brush."

"What happened to Julian, Mary?" Alice already knew the answer.

"Well, child," smiled Mary. "He walked off, all red-faced.

A couple times later, you know, over a few weeks here and there, Julian tries to tell Ol' ugly Mary that he loves me. Starts talkin' 'bout my eyes, my soul, my goodness. I don't know what the hell he's goin' on 'bout, except I keep tellin' him that he's got himself the wrong Mary, either that or some kind 'o brain fever. This Mary here, I tells him, is black as burnt wood and got a face that'd make a horse get up on two legs and jump off a steep rock. So each time he comes for his courtin', I sends him away and he goes, all a sulkin'.

"Now one night while I'm deliverin' mail to Virginia City, I get word at one of the stops that Julian done hung himself, all on account of his lovin' me and bein' rejected. Well, all I could do was cry, but the boys, they all start lookin' at me. So I turned that cry into a mighty laugh for poor Julian.

"Them boys took up the laughter with me. I seen some poor, horrible sights in my day. Menfolk is the ugliest things."

"I know, Mary," Alice motioned quietly.

Basil stirred and got up to use the bathroom. Alice wondered if he'd be coming back. She stared at the wall and thought about Stu.

After Caesar, Alice had met Stu, who took her down to New Orleans. Alice got a job as a saucier at a trendy restaurant in the French Quarter, next door to an old-time pharmacy. The pharmacist had flirted with Alice several times until he realized Alice was in love with Stu. Pale, tall, pudgy, and a sloppy dresser, Stu resembled a giant ear of half-husked corn. After a long romance, Stu promised to marry Alice.

When Alice realized that she loved Stu, she emitted sparks of joy to all who came in contact with her. She stopped to help kids carrying groceries and invited the homeless into the restaurant after it had closed so she could cook for them. Alice worked these small miracles, thinking that love was the cause of all happiness. People were intended to fall in love and spread joy, the opposite of a plague.

"You were so blinded by love that you couldn't see this lunkhead slowly slippin' away. He didn't love you. He was in love with love," advised Mary.

Stu and Alice planned a small wedding, mostly for the benefit of his parents. Alice had no family and was excited to finally own one. She'd thought it odd when Stu told her to meet him at the church for the rehearsal, and, sure enough, she arrived to discover the pews vacant and the church empty. She gazed at the lonely altar for a few hours, wondering if Stu and his family were late or if she'd truly been left behind. Then, the priest's cat, the one that ran from people who came to the rectory, walked up to Alice and rubbed the side of its long body against her ankles. The cat, as if it sensed Alice's profound despair, circled her again and again, reminding Alice of how she kept coming back to the same place in her life no matter how far she traveled, no matter the wisdom she thought she had acquired.

"You should have kept the cat," said Mary. "They're good for comfort when the blue demons come." Then, after considering Alice a bit more, she added, "In fact, you should have taken two of them, like aspirin."

Thereafter, Alice's eyes turned cold; they held the loneliness of a prairie moon. She cursed the heavens for creating this need for men. Need for men? It was as if she were the opposite of a vampire—she would seek men out and give them her very lifeblood.

The screams echoed in her head. "Can't you make him so he won't hate me? So that he won't beat me? So that he won't pay me off to keep our sleeping together a secret from his family? So he won't lie when he says he loves me? So he won't appear sane when he's not? So he won't ask me to marry him when he has no intention of going through with it?"

After Stu, Alice briefly dated the pharmacist next door to the restaurant. Cooking became her life. Her lack of a right index finger kept her from taking on the top-quality work, but she made do. And she continued in her silence. She even created a signature dish that brought her some attention—grilled capon. She thought the dish appropriate. Capons were, after all, castrated roosters.

Cooking suited her, for it allowed a quiet meditation. It also meant that she could think through her problems, over and over, letting them simmer in her mind. As long as she stayed in the restaurant kitchen, her life, her self-imposed exile from the world, worked out fine. She'd intended to live out her life cooking and traveling around from city to city, constantly on the run from intimacy. Until, of course, the day Alfredo had walked into her kitchen.

He swept her off her feet and drove her to San Francisco. Alfredo was rich, beautiful, and romantically foreign. He also wouldn't stop talking. When he'd grasped the implications of her silence, he really began to get some things off his chest. Families, fears, past women, all came up in a stream of verbosity, how he pitied women—their frailties, their unsuitability for the savage world.

Alice, in turn, began pitying Alfredo, thinking she could help him, save him, turn him around. In Nevada, he spoke frankly about what he thought of Alice, her faults, and her physical imperfections. One week of life with Alfredo and his ranting became unbearable. While contemplating how to break off the relationship, Alice, at her local bank, was stunned to discover from the teller that Alfredo had, that very morning, cleaned out her savings and closed the account. His belongings were gone from their apartment; he had disappeared. Alice surprised herself by pursuing him. She had worked too hard for her nest egg, and it was all she had left.

Alfredo, she soon discovered, had had the gall to open a restaurant with her money. Finally confronted, he told her that as far as he was concerned, the time he'd put into their relationship was fair exchange for the money he had taken.

The next day, he burned the restaurant to the ground and collected on the insurance. And still, Alice remained silent.

Basil came back to bed and whispered his most intimate fears and dreams in Alice's ear, quiet as a prayer. She realized that she was the closest he would ever come to a church, and the bed was the altar where he chose to make his confession. Alice wondered if she was capable of giving Basil absolution. In a way, his confessional was a fitting end to her relationship with men. This was the final excursion into their hearts before she launched toward uncharted waters. In her mind's eye, she saw her own confession. She considered mercy for Basil. Then, suddenly, her past swept up before her eyes like a fine cotton bed sheet being shaken out for the first time.

Basil shifted, and Alice focused on what he was saying. His speech had not yet been affected. She glanced past Basil at Stagecoach Mary and thought of her mother, who had died after discovering the child that Alice's father had had with another woman.

"I think someone needs to stop listening to this no-account pisspot dribble on 'bout his sad life and hear the end of my story," said Mary.

Alice reflected for a moment. Ashamed at getting this sweet ghost upset, she looked up from Basil and pleaded, "I'm sorry, Mary. Do go on."

"All right then. So I gets back to town and sure enough everyone's talkin' 'bout poor Julian and how he done kill himself and the circumstance surroundin' it. Cyrus, his boss, comes up to me as soon as I get into town, like he was waiting for me. He hands me Julian's guitar. Says Julian told him he wanted me to have it. Funny thing, though. When he hands me the guitar, Cyrus gets all serious and tells me Julian had a last wish. I says to Cyrus, 'I imagine his wish was to get buried proper or to be sent back to Spain.' But, no. Cyrus tells me Julian wanted me to learn to play his guitar.

"Now I starts to feel bad for Julian and even think that I treated him wrong. Maybe, I'm figurin', he seen somethin' in me I can't see myself, like maybe he had a special mirror. Cyrus goes on 'bout how he'll teach me to play Julian's guitar on Thursday night. Now he knows that Thursday's the night I deliver gold dust to the miner's court over at Rockslide, but Cyrus starts wailin' 'bout how he ain't gonna get into heaven on account he can't fulfill a dyin' man's last wish. I says, 'Fine. I'll learn guitar Thursday night before I head out.'"

Mary became quiet for a moment. The image of this black angel crackled in Alice's eyes like a campfire.

"Alice, Mary here ain't never been much for gettin' attention, but I gotta' say, for once it was nice. Too bad it was comin' from a dead man. There ain't never been anythin' wrong with sweet Julian, I tells myself, except I kept sendin' him away. Sent him to die is what I did. Well, Thursday night comes along, and I park my horses and coach in the back of Cyrus' saloon. Turns out Cyrus don't know a damn thing about guitars. We're in the back room of the saloon and he's tellin' me to hold the guitar like a cello, and even I know better than that. Julian's luscious instrument sounds like we doin' surgery on a goat.

"Meanwhile, I can hear two things happenin'—a fight's breakin' out between Arizona Pete and Red Yeager in the main parlor, and, outside, my horses are gettin' nervous. I take great pride in knowin' my horses. They only make that kind of noise when wolves or men are sneakin' around. So I march through the parlor, avoiding the fight, and go see about my horses. I'm holdin' the guitar in my left hand on account that my right hand is my shootin' hand. I still remember what a cool, clear night it was. The stars were spread out like someone had flung a veil of diamond dust into the air. As I reach for my pistol, I see Julian in my coach lookin' through the mail, lookin' for the gold dust delivery.

"He's got a gun in his holster, but he ain't that quick. Julian looks up and sees me. He knows, and I know, that he didn't give a damn about Ol' Mary, just wanted her gold dust. Fooled the whole damn town, too. Cyrus and Julian were probably plannin' to leave that very night. Julian knows I'm good with a gun, and he seen me kill some road agents tryin' to rob my coach. Still, he takes out his gun, but he's nervous and holdin' it all wrong, like he's cradlin' a baby. He can't hold a gun, and I can't hold his guitar, which should make us about even. Only we ain't close to being even. My only concern is the gold dust and the letters I'm carryin' in my coach. If'n I shoot Julian in my coach, blood's goin' to get everywhere, which ain't fair to the people expectin' these letters. So I walk real slow toward him. He says he wants his gold.

"My left arm ain't my strongest arm, but it did good enough. I crashed that guitar across poor Julian's face. The guitar that his grandfather made for him. The wood splintered, and I kept one of the long wooden splinters as a souvenir. Used it as a toothpick. Julian talked kinda' funny after that. I'd bring him huckleberry pie every Thursday night when I'd visit him in jail, and I'd ask him to tell me about my pretty eyes again."

Alice breathed deeply, watching Basil. He was dead. Finally. She got up and padded over to the kitchen. From her pocketbook, she took out the small vial of meprobromate and placed it on the floor in front of Basil. She was glad that something productive had come out of her dates with the New Orleans pharmacist. He'd told her that repeated doses of meprobromate would slowly turn one's stomach to Play-Doh. The resulting concoction had been her own recipe: meprobromate and scotch, stirred with Mary's guitar toothpick and fashioned especially for Basil on each of their Thursday night dates.

Stagecoach Mary grinned and said, "Come on, girl. You know you did the right thing." Alice knew Mary was right. Alice's mother had died of a broken heart. Her father had run off and remarried another. Alice hadn't found her father yet, but she'd found his son from his other family—Basil. He'd looked just like her father.

When Jilted Alice spoke, she said, "Now where do the rest of them live?"

"I knew you'd get around to askin'," said Stagecoach Mary with assurance.

Alice thought of the stack of maps in her car and of the little red soldiers waiting to join the one on her thigh.

Mary brushed the black hair from Basil's still face and caressed Alice's hands. "Let's go now, child."

And with that, Jilted Alice picked up the huckleberry pie she'd brought over for dessert and Stagecoach Mary's framed picture and left the house, locking the door behind her. She was ready to speak to the other men in her life out in the world.

THE PLUCKY WOOING
OF EMILY

Conway Blitherton—Connie to his friends—was a model London bachelor with plenty of means. The means had arrived as a rather voluminous inheritance from a distant aunt, owing to the fact that Connie's parents had passed away when he was barely out of short pants. Despite this early tragedy, Connie had soldiered on and his life was often described as a "pippin," albeit with one small snag. If one were to crack open the Blitherton ledger and peruse the side *noir*, one would discover that Connie was twenty-four, was moderately fair of countenance, had his own valet, and was in possession of a wonderful flat. The side *rouge*, on the other hand, would be filled with many examples of a diminished inventory of marbles rattling about Connie's bean. Within minutes of his company, one would be quick to observe that there existed a vast wealth of craniums with deeper ridges and less overall smoothness than Connie's. Still, all in all, Connie was a happy man.

However, there was the aforementioned snag. Once it occurred to Connie's elders that the boy was now enjoying his third decade as an unattached bachelor, they began to apply pressure that would have made the bottom of the sea envious. The problem was Connie's complete inability to relate to the fairer sex. No matter how many women he courted, he was never able to connect with the one Eve with whom he was meant to share God's Eden. Putting it mildly, Oedipus had a better go with the ladies.

But all that had recently changed. Connie was a regular at 43 Bond, his favorite restaurant. Once a month, he noticed the most enchanting girl strapping on the old feedbag with an elderly female companion. Connie would later come to know these women as Emily Highurst and her Aunt Paige. From across the restaurant, when he first laid eyes on Emily's dimpled cheeks and brunette tresses, Connie was smitten. It took several months of confidence-building and counsel from his valet, Jameson, but he decided that he would finally make his introductions and ask for Emily's hand.

Connie was almost at Emily's table, wine glass in hand to toast her magnificence, when 43 Bond's chef, Teddy Pringleglass, approached Emily, effectively cutting off Connie's route to victory. Connie was one table away but didn't want to appear to be standing in a receiving line, so he pulled a chair from a nearby table and sat down within arm's length of his distant beloved. Her perfume made him so dreamy eyed, he wasn't sure how much time had elapsed before Aunt Paige summarily dismissed poor old Teddy Pringleglass's advances toward her niece.

"Now, you are to go back into the kitchen," insisted Aunt Paige in an imperious manner to a retreating Teddy Pringleglass. "Emily may be from the country, but, be assured, I am not. One simply doesn't approach a strange girl and profess his love to her. Especially when you're the help." If Attila the Hun had been present, he would have done well to take copious notes on Aunt Paige's tone and body language.

"Oh, Aunt Paige," said Emily in a mellifluous voice that matched her beauty.

"And as for you, my naïve niece, if you'd like to continue visiting me once a month from Illspile-on-the-Vale, you are not to receive such gentlemen."

At this juncture, Aunt Paige stood up haughtily, intending to discuss Teddy Pringleglass's behavior with management, followed by a thorough and robust powdering of the old proboscis. However, the chair upon which Connie was sitting prevented Aunt Paige from completing these tasks; one of the chair legs was resting comfortably on top of the hem of her dress. Aunt Paige's attempted departure caused two immediate reactions. First, there was a great ripping sound as an enormous tear developed in her dress, which could have been equaled only, perhaps, by a tectonic shift in the San Andreas Fault. Secondly, the blameworthy chair tipped over, causing Connie to tip over as well. Most importantly, it caused Connie's wine glass to tip over, splashing the contents directly onto Aunt Paige's artfully made face, bringing to mind the conclusion of a log flume ride.

"Well, I never," said an incredulous, and quite moist, Aunt Paige. She grabbed Emily by the arm and dragged her away, muttering that this would be her last visit to this establishment. Emily glanced over her shoulder at Connie and smiled weakly. Connie smiled back. He knew they would never be together again. They had never even met. He was heartbroken and dejectedly sulked homeward.

"A most unfortunate development, sir," said Jameson, shaking the iced martini tumbler after Connie had concluded a sum-up of the afternoon's misadventure.

Connie sank further into his easy chair, the view of Hyde Park evoking little joy. "And the thing that really frazzles the neurons, if that's the phrase I want, is that Pringleglass selects the very moment of my declaration to pop in and muck it all up."

"It does appear to have been an ill-fated moment, sir," said Jameson, pouring the martini.

"Dash it, I am quite fond of that girl," said Connie. "Oh, Jameson, I fear even you couldn't scale the obstacles that have been placed between me and Emily Highurst."

Jameson raised his right eyebrow an eighth of an inch, indicating that powerful brain of his was in full locomotion.

Jameson had been ironing Connie's wrinkled life for years. He handed Connie the martini. "Sir, I do not mean to suggest any disrespect nor presume beyond my station, but the thought occurs that you sell yourself short."

"I do? Short, do I?"

"I wish to see you happy, sir. I shall give the matter some thought."

"Jolly good, Jameson. That's the feudal spirit." Connie took a sip of the bracing martini and his spirits were restored. "You're right, by Jove, I am made of more fibrous stock than the average dejected lover. Well, I'm very bucked up by this news. I'll leave you to it, then. Eat kelp if you must. Heard it works wonders for brainial maximization, if that's the term."

Connie spent the rest of the day at his club, playing darts with his pal Stilton while thinking of Emily. His dreamy-eyed state resulted in the loss of one quid and the required visit to a doctor by Stilton, owing to three darts thrown by Connie which found purchase on Stilton's mid-leg, back, and rump.

"What-ho, Jameson! Has a plan been hatched, or are you still in the incubatory stage?" asked Connie as Jameson took his hat, coat, and gloves.

"A course of action does suggest itself," said Jameson.

"Excellent," said Connie. "Does it involve Emily?"

"Most assuredly, sir. You will recall that Miss Emily Highurst resides in Illspile-on-the-Vale, a countryside hamlet. I have made inquiries and discovered that the annual county fair occurs this weekend in the very same town. Apparently, the jewel in the county fair program is the farm animal competition. Since you are a distinguished gentleman from London, I have arranged for you to be on the judging panel."

Connie sat attentively, letting the words percolate. It was as if he were attempting to row the Thames, but his oars did not intersect with the river. "I'm sorry, Jameson, what am I doing?"

"It has come to my attention that the Highursts will have

23

several of their animals entered in the competition," said Jameson. "One presumes Miss Emily would be rather impressed by a gentleman's knowledge in such matters."

The oars finally splashed into the water.

"Ah, got it. Excellent. A most inspired scheme, Jameson."

"Thank you, sir."

"I'll take it from here," said Connie, getting up and pacing around the room. The synapses were firing on as many cylinders as possible. "The plan is simplicity itself. Step one: impress Emily and her family with my knowledge of farm animals. Step two: rig the contest so the Highursts win the blasted fair competition. And step three: pitch my woo."

"Very good, sir."

"Jameson, you are a marvel."

"One does endeavor to provide satisfaction, sir."

"And the country air will do us good," said Connie.

"There is one small hitch, sir. If I may explain?"

Connie sat back down. There were always hitches when it came to the fairer sex. "How small a hitch?"

"One is only to listen attentively at the local public house to receive dispatches from surrounding areas."

"Yes, yes?"

"Lord Highurst is very keen on marrying off his daughter, Emily, to a gentleman of means," said Jameson.

"Check!"

"According to the Pig and Frog barmaid, his lordship is, if you will excuse the crudeness, land-rich and cash-poor. He seeks a match for his daughter who can balance the ledgers, if you grasp my meaning, sir."

"Check, check! All cash-rich and land-poor. That's me. Gosh, Jameson, this pudding gets richer by the minute. But do tell, I feel this infinitesimally small hitch looming above like the scimitar of Damocles."

"An apt description, sir. In addition to the suitor's qualities which I have just described, his lordship is very fond of Miss

Emily and wants her future mate to be a man of substance and intelligence."

"What-ho?"

"The phrase, 'No nincompoops need apply,' has been utilized in the past to great effect by Lord Highurst, according to the barmaid."

"Jameson, you are never to frequent the Pig and Frog again. I am suspect of their barmaid's chumminess."

"Very good, sir."

"No nincompoop, I," said Connie, more to convince himself than Jameson.

"It is not a sobriquet which I would apply," said Jameson.

Connie didn't think he could withstand a direct assault from Poppa Highurst. But there was the prize of Emily to fortify him. "Blast it, Jameson, I'll do it. Please make the proper preparations."

That weekend, Connie stepped off the morning seven-fifteen at Illspile-on-the-Vale, dressed in full country gentlemen clothes. "Ah, sir, welcome," said Jameson, opening the door of Connie's room at The Rested Shepherd, the local inn. Jameson had arrived ahead of time to make preparations. "I trust you had a pleasant journey? Now, if I may, there is a small matter that requires your attention."

"Right-ho, Jameson. But first, a bit of a walk, what? Must begin my quest for the love of my life and all that. She's about. I can feel it."

"Yes, sir. Excellent. But first, perhaps, a chat is in order?" A strange honking sound came from the water closet. Connie seemed not to take notice.

"Blast it, Jameson, I'm off. I can't stand to be this close to her and yet so far away. Fingers crossed not to run into her aunt, though. Bit unpleasant, that one. Then again, they're all country mice, and she's a bit of a city rat."

And with the application of his squire's hat upon his head

at a jaunty angle, Connie was off. Jameson sighed his usual sigh.

Connie wandered the fairgrounds. It was a lovely day and the bright green meadow was filled with tents, games, and activities, not to mention the happy local populace. Connie came to the livestock exhibition. There seemed to be a ruckus ensuing.

He collared one of the spectators. "I say, what the devil is the commotion?"

"A chicken, duck, and turkey have been stolen from his lordship. They were sure to be blue ribbon stuff! The turkey is especially troublesome since it was imported from the States."

"Oh my," said Connie, appreciating the loss as if it was his own. "May I be of some assistance? I have been known to lose the old keys from time to time and to retrace my steps until they were found."

Connie was led to the bereaved family. They sat in a circle under one of the exhibition tents. Three empty coops stood ominously nearby.

"I say, sorry to hear of your loss. Bit of bad luck, really. But if I may…." Connie's breath failed him. Sitting there among her parents and younger sister was none other than the fair Emily.

"You," she said, the blush returning to her ivory cheek.

"You," he repeated, stunned to be in her presence again.

"Emily, you know this man?" demanded Lord Highurst. Connie noted that there was about the man a disturbing resemblance in manner and tone to Aunt Paige. Connie quickly checked to ensure that all chairs and wine glasses within proximity were behaving within acceptable practices.

"My dearest Emily," said Connie.

Emily blushed again.

"I beg your pardon?" insisted Lord Highurst.

"Allow me to introduce myself," said Connie, surprised at

his own confidence. "I am Conway Blitherton. Connie to my friends. I've just arrived this morning from London to judge the animal competition."

"And?"

"Yes…right. Excellent observation. Top-notch, really. Now, regarding your daughter. We have never actually met but I have dined at the same restaurant…."

"Enough of this nincompoopery," said Lord Highurst. "I have lived all my years in Illspile-on-the-Vale, as have all these good people. A stranger from London arrives and my prized poultry are missing."

"Sir, what are you suggesting?" said Connie, his voice rising in tone with each syllable.

"Only that the local constabulary will be notified of these developments, and I am certain that your presence will be required with them for further interview," said Lord Highurst.

"What-ho?" responded Connie, weakly.

"Oh, Connie," said Emily in a manner that implied disappointment.

And with that, Lord Highurst grabbed Emily by the arm and dragged her away in a scene all too familiar to Connie.

"Why, this is a disaster," Connie said, pacing about his room as Jameson looked on. "I find myself in the countryside completely de-Emilied. What am I to do?"

"All is not lost, sir." The honking sound persisted from the water closet. It was accompanied by a squawking noise. Connie gave it no heed as he was presently preoccupied with weightier affairs.

"Oh, Jameson, you don't understand. They suspect me of being the Great Poultry Snatcher. How am I ever to live this down? How will Emily accept me now?"

Jameson consulted his pocket watch.

"I believe I can bring resolution to your difficulties, sir, if you'll accompany me to the train station. There is only one evening train that leaves for London from this station. The nine twenty-eight awaits us."

Although Connie was a world-class conflict-avoider, he couldn't imagine a world where he abandoned his love. "What's this, Jameson? Dash off like common criminals? I should say not. And to even imply such a course of action…"

"If you'll just follow me, sir."

"Right. Spot of tea first?"

"We really don't have the time, sir."

"Right. Drop of brandy, then?"

"Sir."

Their arrival at the train station put Connie further out onto the cliff's edge when he noticed that the local police station was located next door.

"Et tu, Jameson? A bit of the old Turn-Your-Master-In, then, is it?"

"If you will endeavor to turn your gaze toward that direction, sir," said Jameson, pointing indiscreetly at a fellow sitting at the train station with three large sacks resting at his feet.

"What-ho? I say, that chappy looks a bit familiar."

"I venture he should, sir."

Connie gave his eyes a squint. "Why, it's Teddy Pringleglass from 43 Bond. What the deuce is he doing here?"

Suddenly, a constable in full helmet nabbed old Teddy. There was a bit of resistance by the chef but the policeman meant business, being a country type that seemed to have been raised wrestling wild pigs and all that. Teddy shouted, "What the devil is the meaning of all this?" Which seemed, to Connie's way of thinking, an excellent and most relevant question. The pig-wrestler and Teddy approached Connie and Jameson.

"Jameson, what *is* going on here?"

With a gleam in his eye, Jameson turned to Connie and whispered, "In a word, sir, turducken."

Emily and her family were gathered in the lobby of The

Rested Shepherd, along with the constable, Teddy, and, of course, Connie and Jameson.

"Now, if you please, Jameson," insisted Lord Highurst.

"Yes, Jameson," added Connie. "Untie this knot."

"Very well, sir. It has already been established that Mr. Pringleglass here had feelings of a romantic nature for his lordship's daughter. When Mr. Pringleglass's advances were summarily rebuffed, he took it upon himself to exact a revenge most foul upon your family."

"And how exactly?" asked the constable, still holding Teddy tight in his grasp.

"By stealing their prized poultry and serving it at his restaurant to Miss Emily's aunt. In one sitting."

"One sitting?" asked Lord Highurst. "Well, I never. My sister has been known to have a bit of a chew at the cud, but she could never eat three dinners at once."

"If I may be permitted to provide further elucidation, sir?" said Jameson.

"Yes, go on."

"Simply put, Mr. Pringleglass is an accomplished chef. When he heard of your imported turkey, along with your other prized poultry, he devised a plan to make turducken. An extraordinary dish, requiring the most committed dedication to the culinary craft, it can take upwards of twenty hours to prepare. In summary, one removes the bones from a chicken, duck, and turkey, then stuffs the chicken into the duck and the duck into the turkey, all the while tucking savory stuffing in between. The entire affair is roasted. Then, being boneless, it is sliced crosswise, each slice revealing six concentric rings of juicy goodness."

There was a long silence as everyone's minds dashed to and fro between the despicable schemes of one Teddy Pringleglass and the saliva-inducing description of this tantalizing feast.

"Good show, Jameson," said Connie, breaking the silence.

"Yes, thank you, Jameson," said Emily. She looked away, tears in her eyes.

"Right," said the constable. "It's a ten quid fine for you." And with that, he dragged old Teddy away.

Connie approached Emily. "Dear Emily, what in heaven is the matter?"

"My animals have departed this mortal plane."

"On the contrary, my lady," said Jameson, "if you would please follow me upstairs." Then, turning to Emily's parents, he added, "With your lordship's permission, of course."

"Yes, off you go," said Emily's father, both glad and confused at these developments.

Jameson led them to Connie's room.

"Lady Emily," said Jameson, "Lord Conway sent me ahead of him with instructions to be on the lookout for suspicious characters during my journey. I spied Mr. Pringleglass in the next compartment during my train ride here. Per Lord Conway's careful instructions, his utmost concern being your welfare, I followed Mr. Pringleglass. Reporting back to Lord Conway, he soon realized the devious plans at hand. Anticipating his treachery, Lord Conway directed me to switch out your targeted fowl with lesser creatures."

"What, what, what?" inquired Connie. "I say, Jameson, what…what did I do?"

"I believe these belong to you," said Jameson to Emily, opening the lavatory door. Out wobbled a disoriented chicken, duck, and turkey.

"Oh, Connie," said Emily. She put her arms around him and kissed him deeply. "These animals mean more to me than anything. How did you know?"

"Well, birds of a feather."

CATCH OF THE DAY

"My father was a seafood lover," said Newberg.

"Obviously," said Valerie, the pretty seamstress, through a mouthful of pins.

"He was always fond of your work," continued Newberg as Valerie finished taking measurements for his tuxedo. "Said it was like you had six hands. That's why I came to you for this fitting."

"Thanks," said Valerie. She couldn't look him in the eyes.

"Also, because you're the only one I know who doesn't mind...my affliction," he said, brandishing the giant pincer he had for a right arm. The feeding claw made a clicking sound with his crusher claw.

She took a deep breath. "You mean...?"

"Yes," said Newberg, a distant look in his eyes, "my shyness."

His eyesight was getting worse by the day. He knew it had something to do with the compound eyes on top of the stalks that grew from his head. He kept them under a hat, but to see correctly, the stalks needed to breathe.

"Well, I mean, you're not the only one who understands my shyness," he continued. "Of course, there's my girlfriend, Elsie. She loves me for who I am."

"How nice for her," said Valerie curtly. She put down her measuring tape, pins, and chalk, and crossed the main room of her tailor shop.

Newberg's parents had passed away a year earlier, leaving him with all their possessions. Newberg's father had been a local Maine fisherman who was rumored to have caught a fabled set of pearls in his day. Yet despite all the nets and lines Newberg's father had set, he was the one finally caught by Newberg's mother. She was the new manager of the town aquarium. His marriage had caused a bit of scandal in the small fishing village because the bride wasn't local. Also, there were rumors that to earn extra money when she was in college, Newberg's mother had volunteered for strange spinal cord injection experiments. Valerie knew the rumors were true; she had recently volunteered for these experiments herself.

"So," said Valerie, returning to finish the tux fitting. "Tell me all about this Elsie and how you two met."

"Not much to tell really," said Newberg. "One day, she came to the docks where I work, and we struck up a conversation. After a few weeks, she invited me to meet her parents. That's what the tux is for."

"And has Elsie told them about your…."

"My what?" asked Newberg.

Valerie looked up at Newberg with a quizzical expression. "You said before that you felt like an outsider," she said. "Since when?"

With a sigh, he confided in her regarding the tractor trailer incident the previous winter. He'd been trudging through town wearing an overcoat during rush hour when he came to a busy intersection. Pedestrians started crowding behind him, waiting to cross the road. The traffic signal changed. Newberg started crossing, then suddenly stopped when he got an itch on his head. He raised his large red pincer claw to scratch it. To the people behind Newberg, the pincer claw appeared to be a large red stop sign being held by a crossing guard. Obediently, they stopped walking. Without warning, a tractor trailer came barreling down the road; the driver would have mowed down a tenth of the town's population if they hadn't been stopped from crossing. After the initial shock, the crowd gathered around Newberg to thank him. As they were patting him on the shoulder, his overcoat slipped off and people saw the pincer claw. Some screamed, but most ran away.

Newberg said he thought it was due to his painful shyness. Valerie nodded but her expression told him she knew better.

She was determined to break the tension. "I once knew a woman who had the head of a badger and the body of a badger, but here's the twist: it was the body of a different badger," she said.

"Either way, wouldn't that make her a badger, not a woman?"

"Seemingly."

"Elsie loves me for who I am," said Newberg.

Valerie smiled blankly, finishing up her measurements.

"And I know she's serious," he continued. "Because she asked me to bring a little gift to each of her parents. She said it's traditional before I ask for her hand in marriage."

"Oh," said Valerie, standing up. "Already they're asking you to shell out money."

"No, it's not like that."

"Right. Well, come back at five tonight. I should have your tux ready by then," she said.

Newberg could tell Valerie was concealing her feelings but couldn't determine what those feelings were. That was the thing about Valerie.

He spent the rest of the day molting and shopping for a gift for his future father-in-law. He knew almost nothing about the man. Elsie had mentioned, in passing, her father's childlike playfulness. Newberg finally settled on a great gift.

Elsie's mother, Mrs. Keller, was described as small-boned and having everything she could ever desire. Newberg knew exactly what would set her heart aflutter.

Newberg returned to Valerie's shop at five. He gave her the gifts to admire as he tried on the tux. It fit perfectly. He thanked her for her exceptional craftsmanship. She smiled her Valerie smile and wished him luck. He turned redder than usual.

Elsie's parents' house was a suburban ranch on a street of identical ranches. Newberg was jittery when he arrived, but then a feeling of joy overcame him at the prospect that someone loved him despite his shyness. Her parents would, in all likelihood, be just as accepting of his handicap as their daughter. Newberg knocked on the door. His back still itched from the six walking legs that had started to extrude from his back. At least the leg-buds were still small enough to disguise beneath his jacket.

Elsie was the first to greet Newberg at the door. She wore a beautiful evening gown and her hair up in a bun. She commented on how handsome he looked in his tux. Her face displayed shock, however, when she looked at his head. He had moussed his hair into dozens of spikes. He told her he read in a magazine that this do was all the rage. He didn't have the heart to explain how he was camouflaging his newly formed eye-stalks.

Mrs. Keller came down the stairs next and greeted him warmly. She looked him in the eye and never looked away. It was as if she was scared to look elsewhere. Newberg took this as a sign that she wanted to help draw him out of his shyness. Elsie called to the next room for her father. Mr. Keller emerged from the hallway in a wheelchair. He greeted Newberg by extending his right hand in a robust manner. Newberg shook it with his left hand.

They adjourned to the living room for cocktails around the cozy coffee table. "The ballet starts in two hours, so we're not in any rush," said Elsie.

Elsie's parents either stared at their drinks or looked directly into Newberg's eyes.

"What ballet are we all seeing?" asked Newburg, taking a sip from his salted water.

"*The Nutcracker*," said Elsie.

Newberg spit water in a giant spray that managed to drench both parents.

"Great Neptune," said Newberg. "I'm so sorry. It's just that I hate the N-word."

"Well," said Mr. Keller, drying himself. "What say I take you for a tour of our little home?"

"Uh, before we do that, Dad…" said Elsie, nudging Newberg.

"Yes," said Newberg. He whispered into Elsie's ear how he was slightly embarrassed by the gift he had picked out for her dad.

"Come, come," said Mrs. Keller. "Nothing to do for that shyness but overcome it."

"Right," said Newberg, standing up. "I'll be right back."

He came back into the house moments later bearing a small wrapped box and an enormous wrapped tube.

"Well, I never," said Mr. Keller, accepting the large wrapped tube. He opened it, revealing a bright red pogo stick. "Odd choice," he said. "We'll get along swimmingly." He laid the pogo stick on top of his wheelchair motor.

"I hope mine's not a mini pogo stick," said Mrs. Keller. She unwrapped the small box and opened it. Her eyes lit up at the treasure inside. It was Newberg's father's Anklet of Pearls. Newberg didn't care much for jewelry but knew his father would have wanted this piece to stay in the family.

The Anklet of Pearls was stunningly beautiful. It glistened even in darkness. "Here, let me show you how they glow," said Newberg. "Do you have somewhere dark we can go?"

Mrs. Keller smiled. "Let's go to the backyard by the pool," she said. Newberg followed Mr. Keller out to the pool, while Elsie and her mother stayed a few steps behind.

Mr. Keller pointed out their cast-iron butter press collection, displayed on a lighted shelf. Newberg shuddered, his pincer claw clicking beneath the voluminous tuxedo jacket sleeve.

His thoughts were interrupted by Mrs. Keller. She cooed as she inspected the Anklet of Pearls in the moonlight. Her smile quickly turned to a grimace as she closed the box with a snap and wheeled her husband into the house.

Newberg, confused, turned around to see Elsie stepping out of her evening gown. She wore a bikini underneath.

"What's going on? Did I do something wrong?" asked Newberg.

"My parents saw how uncomfortable the ballet made you, so they suggested we stay home while they attend. Isn't that wonderful?"

She walked over to the pool cabana and flipped a switch. Suddenly, the Jacuzzi next to the in-ground pool began to roil violently. Elsie stepped into the Jacuzzi slowly as the water heated up.

"Oh, Poseidon," said Newberg, terrified. "That's not what I think it is, is it?"

Newberg's head began to itch.

"Come on, lobster-boy, get in. I promise to make it worth your while."

Newberg didn't know what to do. On the one claw, he had waited his whole life for this moment. On the other claw, every instinct he possessed said to run the other way.

Newberg focused on his itching head. The world slowed down and everything became clear. He was seeing the surrounding world, not through his human eyes but through his compound eyes. Although he was facing Elsie in the boiling water, he could see behind him, and what he saw terrified him. Mr. Keller was slowly and quietly wheeling toward him, a look of menace about his face. Before Mr. Keller could get any closer and push Newberg into the boiling water, Newberg spun around with alarming speed and instinctively swung his pincer claw forward. The claw wrapped around the spring-action of the pogo stick on the back of the wheelchair, then pressed tight and let go. The pogo stick sprang away from the wheelchair, shifting the motor into overdrive and rocketing the wheelchair forward. Mr. Keller was violently propelled into the deep end of the pool. Elsie jumped out of the Jacuzzi and into the pool to save her father.

"That will be quite enough," said Mrs. Keller. She wore a lobster bib and waved a giant rubber band threateningly. "Get into that Jacuzzi," she demanded.

"But I just got out of it," said Elsie.

"Not you," shouted Mrs. Keller. "Up with your hand and claw!" Newberg was speechless. How had the evening gone so wrong? "I was in love with your father," said Mrs. Keller to Newberg, advancing on him as he retreated toward the Jacuzzi. "He was supposed to give me the Anklet of Pearls."

"Well, part of this is news to me," said Mr. Keller, as Elsie pushed him to the shallow side of the pool.

"You think your fate is cruel?" Mrs. Keller asked Newberg. "I was a scientist conducting experiments on longevity in humans and lobsters. Your mother volunteered. I injected a serum into her spinal cord made up of lobster DNA. Your father married her anyway. But it all worked out. My little experiment created you, and Elsie made you bring me the pearls!"

There would have been more to hear were it not for the interruption of a loud, metallic clang, emanating from the cast-iron butter press, which had come into direct contact with Mrs. Keller's head. The sound echoed into the night. At the business end of the swinging butter press stood Valerie.

Valerie grabbed Newberg's claw and pulled him toward her. "Come on, surf and turf, let's get the hell out of here."

They ran two blocks to her waiting car. Before they got in, Valerie put a hand on Newberg's claw.

"Are you okay?" she asked.

"I've lost the two most important things in my life: my girlfriend and my father's pearls."

Valerie reached into her purse and pulled out the Anklet of

Pearls. "I switched them when you were trying on your tux. These were phonies." She kissed him hard on the lips. "And just one more surprise," she said as she wrapped her recently sprouted six legs around him.

THE JOHN HOUR

June 30, 1979
Four and a Half Hours Until Curtain

Dave Wilson was always nervous riding into Manhattan. He was a country boy at heart and had lived his thirty-one years sequestered away within the white pines of Upstate New York. If it was up to him, his husky frame and brown, wavy hair would never get blown by a New York City breeze. The city folks just didn't seem to know how to live. They spent their whole lives with their arms tucked close to their sides, afraid to touch their neighbor as they hustled from busy Point A to frantic Point B. They were always thin, afraid to take up any more horizontal space than was absolutely necessary, but free to be as tall as they pleased. New York City was all about the vertical space. The horizontal space had a premium markup. Dave liked where he lived in the quiet, spacious land in the Adirondacks. A fellow could breathe there. A fellow could slowly build a law practice there and marry his aspiring dancer of a girlfriend. Still, Dave found himself this Saturday night on a train that was taking him and his fiancée, Janis, right into the heart of Manhattan.

He looked over at Janis and gave her a goofy smile, hoping she wouldn't notice his agitated state of mind. It was bad enough that they were going to be set free in the city, but Dave was also going to meet Janis's father for the first time. Janis, who was twenty-seven, taught dance at the local college. Disco was her most popular class. Her dream was to stop teaching people how to do the Bus Stop and become a professional dancer, preferably on Broadway. She had a beautiful face, framed by short brown hair, and a long, thin, line of a body, natural for a dancer. Dave had dated her for four months before he got the nerve to ask her to marry him. He was shocked when she agreed on the spot. He felt she could do much better. Now, his life was dedicated to making her happy.

Presently, making Janis happy meant getting tickets to the Broadway show *Got Tu Go Disco*. Janis had heard that the show had the best disco dancing on Broadway, and she felt certain this was a sign. Dancers on Broadway were always getting hurt or moving on to other gigs. If she could successfully audition for the part of one of the replacement dancers, it would be her entry into professional dancing. She would move into the city with her fiancé, live close to her dad, and start her Broadway career. It all hinged on getting to see *Got Tu Go Disco* so she could learn the steps for her audition. The fact that she didn't know a single person even remotely associated with the show hardly caused her a moment of despair.

"What theater is it playing at again?" asked Dave as the train pulled into the station.

"The Minskoff," said Janis, barely able to contain her excitement. "It starts at eight-thirty sharp. We can have a drink with my dad afterwards."

Dave had promised her he would take her to see this show. The rest of her plan—moving into the city—did not sit well with Dave. Employed as a local assistant district attorney in his small town, he had plans to open his own law practice in a few years. Janis's father, Earl, happened to be the Manhattan district attorney, which Janis took as another sign that they should be living in the city. Janis had talked to her dad about getting Dave a position on his team. Dave cringed when he thought about the massive caseloads and the stressful energy and pressure associated with Earl's Manhattan DA's office.

The thing to do, Dave reminded himself, was to focus on getting tickets to *Got Tu Go Disco*. One problem at a time. He had been unable to get tickets ahead of time, which was not uncommon. His city-going friends typically waited until the day of the show and bought theirs from one of the dozens of ticket brokers throughout the city.

Dave grabbed their suitcases and left the train, shuffling along the dirty platform to the escalator. It was a slog with hundreds of people around them, all trying to do the same thing, all trying to fit through a door manufactured to accommodate one person's width. Dave and Janis stepped off the crowded, grimy escalator and were met by a sea of people, all locked into some sort of knot that seemed inescapable. They moved by inches, bumping into people and getting stepped on, all pressed up tight against one another. Dave spotted an exit sign and wiggled his elbow to get Janis's attention.

Dave took a giant breath once they left Grand Central Station. It was the kind of breath that he imagined submarine sailors took when they reached the surface and flung open the hatch. He took a different kind of breath when he surveyed the street and realized that the crowds outside the station made the inside seem like a deserted island. Dave never felt less like going to a disco show, but he hoped the bother was worth it to keep Janis happy.

Janis tapped Dave on the shoulder and pointed to a black car a block away. The driver, a man in his fifties and wearing a brown suit, was holding an oak tag sign with Dave's name on it.

"I'm Dave Wilson," Dave said as they approached the driver.

"Hello," said the driver. "I'm Harry, an assistant at the DA's office. You must be Janis. Your dad sent me to pick you up."

"Thank goodness you're on time," said Janis, loading her bag into the trunk.

They got in the car and headed out into traffic. Before long they pulled up to Earl's apartment, a stately building of at least forty floors. Dave wondered how people lived like this.

They thanked Harry while a uniformed doorman retrieved their luggage. The doorman escorted them to Earl's apartment and handed them the key.

After depositing their bags in the guest bedroom, Dave sprawled out on the bed, ready for a nap.

"Aren't you forgetting something?" said Janis.

"What? The show isn't for almost four hours."

"Tickets?" said Janis.

Dave sprang from the bed. Crap. He still had to get tickets.

"Okay," said Dave. "Here's the plan. I'll go to the ticket broker and be right back."

"You might be right back, but I won't be here to greet you."

"Why not?" said Dave.

"I'm going dress shopping for tonight. I'll meet you at Bigelow's in a few hours. I love you!" And with that, she kissed Dave and was off. He smiled in the goofy way he had done ever since meeting her.

Dave then dialed the ticket broker his friends had recommended. "Hi," said Dave. "I'd like to get two tickets for tonight's performance of *Got Tu Go Disco*, your two best seats."

"*Got Tu Go Disco?*" said the broker.

"Yes, two tickets, please."

"Oh, honey, you're out of luck. Didn't you hear?"

"Hear what?' said Dave. "What is there to hear? They all moved to Funkytown?"

"They're closing tonight. Last performance."

"But the show just opened four days ago."

"You're telling me," said the broker, slightly annoyed. "I know when it opened. Four days ago. And it closes tonight. Lousy show, lousy ticket sales."

"Well, do you have tickets for tonight? I mean, if it had lousy sales, maybe…"

"No tickets," said the broker. "We dumped them all to other carriers. Can I get you tickets to another show?"

"Any other hot disco dance shows?"

"Honey, they all moved to Funkytown."

Dave hung up the phone. He tried three other brokers with the same results. Apparently, no one had to go disco.

Three Hours and Forty-Five Minutes Until Curtain

Dave couldn't find a phone book at the apartment, so he headed to the nearest coffee shop. The back of the shop had a bank of pay phones with half-wall dividers. There was no privacy, but at least the pay phones had phone books chained to the wall.

The coffee shop was small and busy, populated with a few tables and a brisk counter service on bar stools. The smell of greasy coffee hung in the air. Dave looked up another ticket broker and explained his situation. For the fifth time that day, he was told that *Got Tu Go Disco* was closing that night and no tickets were available.

Dave hung up, dejected. He was trying to figure out how he was going to break this to Janis. Maybe he could just take her disco dancing at one of those clubs. Dave wasn't much of a dancer, but no one watched him when they danced anyway. All eyes were on Janis.

"As they say in the trade, my friend, you are in a pickle," said a gruff voice.

Dave looked up to see a short fire hydrant of a guy with a huge top hat. He wore a dusty sweater and vest, despite the June heat. He looked as if he hadn't shaved in a while. Dave guessed him to be about forty-five. "Pardon?"

"I couldn't help but overhear your predicament," said the man in the top hat.

"Yeah," said Dave, getting up to leave. He had no time for chitchat with strangers, and this guy looked like a pickpocket.

"You are trying to arrange for services, and no one is providing you satisfaction. That is a pickle. Allow me to introduce myself. I am Sugar Sam." He stood up and didn't seem any less compact. He put out a meaty hand for Dave to shake. "Sugar Sam to my friends."

"Sugar Sam?" said Dave, shaking his hand.

"Because I am going to get you a sweet deal. We're talking sweet." Sugar Sam smiled and revealed yellowing teeth and terrible fishy breath. He brought to mind a zombie Oompa-Loompa. "I know a girl."

"I have a girl. That's who I'm trying to get tickets for," Dave said as he turned to leave.

"Of course, you got a girl," said Sugar Sam. "But not like *my* girl. My girl can help you with your pickle."

"My pickle?"

"Whose pickle if not yours? Here." Sugar Sam handed Dave a stained piece of paper with an address scribbled on it. "And you pay her in cash. I get my cut from her later."

Dave stood up straighter. "You mean she can get me into *Got Tu Go Disco?*"

"If that's your pleasure."

Dave thanked Sugar Sam profusely and ran off. Things like this never happened to him. And certainly not in the city. In the city, people tried to take advantage of you, not help you out of a pickle. Dave decided that Sugar Sam was more like a city leprechaun.

Three Hours Until Curtain

The office was in the back of a bodega that looked as if it had been put up five minutes before. Dave arrived after running a few blocks and getting lost for several more. He'd checked the address again to make sure. He checked his wallet for the third time to make sure the cash he needed was there but also to make sure his wallet was still there. He didn't like the look of this neighborhood.

The young girl behind the bodega register, lost in some teen magazine, nodded her head, beckoning Dave to knock on the door at the back of the shop. The things he did for

Janis. A woman answered the door and stared into Dave's eyes. She was in her twenties, thin and athletic from what Dave could tell, and wore a denim shirt, denim vest, and jeans. A denim bandana was wrapped around her head. She continued staring without saying a word. She smelled vaguely of lavender.

"Um, Sugar Sam sent me," said Dave. "I don't know how this works."

She invited him in and closed the door behind him. It was a shabby office in a small room, with a small desk, a closet, and a large couch. The window had a gravy-brown film that looked like it hadn't let in sun in more than twenty years.

"I am Brilda," she said with an unplaceable accent. "And you have money for me?"

"Oh, I see," said Dave. He fumbled for his wallet. "Sugar Sam said you could help me. I gotta go disco!" He laughed in hopes that it would make this transaction less awkward. "So you can help me?"

"Brilda help all who have money for her. So you tell Brilda what you need, yes?"

Dave managed to pull his wallet out. "I need two for to-night. *Got Tu Go Disco*. Whatever you have."

"I have the best. But first you tell me your name. I like to know who I am providing service to."

"Dave Wilson," he said, relieved beyond measure that he was going to be the hero after all. Plus, he would have a great story to tell when they got back home about pickles, leprechauns, and denim gypsy women.

"David Wilson," said Brilda, rolling the name around in her mouth like a Life Saver. She put out her hand to take his. Dave stuffed a twenty-dollar bill in her hand. She looked down at the money, then let go of his hand and turned around. She took off the denim scarf around her head and laid it out on the couch. She unzipped her vest.

It was the zipping sound that finally made Dave realize

what he had gotten himself into. How could he be so stupid? His friends had kidded him about stuff like this. This woman was a prostitute. A denim-wearing prostitute. With a name like Brilda, what else could she be? What kind of name was Brilda? Clearly it was a fake name. She might as well have called herself Slippery Sally. Before Brilda turned around, Dave opened up the office door and ran out, bolting past the confused bodega cashier girl.

Dave sprinted down the street, not sure of where to go next. He couldn't believe how easily he had been duped. A prostitute! Why a denim bandana? Why was he fixated on that? What would they say back home? This would do wonders for his law career. Or what if she was a cop? Her and that squat, creepy, gnome character. What was his name? Pepper Pete. No, wait. Sugar Sam. He'd heard about these sting operations. They were going to find him and arrest him. He continued running downtown, dodging others on the sidewalk. He was a fugitive from the law.

Two and a Half Hours Until Curtain

Dave was out of breath and couldn't run anymore. He saw an open bar and ducked in. It was a classic dive like those he had seen in the movies with the wraparound wooden bar. The place was crowded but everyone was oddly quiet. The bartender—hunched over a radio with the patrons leaning in, listening attentively—motioned to Dave to wait a moment. Dave found an empty bar stool, relieved to sit down.

Then it occurred to him. What if they were broadcasting an all-points bulletin newsflash to the citizens of New York? *Be on the lookout for a slightly dim-witted lawyer from Upstate New York who answers to the name of Dave, who is definitely not going to see a Broadway show with his fiancée tonight.* Could the authorities have organized a manhunt for him already? The broadcast ended, the customers resumed their chatter. Clearly, whatever was on the radio had lost their attention. Good, thought

Dave. Maybe they wouldn't turn him in after all.

The bartender came over to take Dave's order.

"What was that you were all listening to?" said Dave.

"You didn't hear?" said the bartender. "It's the *John Hour*. Can you believe what they're broadcasting? Freakin' *John Hour*."

"What is that? A show about fixing toilets?" said Dave.

"Here," said the bartender, sliding over the *Daily News* to Dave. "Be my guest."

Dave scanned the article. Mayor Koch was requiring WNYC, the city-owned public station, to read the names of all men who had been arrested for soliciting prostitution that day. Koch intended to use this public shaming, dubbed the *John Hour*, as a tool to reduce prostitution. The broadcast was scheduled to go live at six. Dave checked his watch. It was a few minutes after six. Everyone at the bar had just been listening to the list of names.

"Why did they stop listening?" Dave asked the bartender.

"They're just keep repeating the same nine names over and over. That's how they're filling an hour. Can you believe this sleazy city?"

Dave started shaking. He asked if the bartender could bring over the radio. He cautiously put his ear to the speaker, knowing that the entire broadcast was insane, some sort of practical joke. But he heard the WNYC radio station manager run through the list of names alphabetically. After eight names were read, the radio station manager announced, "David Wilson," and started from the top again.

Two Hours and Fifteen Minutes Until Curtain

"I'll have the tallest scotch legally sold in the city," said Dave to the bartender. Later, he wouldn't be able to recall how big the glass had been or the volume of single malt Highland scotch it had held. It was not in front of him long enough. Three deep pulls from the glass and the scotch had settled in his belly. The bartender took away the glass swiftly, knowing a repeat customer when he saw one. By his third drink, Dave was calm enough to try and salvage what remained of his dignity. He had at least stopped shaking.

He took stock of his life. Now this: this was a pickle. His reputation lay in tatters, flapping in the wind like yesterday's sandwich wrapper. Word of this would certainly spread quickly. This was the crazy kind of story that the rest of the country loved to repeat. The filth and brazen politics of New York City would certainly titillate everyone. And it was easy to imagine that the names of the nine johns would be included in the story. How could he ever go back home? How could he show his face to Janis or her dad? Who would believe he was innocent? Yes, he had given Brilda the money, but no services had been exchanged. Wouldn't a jury see his side of the story? He was so screwed.

Then a thought occurred to him and he slipped off his barstool. The broadcast had reported that nine johns had been convicted. He had never gone through due process. Which meant one thing: Earl had something to do with this. Earl had somehow mixed up Dave in this fiasco. Maybe Earl didn't like the idea of his daughter marrying a small-town country lawyer. Maybe this was a gambit to try and break them up. Well, goddammit, things weren't looking great for ol' Dave right now. And he could kiss any marriage prospects goodbye if he didn't unravel this Gordian knot fast!

He was supposed to be meeting Janis in forty-five minutes. In that time, he had to avoid the wrath of Earl by not being arrested, prove his innocence, and still find the damn tickets to the damn show. He didn't know why it was still so important to him to get the tickets. He supposed that running around Manhattan, looking for two on the aisle for the last performance ever of *Got Tu Go Disco* was the least insane thing he could do today. He paid for his drinks and asked the bartender for some change. He dropped a dime into the pay phone in the back of the bar. WNYC's line was busy. He waited a few minutes and tried again. Still busy.

Dave left the bar a bit wobbly but still vertical. As he stepped out into the bright sunlight of a late June afternoon, a crosstown bus stopped in front of him. He asked the driver if the bus was going in the direction of WNYC. The bus driver told him to get in. Dave would have to transfer to another crosstown bus, but he could be there shortly. It was the first thing that had gone right all day.

Dave sat on the crowded bus, feeling the heat of everyone's eyes on him. Clearly, everyone had heard the broadcast, which had been invariably followed by photos of the nine perps. He buried his head in a discarded newspaper, hoping the angry mob wouldn't recognize him and pounce.

Two bus rides later, Dave stood in the lobby of the WNYC radio station. He approached the young receptionist, who appeared enthralled with a paperback novel and didn't look up when he said hello. Finally, frustrated by this interruption, she glanced up at Dave.

"I'd like to speak to the station manager," said Dave.

"You can't," said the young woman with a nasal pitch that spoke of future deviated septum surgeries.

"I most certainly can and will," said Dave. "I want a complete retraction broadcast..."

"Station manager quit. Just walked out right before you got here."

"What?"

"It was that *John Hour*," said the receptionist. "The whole crew up and quit. They're re-running an old pledge drive with Beverly Sills."

One and a Half Hours Until Curtain

Bigelow's was an old cosmetic shop that had avoided the trends of time. It was still handsomely appointed with mahogany columns, a second-floor wraparound balcony that could be accessed by a sliding brass spiral staircase, and staff in white lab coats. Thousands of bottles shimmered in the light, giving off the glow and aura of a child that had been produced by the mating of a chemist and a lighthouse.

Dave couldn't find a cab and had taken a bus to Bigelow's from the radio station. He wandered up and down the aisles of pharmaceuticals, unguents, and lotions, craning his neck over the top-shelf displays, looking for Janis. Finally, he spotted her in front of an elaborate arrangement of old-fashioned foot cream. She was barefoot.

He approached her cautiously in case the cops were hiding, ready to spring forth from the perfume aisle. She saw him and smiled. "You'll never believe what happened," she said.

"I'll see your mishap and raise it," said Dave, kissing her. It lifted his spirits to be with her again. They never should have gone their separate ways in the city.

"I couldn't find a cab so I walked here. Sixteen blocks, I walked here. My poor feet."

"Oh, honey," said Dave, consoling her.

"One shoe broke and the other started hurting like hell. I didn't pass one shoe store. So a lady in the back said she would try to fix my shoes. And here I stand contemplating foot cream. It's been a horrible afternoon. How was yours?"

"Fine," said Dave.

"I don't trust a new pair of shoes in the city anyway. Too uncomfortable breaking them in. I need good shoes for disco dancing." She started toward the back of the store where the cashier waited for her behind the counter. The cashier handed Janis back her shoes. The left heel was broken and swung menacingly on a hinge of leather.

"I'm sorry, miss," said the cashier. "But she couldn't fix the shoes. No tools in the back. I have some glue as a temporary fix." She handed Janis a half-filled, lumpy tube of glue.

"Gotta love the city," said Janis to Dave as she repaired her left heel.

"It's not for the meek. Maybe we should just head back home?"

"That's what I was thinking," said Janis as she headed out to the street. Dave was overjoyed.

"So we'll grab a train out of Grand Central?" said Dave

"What? No. My dad's apartment. We can grab a cab there, and I can borrow a pair of my mother's shoes. Five years divorced and the woman still keeps clothes at his place." She walked to the street corner and stuck out her hand to hail a cab.

Nervously, Dave followed her to the corner, shielding his face from the street as cop cars drove by. He was hoping reporters wouldn't suddenly lunge out from behind the hot dog cart. No cab came so they walked a block very slowly, Janis favoring the unbroken but uncomfortable shoe. They waited at the next corner. Dave felt like a sitting duck.

A man in a shabby overcoat passed them and noticed Janis sticking out her hand.

"Hey, lady, don't you know there's a cab strike going on? Cabbie ain't coming to pick you up now." He proceeded on his merry and sober way.

"This city," said Dave, shaking his head, hoping to convince Janis that Upstate New York would clearly be the best bet. Although he knew humiliation awaited him there too. Janis asked Dave for a dime and went into the phone booth on the corner, closing the door behind her.

A minute later, she walked over to Dave who had buried his head in the newspaper, hoping to avoid detection.

"No answer at my dad's. But I called a friend I know for a ride. I can't walk anymore, even to the bus stop."

Dave nodded, still invisible behind the paper.

One Hour Until Curtain

A 1967 rusty station wagon sputtered up to the curb and honked its horn. The driver, vaguely seen through the filthy windows, appeared to be motioning Dave and Janis to step in.

"You didn't," said Dave.

"What other choice do we have?" said Janis, opening the back door and climbing in.

Dave hated Janis's old boyfriend, Reed. Reed was a leftover hippie living as if it were the sixties. He tooled around town in his station wagon, selling weed and trying to score tickets to the next Woodstock. As a sideline, he followed the Grateful Dead around the country and sold crossword puzzles to the other Deadheads before and after their concerts. The answers to the puzzles were always words that Jerry Garcia had used the week prior.

"There's room for you up here, baby," said Reed to Janis. Then Reed noticed Dave getting into the backseat next to Janis. "Who's the square, man? You a narc?"

"Reed, that doesn't even make sense. Dave is my fiancé. You know this. I told you on the phone."

Dave stretched out his hand. "Good to see you again, Reed."

Reed ignored him while the car idled. A car behind them honked their horn. "I thought you were joking, Janis baby. Didn't know you were actually gonna get hitched with the man over here," said Reed in a grumbling tone. He put the wagon into drive, and it lurched forward. "Still, Janis baby, you look fine."

"Reed, I appreciate the ride, but it's not going to happen," said Janis.

"What's not going to happen?" said Dave. He was distracted by his troubles but realized he really should focus on the car's driver.

"Sex," said Reed. "Sex with your old lady. She's saying she and I may not be getting it on."

"What?" said Dave.

"Reed, you're disgusting. It's not going to happen. Now

if you're going to be like this, you can just drop us off right here," said Janis. Dave heard the irritation in her voice and didn't like it.

"All right, all right," said Reed. "Jeez. Guy can't even pay a compliment to his former old lady. Now where we going?"

Janis gave him her father's address. "It's just a few blocks ahead and to the right."

Dave took a deep breath, grateful for a moment's peace.

"Everyone I know back home is talking about the show," said Janis.

"The show," said Dave, bolting up and hitting his head on the ceiling. "What show?"

"Hey, careful with the car, man," said Reed. "It's a classic."

"A woman sells disco clothes and hates disco music," said Janis. "Until her boyfriend takes her to the local dance club where she becomes the disco queen. Gotta love it."

"Sounds groovy," said Reed.

Thank God, thought Dave. It sounded like the polar opposite of the *John Hour*. "Speaking of," he said, trying to stall any further conversation until he could clear his befuddled mind. "Can we have some music?"

"Now you're talking my lingo, man," said Reed. "You're all right, man."

Reed turned the knob and the news came on. An irate editorial on-air panel was debating the aftermath of the *John Hour* broadcast. "Oh, this crazy story again," said Reed. "It's all anyone can talk about today."

"Turn it off!" Dave yelled.

"Wait," said Janis. "I don't know what's happening. I haven't heard this yet. Keep it on."

Reed's loyalties clearly lay with Janis, and so the broadcast continued unabated.

"This week's premiere of Mayor Koch's *John Hour* is still causing an uproar over the airwaves," continued the man with his editorial. "The public station, WNYC, was forced to broadcast the names of nine convicted customers of prostitutes. It was a shabby show, in no way redeemed by its brevity. City-employed announcers read the names over city-owned radio and television stations. And it was a mighty misuse of government power."

"That's horrible," said Janis.

"Horrible," agreed Dave, praying they wouldn't repeat the names of the johns. He prayed so hard, he felt as if his veins were going to pop out of his head.

"Yeah, I know what you mean, man," said Reed. "Want to come back to my place and get high?"

That frustrated look crossed Janis's face again. "No, we do not want to go back to your place to get stoned. Reed, stop the car right here. We'll walk the rest of the way."

There must have been something about Janis's tone that reminded Reed of his scolding mother, because he obediently slammed on the brakes. The car came to a screeching halt. Or maybe this was the way Janis always talked to Reed. Or maybe this was the way everyone talked to Reed.

"I'm so disappointed in you," Janis said to Reed as she stepped out of the car.

"Let me know when you're in town again and we'll party," said Reed, oblivious to her anger. "Later, narc man," he said as Dave slid across the backseat and out of the car.

Dave watched Reed's car pull away and was gratified at the sight. He turned around and saw Janis heading into the building in front of them. It was a police station.

Crap.

Forty-Five Minutes Until Curtain

"Hold on a minute," said Dave, grabbing Janis's shoulder. "Where are you going?"

"I need to sit down," said Janis. "My feet are killing me. I can't walk anymore. You know my feet are my livelihood."

Dave's mind raced as they stood outside the police station,

the pedestrian traffic growing every minute as rush hour approached. "Okay," he said. "You wait inside. You go in there and tell the desk sergeant who your dad is. They'll let you wait there, while I go get train tickets for us. Be right back."

"Train tickets?" said Janis.

"I meant theater tickets. You know, with all the hustle and bustle, I got confused. Theater tickets."

"You haven't gotten the tickets yet?"

"I did get them. Yes. How could I forget that?" said Dave, hoping she was buying what he was shoveling. "I have the tickets. How stupid of me. I meant shoes. I will go buy you a pair of shoes. Now you wait right there." And he took off down the street so as not to give her any more opportunities to question anything else about his day or his motives.

Thirty Minutes Until Curtain

Dave thought of just running off by himself. It would have been easy enough in New York City to take a train anywhere. And from there, an airplane to the other side of the world, where they had never heard of the *John Hour* and this damn mayor and his tyranny against innocent men.

But just two blocks from the police station, he stopped short of living out the rest of his life in Afghanistan. He thought of Janis and how, more than anything else, he wanted to be with her. If he left now, she would always think he was guilty. He had to go back and fight for her, to prove his innocence and win her back—after she found out what he had done. Even if *he* was completely mystified about what he had and hadn't done.

Dave scanned the street for some kind of sign. Something that would guide his next step. The sun finally went down and the street lights came on, and with the street lights, the neon store signs. And the sign that shone brightly right in front of him read Thom McAn. They had the same shoe store back home.

A few minutes later, Dave ran into the police station, clutching a box of size six sandals like a football.

"Dave," said Janis, getting up to meet him. She had been seated in the general waiting area. "You got me shoes." She wrapped her arms around him and kissed him with gusto and appreciation. "My hero."

It was the best part of Dave's day. He put his arms around her waist and whispered, "Let's get out of here."

His intent was to get her on a train heading home as soon as possible and never return to the city. He'd explain it all to her at some point in the next ten or twenty years. She happily followed him to the police station door.

"Hold it right there, mister," said a commanding voice from the back of the station.

Dave slowly turned around, putting his hands behind his back, wondering if they allowed conjugal visits at Rikers Island. A bear of a man in a crisp wool suit approached Dave and Janis. All the police officers stood at attention and stayed out of his way.

"Who do you think you are?" said the man to a now quivering Dave.

"I...I don't...I never..." was all Dave could manage.

"Trying to avoid your future father-in-law already?" said the man in a booming voice. His face broke out into a smile, which seemed to relax everyone but Dave. Dave and his sphincter muscles remained incredibly clenched.

"Oh, Daddy," said Janis.

"Nice to finally meet you, sir," said Dave after much effort. "I'm really looking forward to getting to know you. I love your daughter very much." He placed his suddenly small hand into the pot roast that was Earl's hand.

"That's good," said Earl. "Janis seems very happy to...."

"I'm sorry," said Dave. "But we have to go. Now."

"Why?" said Earl.

"Yes, why?" said Janis.

The police station was deadly quiet. There was a pause Dave would think of the rest of his life as "The Pause."

"We have tickets for *Got Tu Go Disco*," said Dave. "And we got to go see it."

Janis turned around and gave Dave another big kiss and hug. "Oh, honey. I thought you were kidding about having tickets. You found tickets! I can't tell you how excited I am!"

Janis kissed her dad on the cheek. "We'll see you after the show, Dad! Love ya."

Dave took Janis's hand and led her out of the station. They made it as far as the sidewalk.

"Hold it," said Earl.

Dave knew he was busted.

"Don't you know there's a cab strike going on?" said Earl. "I'll give you a lift."

Twenty Minutes Until Curtain

They chatted from the backseat, while Earl drove the few blocks to the theater district. Dave tried to keep it mostly to small talk. He still didn't know how he was going to break it to Janis that he didn't have tickets, or how he was going to avoid being arrested and prosecuted by Earl.

They sat in silence for a few minutes which delighted Dave. Then Janis said, "Oh, Dad, did you hear about this *John Hour* thing?"

"Hear about it?" said Earl. "Koch's office is going bonkers doing damage control. I know what I'll be doing for the next few weeks."

"What's that, sir?" said Dave, prepared to meet his maker.

"Making sure that the rights of those poor, stupid bastards are protected. Imagine being one of those guys who goes to a prostitute and gets his name read aloud to the public. It ain't right, I tell you."

"Dad, those men are scum."

"They may be scum," said Earl, "but they still got rights. What do you make of all this, David?"

Dave stared into Earl's eyes through the rearview mirror. "I think you're not going to arrest me, sir."

Janis and Earl laughed. It was a healthy, non-threatening laugh. Not the kind of laugh you laugh as you commit someone to jail. Dave almost wept with relief.

"You know, David," said Earl. "There's a job waiting for you in my office if you want to bring my Janis back into the city. I mean, you'd have to apply and all that, but the job is basically yours. Think about it."

"Thank you, sir. I will."

Earl dropped them off in front of the Minskoff. There was a small crowd smoking outside. Most of the ticket holders had already gone in. Giant closing banners ran diagonally across all the show cards and posters.

Dave shook Earl's hand, which didn't seem as monstrously huge as it had before. Janis kissed her dad goodbye.

"He's a good guy," said Dave.

"I always thought so," said Janis. "Got the tickets?"

Eight Minutes Until Curtain

Dave was at a complete loss as to what to do. He didn't want to disappoint Janis. Not after that nice family moment. But he was completely out of gas. His thoughts were interrupted by obnoxious laughter. Dave looked past the theater-goers milling about and saw that the laughter was coming from the box office. He made his way to the box office window.

Three uniformed teenagers, two females and one male, sat in the box office, beside themselves with laughter. They were in a very merry mood considering the theater where they worked would be vacant now that the show was closing. They were roaring with laughter, and it became apparent to Dave that they were drunk.

"Dave," said Janis catching up to him. "Give them our tickets so we can go in. The show's about to start."

Dave suddenly realized what the box office teenagers found

so amusing. They were laughing at the *John Hour* broadcast. Someone had taped the show, and the box office teenagers had gotten their hands on the tape. They were playing it over and over again on their tape recorder.

Three Minutes Until Curtain

"The *John Hour*," the broadcast began, interrupted by bellows of laughter from the teenagers. "…David Wilson." Followed by more laughter.

"David!" said Janis. "Did they just say your name? Is that why you've been acting so bizarre all day?"

"Janis," he said, taking two steps back and girding his loins. "How could I have gone to see a prostitute with everything else I've been doing today?"

Except he was lying. He might have gone to see a prostitute today. It was definitely something he might have done.

"David Wilson, what is going on?" demanded Janis.

"David Wilson?" said one of the girls in the ticket office. She wore a name tag that said Kimmy. "Like in the *John Hour*?"

"No," started Dave. "I…"

"We have your tickets," said Kimmy.

"My tickets?" said Dave.

"That's what was so funny," said Kimmy. "Guy on the radio had the same name as someone going to see this show. I mean, who goes to see a prostitute and then a Broadway disco show? That wasn't you on the radio, was it?"

"Of course not," said Dave, looking at Janis. "How did the tickets…."

"Lady named Brunilda or Brillo Pad or something dropped them off for you," said Kimmy.

"Brilda," said Dave. "So she wasn't a prostitute."

"Excuse me?" said Janis.

"Kidding," said Dave. "She's my ticket broker. Good old Brilda."

One Minute Until Curtain

Janis smiled, and they went in to see the show.

Which was awful. Realization-that-you-never-want-to-be-a-disco-dancer awful.

A month later, Dave and Janis were married.

Three months later, they moved into the city.

After one broadcast, the *John Hour* was discontinued.

A LOVE SUPREME

ACKNOWLEDGEMENT

Mildred Garrison was wiping down the counters of her coffee shop for the fifth time when she noticed she would be late for her blind date. She had owned Brew-Ha-Ha for seven years and had never closed early before tonight. Her back was aching by the time she topped off the last cup of coffee, rang up the last check, and said goodbye to her last customer of the evening. Then, she told her three employees they could go home early.

Her plan was to quickly scrub the kitchen and wipe down the counters so she had enough time to get ready for her date. She knew that the older she got, the more time she would need to make herself look younger. But the counter refused to give up its coffee rings, grease stains, and apple pie crumbs, and Mildred wiped down the counters again and again as the hours dripped by. When she was satisfied that there were no more germs, mold, or stains remaining, she wiped the counters one last time with a clean, soapy cloth just to be safe.

Mildred made sure the Closed sign was facing out onto Hickory Street and locked the coffee shop door. It was a beautiful summer night in Upstate New York. The sun was just going down and the air smelled fresh and clean. She drove her six-year-old car home, just a few miles away, and went up to her apartment to get ready for her date.

An hour later, she was back on the road, grateful that this was a late date. She was excited about being out late on a school night. She thought about her dating banter and what she might reveal about herself during the course of the evening. She checked her eyes in the rearview mirror at a red light and noted she needed to apply some more makeup when she pulled up at her date's apartment building.

Needing a confidence boost, Mildred called her ex-boyfriend from her car to ask for advice on how to behave on a blind date.

Carl answered on the first ring. "Hey, Mildred, you there yet?"

"Almost, Carl. I hate blind dates. I'm getting a really bad feeling in the pit of my stomach. Maybe I should just go home."

"Were you this nervous on ours?"

"It's been so long, I don't remember," she said.

Carl was Mildred's mailman. He had left an anonymous note in her mailbox asking for a date. Mildred, feeling lonely, agreed to meet somewhere public and during the day to be safe. She and Carl dated a few times, but it didn't go anywhere. They remained friends, but Mildred suspected that Carl was still interested in her romantically.

"Remind me again why you're going to this guy's apartment when you don't know him?" said Carl.

"I know, right? Strike one with this guy is him making me feel like an escort."

The silence on the phone reminded Mildred of the awkward situation she had gotten into by dating Carl. But he was always there for her, and Mildred felt that she needed that in a relationship. "Thanks, Carl."

"Call me when you get home," he said. "Take care of yourself." Before she could respond, he hung up.

Mildred's GPS told her she was a few minutes away from her destination. She thought about Carl and how the only days in her apartment building that weren't awkward any longer were federal holidays when there wasn't any mail.

She pulled up to the luxury condo building. She looked up

at the building as she got out of the car and handed her keys to the valet. She had only seen the condos from a distance since she seldom visited the best part of the city, with its great view of Onondaga Lake.

"Tyler McCoy," she told the security man who sat behind the polished walnut reception desk.

He looked at his computer screen and smiled. "Ah, yes," he said. "Mr. McCoy is waiting for you in 1208. Elevator's just to your right."

The security man smiled again, as if he had a secret that Mildred was insufficiently privileged to know. She rang the bell at 1208 and took a deep breath. She straightened her skirt and felt her hair to make sure it wasn't sticking up. The panic button app on her phone was open to automatically text Carl and the police in case things went awry. Help was just a button away.

The door opened and a handsome man about Mildred's age stood inside. He had broad shoulders that were accentuated by his suit. His hair was slightly gray, but Mildred noticed it was dyed to look less gray. He also had a mustache that made his face look pudgy. He seemed safe, but vain. "Mildred?"

"Tyler," she said, walking into the apartment. He took her coat and hung it in the closet while she admired the beautifully appointed room and its grand view of the city.

"Thank you so much for meeting me here," said Tyler. "Can I get you a drink?"

While Tyler went to the kitchen to make Mildred a gin and tonic, she sat on the loveseat and noted that they were quite alone. No staff. She kept her hand in her purse, her finger on the panic button of her phone.

Tyler returned and handed her the drink. He had a scotch in his other hand.

"This isn't your apartment, is it?" she asked.

Tyler slowly smiled and looked around. "What gave it away?"

"The furnishings. They're at least two decades old in their style. And you seem very fashionable."

"Bob told me you were very smart," said Tyler, sitting across from her on the couch. "You probably recognize me by now."

"Also," said Mildred, "there are photos on the bookshelf of a family and you are in none of them."

"That's Bob's family. You remember Bob."

Mildred stood up and put her drink down.

"Now before you freak out," said Tyler, "there's a reason for this. It's fine. Bob's out of town right now."

"Did you tell Bob to come to my coffee shop and ask me out on a date for you?"

"He said you were my type. He's a good friend."

"I think I'm going to leave," said Mildred. She said it in a way that she hoped sounded chilly and aloof.

"Now just wait," said Tyler, getting up. Mildred backed away, her finger still on the panic button. "I met you here because of them." He pointed his chin over toward the television.

"Them?"

"The paparazzi," said Tyler. "The media. They would love to get a glimpse of my social life."

Mildred took a step closer and looked into Tyler's eyes. "Wait. You're the guy. Now I know you. You're...."

"The Pajama King," said Tyler proudly.

"Yes!" said Mildred. "Oh my God! The Pajama King. All those bus ads and commercials. Tyler McCoy. The Real McCoy."

Tyler smiled and Mildred could see all his teeth were new. "I haven't used Real McCoy in a few years. I like Pajama King much better. Especially since I'm going global now."

Tyler owned a chain of pajama stores called Cozy Dozy that had just gone national. He still did his own commercials, which was part of Cozy Dozy's charm. He had grown into quite a local influence because he had kept all his manufacturing in Upstate New York. He was a popular public figure who had created hundreds of jobs. Mildred had just heard on the local news that morning that he was thinking of running for office.

The ice in her glass clinked as it melted a little. She sat back down. "So this wasn't exactly a blind date for you, was it?" said Mildred. "Bob probably showed you a picture of me and told you what I do?"

"Running a small business is hard work," said Tyler. "Nothing to be ashamed of. He tells me you started the business a few years back. Very nice." He got up from the couch and took a few steps toward her. "Do you mind?"

She nodded her head, and he sat next to her on the loveseat. "It's nothing like your business," she said. "I mean, where do you even get the idea for something like Cozy Dozy?" She moved a little closer to him and took her finger off the panic button.

"It's a long, boring story," said Tyler. "Short version is I came up with the concept, the design, and I just kept selling it until it became this huge thing." Tyler moved closer to her. "But enough about work." Tyler leaned in close enough that Mildred could smell his minty breath. "Are you hungry?"

"Starving."

The next morning, Mildred got to see the apartment's view of the city and lake in the sunlight. Tyler had gotten up a few minutes earlier and gone to the bathroom. She took a relaxing breath and stretched in bed.

Tyler had put on his Cozy Dozy pajamas. He got back into the king-size bed, rolled over, and patted Mildred on the hip.

"Oh my god!" Mildred screamed. "You're married!" She jumped out of bed and began dressing.

"What, what?" said Tyler.

"This morning it all came back to me. You do those

commercials with your wife!" Cozy Dozy commercials, she now recalled, always featured the Pajama King happily plugging the flannel loungewear he wore while standing next to his wife, the Pajama Mama. "I'm out of here," said Mildred.

"Stop with the high-and-mighty routine," said Tyler. "Of course you knew I was married. The moment I opened the door, you knew I was married. Who doesn't know me?"

"You're a shithead."

"A shithead you're going to have dinner with tonight. I come stocked with a lot of perks."

"You're disgusting."

"I don't see you leaving," he said.

"Does this work on the other women?"

"Let's focus on you and your future," he said.

Mildred stared hard at the magnificent view. She thought of her coffee shop and the back-breaking hours. After a respectful minute, she said, "Lifestyles of the rich and famous, huh?"

She stayed for dinner. And the perks. Tyler appeared both smug and surprised when she agreed to a second date.

From then on, they always met at Bob's apartment, although once he flew her to California for a Napa Valley wine tour. Tyler seemed very comfortable around her and she would have said she felt the same.

A few months later, Mildred rang his bell at the usual time. Tyler opened the door and smiled. "It's so good to see you," he said, taking her coat. "I've been filming a commercial and the hot lights made me so thirsty. I couldn't wait to have a drink with you...."

"I'm pregnant," said Mildred, flopping down on his couch.

Tyler froze. He looked at her, the welcoming smile slowly sunsetting away. "What?"

"You heard me, Real McCoy," she said.

Tyler poured himself a scotch and downed it. "You can't be pregnant," he said. "I'm married."

"I don't understand how your making a vow to another woman makes me infertile."

RESOLUTION

Tyler McCoy turned down his street in his vintage Audi, his heart pounding. He had already sweat through his undershirt and shirt. His phone rang. "Tyler, sorry it took so long to get back to you," said Bob.

"Bob, what the hell? How could you hook me up with this crazy woman?" As far as Tyler was concerned, he had been nothing short of a gentleman throughout this affair.

"Look, these things happen," Bob replied. "We'll take care of it."

"Well, they don't happen to me!" shouted Tyler. "I'm about to go global!" He pulled into his garage. His wife's garage space was empty. Thank God.

"Let me—" Bob began.

Tyler saw his wife's car pulling into the garage next to his. "I have to go," he said. He hadn't thought about how he was going to handle this situation with Grace. Their marriage was already tenuous at best. She had been a chemical engineer just starting her career when they married. When she failed to get a good job, Tyler swooped in—she was ripe for the picking, he'd thought. At the time, she had been happy not to worry about her career and concentrated on his instead. Tyler thought that was the way it should be anyway.

Over the years, Grace had yelled at him for demeaning her, but Tyler never saw it that way. She had a supporting role to fill in his life, and he was insistent that she perform it to the best of her ability. It was her obligation, after all. She was the Pajama Mama. She'd insisted on keeping her last name, Shepp, when they married. It had been her only act of rebellion.

Tyler hated Grace a little for giving up on her life so easily. She had endured a previous marriage where her ex had treated her badly. He'd left her cold when he saw an opportunity to trade up to a more influential woman, one who would ease his path to becoming a big-time attorney. Grace never had a bad thing to say about her ex. She always tried to see the good in everyone. Maybe she would be understanding about this matter with Mildred. Or Tyler would have to figure out a way to deal with Mildred so that Grace never found out. Or, failing that, he'd have to break it to Grace very gently and strategically. She owned half his company. Damn New York laws.

As Tyler climbed out of his car, the structure of a plan started to form. He'd get Bob to handle Mildred. Pay her off. He had paid Bob handsomely for jobs like this before, and he'd helped Bob out of a couple of jams as well. This way, Grace would never know what had happened and his life could continue to improve with his dutiful wife by his side.

"Why are you seeing that bitch?" Grace demanded, slamming the car door.

"Honey—"

"Don't bother denying it," said Grace. "I followed you today. I've been following you for the past few days. You're sleeping with her, for Christ's sake."

Shit. Tyler leaned against his car, hoping it would act as some kind of barrier. He saw his career imploding. His wife going public with his affair would ruin him. Down went his burgeoning political career. Down went his public persona as the family values guy. Down went his business that Grace would take in the divorce.

He thought of a way to calm Grace down, to make her think that this was all some kind of cosmic misunderstanding. His wife stalked furiously toward him, the heels of her boots making clicking sounds on the cement garage floor. She was taller than Tyler and could use that to her advantage when she wanted to. She had been told her whole life that redheads were crazy, and today, she was fully embracing the red-haired crazy. Tyler had never seen this expression of rage and determination on her face before. He had to keep the truth from her.

"Do you love her?" she asked.

"She's pregnant," he blurted out, suddenly scared for his personal safety and health.

"You're such an idiot. I mean, you think I'm stupid, but at least I stick to my role," she snapped. "Do you love her?"

"No," said Tyler, looking at the oily floor. "It was never love."

Grace walked past Tyler and into their house. He waited thirty minutes before following her. Inside, Grace was pacing the living room with a drink in her hand.

"I hate her," said Grace. She took another step toward Tyler, and he instinctively put his hands in front of his groin for maximum protection. "I hate that woman," she repeated. "She has to be stopped. She's gotten in your head. Messed up how you think. Tried to take you away from me. That woman has to be stopped."

"I know, she...wait, what?" Tyler's hands moved away from his groin.

"We have to get rid of her. I have to get rid of her. You can't be involved."

"Grace," said Tyler, confused. "You're angry. Hurt. Maybe you should..."

"I should what? Think about you in all this? Is that what you want?"

Who was this woman? Tyler didn't know, but he loved her more than ever.

"It's probably best if I'm not involved. Don't even tell me anything," said Tyler.

"I hate that woman," said Grace. Her demeanor had calmed, and Tyler could see she was plotting something.

"Wait," said Tyler. "I have a friend. He can take care of this."

"This is not the kind of thing you send in a man to do. I have to do this. Look at me. You're going to know I did this. And you will owe me for the rest of our lives." Grace stared at him, intensely calm. The ice in her glass clinked.

"I love you," said Tyler weakly.

"Sure you do. She deserves a slow death. Painful. Poison, maybe."

"Well, I'll leave you to it," said Tyler, starting up the stairs. "I can see you have a busy afternoon ahead of you."

In his bathroom, he looked at himself in the mirror and realized that Grace would never leave him. His career was on the rise and that afforded Grace the grand life she loved. This would help their marriage.

This was fantastic, he thought. Grace would resolve this little matter, grow ever closer to him, and be more beholden to him all at the same time. Cozy Dozy.

PURSUANCE

Mildred was in the middle of a desperate call to the police. It was late at night, about two weeks after she had told Tyler she was pregnant. Earlier, she had closed Brew-Ha-Ha and performed her ritual counter-wiping. Now, as she spoke to the police, she wiped her dining room table in slow circles.

"Why won't you believe me?" asked Mildred.

The sergeant on the line hadn't explicitly said he didn't believe her. He just kept asking her to repeat her story over and over again. It wasn't a complicated story.

"A few nights ago," Mildred repeated to the sergeant, "I closed my coffee shop and left work. I noticed this pungent smell around my car. I went to open the driver's door but there was a strange orange stain on the door handle. I'm a stickler about that sort of thing. Overly cautious. And the orange stuff had this weird smell."

"Look, it was probably—" started the sergeant.

"No, listen to me. I'll say it again. When I got home, that

same smell and orange oil was on my apartment doorknob too. And on my mailbox."

"And you think—"

"Isn't it obvious?" said Mildred in desperation. "Someone is out to poison me. I know that sounds crazy, but nobody I know would do this as a joke."

"Look, miss, there's nothing we can do right now. I'm sure no one is out to get you. If you see any unusual activity around your place, you be sure to contact us. Goodbye."

Typical, thought Mildred. Goddamn typical. She poured herself a glass of wine and had a few sips. She picked up the phone.

"Hello, Carl?"

"Mildred, are you okay?"

Mildred told her story to Carl. He understood immediately and offered help. He said he wasn't sure what he could do but it was clear to him that someone could be after Mildred.

"Thanks," said Mildred. It then occurred to her that Carl might have ulterior motives.

The next day Carl rang Mildred with an update. "The local postmaster owes me a favor," he said. "I convinced him to allow me to do a little light video surveillance around your coffee shop and apartment for a few days."

"You're the best," said Mildred.

The video surveillance would start the next day, right outside Brew-Ha-Ha, where Mildred parked her car, and at her apartment and mailbox.

Anthony, Grace's ex-husband, walked back into his well-appointed office where Tyler and Grace sat waiting for him. Anthony was wearing an expensive suit and looked as if he was prepared to argue in front of all the TV cameras in the world. Anthony always looked like that. Tyler and Grace were both fidgety, each for their own reasons. Tyler didn't like having to go back to Grace's ex for legal advice, but it was the safest way to secure this information and make sure it didn't go public. Bob had offered him some legal advice as well, but Bob was a business guy, and they needed criminal legal help. Anthony, at least, was loyal. Tyler suspected that Anthony still had a thing for Grace and might use this situation to his advantage somehow.

"Well, things are not good," said Anthony, sitting behind his desk. His leather office chair made a loud whooshing sound as air escaped the cushion. Tyler felt deflated as well.

"How bad is it, Anthony?" said Grace.

"Pretty goddamn bad. Look," said Anthony. He swung his laptop around so it faced them. "The document you're looking at is a lab report for three wipe samples collected from Ms. Mildred Garrison's car door handle, apartment doorknob, and mailbox. All were collected appropriately using standard protocols. The chain of custody and methodologies for sample collection and laboratory analytical procedures are impeccable."

"English, Anthony," said Tyler, his voice quivering; his usual bravado had been checked at the door.

"The lab report shows trace levels of batrachotoxin. We're talking orders of magnitude above safe levels."

"And this stuff is—" Grace began.

"Toxic. Poison. Really nasty stuff, too. Not acute poison. Not, you know, one whiff and you fall dead. No, this stuff is more chronic. Insidious. It slowly eats away at your organs over weeks until you die. And then, it's almost untraceable."

"Holy crap," said Tyler. "You're fucking crazy."

"Hey, it wasn't me who got that whore pregnant," batted back Grace.

"This toxin," continued Anthony in a businesslike tone, "is banned from this country. And for good reason. It's a really nasty customer. Now, Gracie—"

"It wasn't me. Come on, Anthony. You know I would never…."

Anthony swung his laptop around, clicked a few buttons, then swung it back to show Tyler and Grace a video. The surveillance video showed Mildred's car parked outside the Brew-Ha-Ha. Grace slunk into view. Though she wore sunglasses and had her red hair pulled tight in a bun, it was clearly her. She was carrying a plastic bag from which she produced a rag. She rubbed the rag over Mildred's car door handle, then stuffed the rag back into her bag and casually sauntered off.

The video lapsed to a few hours later, showing Mildred walking toward her car. She reached to open the car door, then stopped. She went back into her shop and returned with a paper towel, which she rubbed over the door handle. She brought the towel to her nose, then hurried back inside.

"Jesus," said Tyler. He saw his entire future slipping away.

The next surveillance video footage was outside Mildred's apartment where the same scene repeated itself: Grace and her rag, followed by Mildred smelling what Grace had left behind and running off.

The video ended, and a stunned silence pervaded the office. Finally, Anthony spoke. "As your counsel, I strongly advise you to speak to no one but me."

"Grace," said Tyler, "what were you thinking? You've ruined me."

"Oh, come on," said Grace. "You knew what I was doing."

"Never in my wildest dreams," said Tyler.

"Anthony," said Grace. "You know me. Isn't there some explanation we could use? Something we could say? Like it was a prank that got out of control or something?"

"Grace, you know I would love to help you out here. See you walk out of here a free woman. This chemical, well, I don't even know where you got it. But the jury will know that you're a chemical engineer and could have manufactured it yourself. It's been banned from this country. Legally banned. This is serious stuff."

"So now what?" said Tyler. "We make a deal and all this stays quiet? Pay a fine? Grace stays under house arrest? Something like that?"

"Not quite," said Anthony. "First, the police are coming to my office to arrest you, Grace. It will all be done quietly with no media around."

"Oh my God," said Grace. "This is like a fantasy for you, isn't it? For both of you."

"Grace," said Anthony. "This is a horrible situation for everyone."

"Only you, Gracie, could try and poison this broad and blame us for inconveniencing you," said Tyler.

"Tyler," said Anthony, "this isn't the time. I'll try to argue for bail and house arrest, but the chances are slim. The state prosecutor is really hot for this case. He's up for reelection, and besides being an attempted murder charge, this is also a chemical weapons treaty violation. We'll see how far we can push this."

The next day, with Grace sitting in the county jail, Tyler was having breakfast alone in his house when he got a call from Bob. "I'm so sorry for all this," said Bob.

"I know you are. At least it's just local. For now," said Tyler glumly.

"Don't worry," said Bob. "You've still got national appeal."

Tyler peeked through the blinds at his front lawn. The news vans and reporters were still camped there. Their numbers might have doubled overnight. Tyler thought he saw a news channel he didn't recognize. Probably some college station reporting on the freak show. He just needed to wait them out. This kind of thing flared up and died down as soon as the next news story broke. He was hoping for an airplane crash or a kid trapped in a well. That would be the best news for Tyler.

His business would suffer locally, but he hoped his out-of-state stores wouldn't be too badly affected. As for now, the

Pajama King would have to lie low. It wouldn't look good for the family values guy to show up to work or appear in his ads without the Pajama Mama. Maybe he could stick to print ads and they could Photoshop her in. He scribbled a reminder to ask his secretary about that.

It didn't take local reporters long to dig around and find Mildred. Locally, the story broke big that the Pajama King was having an affair with the coffee shop lady and had gotten her pregnant. There were protesters outside his office and local Cozy Dozy stores. He was a laughingstock, but at least the story hadn't made it out of the state.

Tyler buried his head in his pillow. How could he have been so stupid? He swore that he would never again marry a woman with a college degree. They thought too much. All that chemical engineering mumbo jumbo had scrambled Grace's head. She should have been happy just being married to him. She shouldn't have followed him to Mildred's that night. Now he was screwed.

A few weeks later, Tyler dragged himself over to the county jail for a meeting with Anthony. Grace sat in handcuffs, smiling. Anthony sat across from her in a new suit. Armed guards stood at the ready outside the small office. "Hello, Tyler," said Grace. "Nice of you to visit."

Tyler hadn't seen her since she'd been in jail. Too much publicity. Why throw gasoline on this dumpster fire? he'd thought.

"Anthony has good news for me," said Grace.

"Well," said Anthony. "I said there was progress. Good news always has bad news chasing it."

"I'm not in the mood for riddles," said Tyler. "What is it?"

Anthony looked at the two of them and took a breath. "Okay, the state has decided to drop the case."

Tyler fist bumped the table in jubilation. "That's fantastic!"

"Well, hold on there, Tyler," said Anthony. "The state doesn't want to prosecute. It would be bad politics. Your chain employs a lot of people. Other businesses are looking to move into the state. They think if they try this case, this story won't go away, and the state will become a laughing-stock. Bad for business."

"Great! So the story just goes away. And what, we just pay a fine?" Grace said, relieved.

"Sure," said Tyler, the reality hitting him. "After everyone found out I was having an affair. I'm still ruined."

Grace smiled. She looked as if she wanted to celebrate. "Oh, Tyler, it's not that bad. You're not the one with an arrest record."

"No," said Anthony. "I mean, it's good news that the state won't prosecute. But this doesn't go away. The federal court believes this case to be under their jurisdiction now. The chemical weapons treaty ban is a federal law. They want to prosecute Grace for deploying chemical weapons in viola-tion of this ban."

"What?" screamed Grace.

"That's ridiculous," said Tyler.

"You're being moved to a federal prison," said Anthony. "I'm sorry. I'll keep fighting."

Tyler sank further into his chair. "You mean this is going national after all?"

"I'm afraid so," said Anthony.

"That's impossible," said Grace. She looked clear-eyed and determined. "Those chemicals weren't really poison. I used non-toxic orange oil."

PSALM

The case was the most talked-about national news item that week. Every news channel and outlet was covering it. Even the BBC and Vatican radio couldn't get enough. Every day there was more air time dedicated to the story. A typical story started with one of the dozen ads showing the Pajama King and the Pajama Mama shilling for Cozy Dozy.

Over the commercial, a narration ran that usually started by covering the basics: the audio of the federal court hearings with Mildred accusing Tyler and Grace of trying to poison her and Grace denying it. The video would then be played, showing Grace rubbing the poison on Mildred's car door handle. Then there was the revelation that Mildred had, at one time, been a low-level designer at Cozy Dozy. That part of the story went nowhere, because no one could recall that Mildred had even met Tyler in her brief stint at his company. The narration would then switch gears, describing the manner in which the state court system was fighting to claim jurisdiction, since it was, after all, a local matter.

These media blasts went on for several months, in a heated cultural frenzy, until the Supreme Court had to decide both the federal-versus-states'-rights issue and the applicability of the chemical weapons treaty ban in this matter. The news stories usually ended with the solemn speculation that this case could result in the most important decision on the country's treaty power since the 1920s, when Justice Oliver Wendell Holmes presided over a case involving the shooting of game birds. Protesters on both sides grew in numbers each day, and the slogans on the signs they carried grew increasingly threatening.

Grace was transferred to the federal courthouse to await further testimony—the case was expected to be decided in the next few days. Tyler had booked himself into a nearby hotel, where he spent the afternoon watching cartoons, eating cheese puffs, and contemplating suicide.

Mildred climbed the steps of the federal courthouse. The building was grand, having been built in an optimistic era. After she got through the paparazzi and security, Mildred was escorted by an officer down a sickly beige hallway lit by fluorescent light. The only sound was the nervous clicking of her shoes as she approached the room where Grace was being held. The officer stopped at a steel door, without window or peephole. It was an imposing door, manufactured to scare off anyone who thought of opening it and releasing whatever evil lurked on the other side.

The officer turned to Mildred, asking her the same question he had asked her before she'd signed all those forms. "Are you sure about this, ma'am?"

"I'm sure," said Mildred.

The officer pushed a button on the intercom next to the door. He held up a badge with a barcode on it for the hallway camera to scan. After a series of clicks and the sounds of sliding metal bars, the door unlocked.

"You have five minutes," said the officer. "You're on camera. I'll be here the moment you signal me."

"Okay," said Mildred. Her voice was so soft and quiet that she hardly recognized it as her own.

Grace sat at a steel table that was bolted to the floor, her hands cuffed to a thick metal bar welded to the table. She looked as if she'd lost twenty pounds the hard way. She looked away from the door when it opened, staring at some dust bunny in the corner of the room. Mildred couldn't quite tell if Grace was scared or bored. She'd worn the same expression the first time she and Mildred had met. It had been the morning after her first date with Tyler. Mildred had driven over to Tyler's house after they'd said goodbye at Bob's apartment. She'd explained to Grace that she had been duped into thinking that Tyler was available. Grace had not been surprised by the revelation. She went on quite a tear. Tyler had been unfaithful before, she'd told Mildred. And that was just the one time Grace had known about. Grace had ranted aloud, plotting her revenge. Tyler was like all the other men out there, she'd raged. Mildred gave her a hug, and together, in the late morning on the back porch, they'd implicitly agreed to topple the patriarchy.

Grace and Mildred had gotten together several times that

week, bound by an oath of loyalty to get back at Tyler, to teach him a real lesson about the perils of using women. They wanted to expose Tyler as a hypocrite and reveal the hypocrisy of the system that supported him, and together they devised a scheme that would do it simply and easily.

With Grace's chemical engineering background and Mildred's penchant for OCD behavior, they formulated a plan in which Grace would use non-toxic chemicals on Mildred's doorknobs and mailbox, and she would be sure to be caught in the act. The resulting hubbub would catch the attention of the local media and Tyler's affair would be exposed. Tyler would be publicly humiliated and forced to step down from his position. Grace would cash in her half of Cozy Dozy and leave Tyler for good. Mildred wanted to topple the patriarchy, to take Grace's anger, multiply it a millionfold, and redirect it at all men. Grace had quickly gotten behind such a notion, but they had never expected things to spiral out of control so far, so fast.

Now, in the steel room with no windows, Mildred stared at Grace and Grace stared at the dust bunny in the corner, her wrists red from the handcuffs.

"I came to say goodbye," said Mildred. "I didn't mean—"

"Sure you did," said Grace, in a detached voice.

The officer came to escort Mildred away, the door slamming hard behind them. As Mildred walked back to her car, the paparazzi caught her every movement in the bright flash of photographic bulbs. She wore her sunglasses and tried to focus only on driving away, but she kept thinking about Grace's words. *Sure, you did.*

Did Grace know that Mildred had watched her? That she had watched Grace rub the non-toxic chemicals on the Brew-Ha-Ha doorknob, on Mildred's apartment's doorknob, and on her mailbox? That she waited for Grace to drive away each time and then had rubbed toxic chemicals on those very places? The same toxic chemicals that Carl had previously confiscated from the Postal Service Import Detention Center? Or had Grace discovered that Mildred used to be a fashion designer years ago? It wouldn't have been difficult to discover. But would that search have made Grace aware that Mildred had been the one to come up with the idea for the designer adult pajamas months before starting with Cozy Dozy? Or how Tyler, desperate to make his company successful, had gone through Mildred's design notebook at her work desk after she'd left for the night? Or how he had brazenly stolen her ideas and made them his own? And how he had not only never given her credit for the ideas or the resultant success of his company, but he had fired her for no damn good reason?

That was many years ago now. When Mildred had shown up for her blind date with Tyler, he'd failed his final test—he hadn't remembered her. Ultimately, she'd been nothing to him other than someone he could use. Mildred had felt the full force of his corruption that night and started to plot her revenge. Then she saw how crazed Grace was about getting even with Tyler, how her rage had built over years of humiliation, like pajama flannel that chafed one's thighs.

Ultimately, Mildred wanted control over Cozy Dozy. She considered that it essentially belonged to her, since its success was founded on her own designs. With Grace in jail and Tyler humiliated, Mildred would drop all charges if Tyler gave her ownership of the company. When she'd found out that Tyler's friend Bob hated Tyler almost as much as she did, she enlisted his help in putting the gears in motion.

Still, the thought of Grace spending the rest of her life in the federal penitentiary troubled Mildred. At most, she'd thought Grace would spend a few months in the local clink.

A few days after seeing Grace, Mildred's attorney called. The Supreme Court had made its decision. Mildred took a cab to her attorney's office, and together they watched CNN with the rest of the world. The Supreme Court unanimously decided to dismiss the case. The justices said that federal laws meant to prevent the international use of chemical weapons couldn't be applied to a woman who'd tried to poison her husband's mistress.

Mildred's attorney told her that as long as Grace spent six months in jail and Mildred dropped the charges, everything would be dismissed. Mildred told her attorney she would think about it. She then called Tyler. When he answered, she could hear the TV in the background.

"I want Cozy Dozy to be signed over to me," she said, "then I'll make all this go away. Otherwise, I will keep humiliating you in public with my pregnancy."

"I'm off to my press conference. Besides, you're not even pregnant," said Tyler.

"What makes you say that?" said Mildred.

"You're trying to bullshit a bullshitter," he replied. "And you don't get anything. Not the store, not me, not anything."

"I don't want you," she said, putting him on speaker. "You're right, Tyler. I'm not pregnant."

"Ha!" he said, vindicated. "You lost. You don't get anything, especially my company. This will all pass. People will forget this and keep buying my pajamas. In a few years, I can still run for office. Now if you'll excuse me…" He may have been a laughing stock, Tyler knew, but the Pajama King was still beloved. And men had built empires on less than that.

"I'm sending you an email," Mildred said. "Open it."

His press conference began ten minutes later. He had a prepared statement, but the press didn't want to hear it. What they wanted to talk about was the photo they'd received in an email from Mildred. It was a picture of Tyler sleeping naked next to Mildred. She wore the flannel pajamas that she had designed and sold under the Cozy Dozy brand.

"You're done," she thought to herself. "If I don't get the empire, no one gets the empire. The Pajama King has no clothes."

HAROLD DOESN'T DATE ANYMORE

Harold stood tall for his age. That's wwwhat everyone said. They also said that Harold's brain wwwas special after the wwwar. Harold didn't remember much from before the wwwar. Harold prized tidiness. Harold prized organization. Harold prized predictability. The only thing Harold thought special about Harold wwwas that he liked to speak of himself in the third person.

After the wwwar, Harold lived alone in his parents' basement. He spent all his time on his computer. Harold had amassed a considerable Matchbox collection through eBay. Modern life allowed Harold to exist outside the social fabric by earning his keep through Internet transactions. Harold chose to live wwwith minimal human contact and had made enough money over time to even purchase his prized possession: a green Matchbox 1973 AMC Gremlin wwwith a wwworking sunroof.

One day Harold decided to get a girlfriend online. Harold had never had a girlfriend before. Harold ordered a pleasant-looking lady through a reputable internet site that had 187 positive user reviews. The lady introduced herself as Laredo and shared a photo of herself with Harold. She had curly brown hair. She had bumpy bits that momentarily made Harold stop thinking about his green Matchbox 1973 AMC Gremlin wwwith a wwworking sunroof. Harold asked her to come over every Friday night.

Each Friday night, Laredo came over and sported Harold

after she swiped his credit card. Once, Harold explained to her about his Matchbox car collection. He told her that his Matchbox car collection had been appraised for $100,000.

One night Laredo asked Harold if she could sleep over. Harold said he had never had a sleepover before. Harold decided it was okay, as long as she didn't touch Harold's Matchbox car collection. They lay closely together, because Harold had only a twin bed. Harold liked the smell of her breath wwwhile she slept.

Harold awoke the next morning and couldn't find Laredo. Also, Harold couldn't find his green Matchbox 1973 AMC Gremlin wwwith a wwworking sunroof. On Laredo's pillow wwwas a note. Harold picked up the ransom note that Laredo had left him. The note said that Harold's green Matchbox 1973 AMC Gremlin wwwith a wwworking sunroof might be returned to him at the state fair in one month in exchange for $100,000. The note also said not to tell his parents or to call the police. Harold decided that Laredo's sweet breath wwwhile she slept had turned to dragon fire wwwhen she wwwoke up.

Harold memorized the note and then ate it. He needed his green Matchbox 1973 AMC Gremlin wwwith a wwworking sunroof back and felt compelled to follow the instructions on the note.

It wwwas a difficult month for Harold, but he wwwaited as he had been told. One month after Laredo's breath had turned to dragon fire, Harold arrived at the state fair. He had not been out in public in a long time. He had never seen so many people. His first backpack held the $100,000, which he had made from selling his Matchbox car collection and some savings bonds. His second backpack contained his travel belongings.

Harold didn't know wwwhere to go once he got to the fairgrounds; the ransom note didn't specify a location. People always made fun of Harold and how Harold presented himself to the world. Some people even asked if Harold belonged in the sideshow. Harold just kept looking for his green Matchbox 1973 AMC Gremlin wwwith a wwworking sunroof. Harold investigated the midway, the tractor pull, the magic show, and the lumberjack competition. The entire time Harold avoided eye contact with the throngs of people who crowded the fairgrounds and thought about the shiny upholstery in the tiny sunroof that flicked open and closed on his green Matchbox 1973 AMC Gremlin. Harold had flicked the sunroof open and closed 2,078 times since he had owned it.

Finally, Harold wwwas exhausted and decided to sit down on the crowded metal bleachers of the mid-sized oval arena wwwith everyone else to see the daredevil motorcycle show. There wwwas loud music, a bang, and a billow of smoke. The biker appeared in the arena and drove his motorcycle through a ring of fire. Harold couldn't see the biker's face because of the helmet. Everyone cheered, but Harold kept looking in the crowd for Laredo and his green Matchbox 1973 AMC Gremlin wwwith a wwworking sunroof.

A curtain rose in the middle of the arena and the biker revealed 12,000 Matchbox cars all lined up in twelve rows of 1,000 Matchbox cars each. A motorcycle ramp had been set up for jumping at each end of the cars. Harold immediately stood up, scanning the 12,000 Matchbox cars lined up in twelve rows of 1,000 Matchbox cars for his green Matchbox 1973 AMC Gremlin wwwith a wwworking sunroof. Harold thought that he should have brought his binoculars in his second backpack. Harold grew nervous that his green Matchbox 1973 AMC Gremlin wwwith a wwworking sunroof might be one of the cars in the mid-sized oval arena. If the biker didn't make the jump, he might land on Harold's green Matchbox 1973 AMC Gremlin wwwith a wwworking sunroof.

The crowd cheered and finally sat down. They wwwere

all giddy and saying that something great wwwas going to happen. Someone told Harold to sit down. He called Harold by the wrong name. Harold turned around and said that his name wwwas Harold, not Rain Man. Harold sat down and tried to calm himself. He counted the Matchbox cars and calculated the average number of treads on the type of tire for those cars if they had been full-sized, multiplied the number of cars by four, and then multiplied that number by the number of treads to get the total number of treads in the arena. Harold added the treads on the motorcycle. This exercise helped calm Harold down. Also, the arena was an oval shape, wwwhich reminded Harold of eggs and Harold liked eggs.

The biker's motorcycle roared as it made a wwwheelie and approached the ramp. Suddenly, the biker appeared to be suspended in mid-air. Harold blinked his eyes quickly to make the motorcycle go faster, as if it wwwere in a movie. Harold held his breath and kept blinking. Finally, Harold put his fists over his eyes.

The crowd around him started cheering. Harold opened his eyes. The biker made it over all the cars and landed hard on the ramp but started spinning out of control toward the wwwooden fence that held a giant sign for an insurance company that read, "Life Got You Down?" The motorcycle crashed through the wwwooden fence with the giant sign for an insurance company that read, "Life Got You Down?" and straight into the chicken coop. The biker's helmet had flown off during the crash. Everyone grew quiet, and then stood to see if the biker had been hurt. Harold wwwondered momentarily if life had gotten the biker down.

And then the biker slowly rose to his feet, wwwiped the chicken coop poop off his boots, and smiled for the first time. The crowds cheered even louder. Harold banged his fists on his ears and squinted his eyes to try and make them stop. After all the camera flashes died down, Harold opened his eyes long enough to get a good look at the biker. It ww-was Laredo.

Harold shook his hands at her but she didn't see him. Harold tried to run down to the egg arena floor to find his car, but the crowds held him back. It took Harold half an hour to get to the egg arena floor, but by then all the Matchbox cars had been removed to make room for a hedgehog that rode a horse and did tricks to the tune of a polka song that Harold didn't know.

Laredo stood behind a rope and two large cowboys stood next to her. People stood in line to get Laredo's autograph. Harold got in line. Harold rocked back and forth. Harold's groaning got so loud that people in line asked him to stop. Next door they wwwere selling honey from a local farm. Someone poured honey on his hair wwwhile he wwwas in line, and everyone laughed. Harold didn't care.

Harold's turn came up. Harold ignored the two large cowboys. Harold handed the first backpack containing the $100,000 to Laredo and asked for his green Matchbox 1973 AMC Gremlin wwwith a wwworking sunroof. She told him that the car remained hidden somewhere on the fairgrounds. She grabbed the backpack containing the $100,000, turned around, and left. The two large cowboys didn't let Harold follow her.

Harold wwwalked away wwwhere there wwwere no people. He saw a big tree wwwith some shade and decided to go there and think this through. He hoped he wwwouldn't step in any chicken coop poop. All the wwwhile, Harold groaned. He sat under the tree in the shade and rocked and groaned. Harold's groaning became louder. He didn't know wwwhat to do. He could have stayed there forever except for the...

BEES!

The bees flew around Harold's head, attracted to the local honey, which someone had poured on his head. Harold started to run frantically in one direction, then the other. Despite wwwhat the doctors had told him, Harold knew he remained fatally allergic to bees. There were thousands of bees. Harold kept running but some of the bees followed him. Harold escaped into the dairy exhibition building. The bees stayed outside.

Harold stopped as soon as he saw the rotating butter sculpture inside a giant refrigerated display case. The sculpture stood ten feet tall and portrayed a cowgirl swinging a lasso in her right hand and holding a Colt .45 revolver in her left. He remembered his gun training during the wwwar. Harold knew immediately that his green Matchbox 1973 AMC Gremlin wwwith a wwworking sunroof lay inside the butter Colt .45 revolver. Harold's wwwar training told him that the butter Colt .45 revolver trigger needed a metal base to support it, and only the flipping action of the sunroof of a green Matchbox 1973 AMC Gremlin could provide that support. And he knew that Laredo had placed it there for Harold to find. And he knew how to get it.

Harold took his scissors out of his backpack and found the bathroom. He cut off all his hair so as not to attract any more bees. Then Harold found the sideshow exhibit. The large clowns let him past the rope for the sideshow performers. Harold hid behind the sideshow dressing room until dark. Once everybody had gone, Harold sneaked back into the dairy exhibition building and over to the butter sculpture. The refrigerated case had been left on all night, so the butter sculpture stayed cold.

Harold found a ladder, pried open the refrigerated case, and climbed up until he stood next to the butter Colt .45 revolver. Harold reached into his backpack and took out six pieces of toast and a butter knife. He scooped up some butter, spread it on the toast, and ate it. He repeated this five more times until the toast was gone. Harold thought of the egg arena and thought it wwwould be nice to have hard-boiled eggs with the buttered toast. Harold liked eggs.

Dan Kopcow

When he was finished, Harold could see the green Matchbox 1973 AMC Gremlin wwwith a wwworking sunroof wwwithin the butter crater he had made in the statue's hand.

Harold heard someone knocking on the dairy exhibition building door.

He snapped off the statue's hand and began to lick off the rest of the butter. Harold heard the door open. Harold swallowed his green Matchbox 1973 AMC Gremlin wwwith a wwworking sunroof and put the remainder of the butter hand holding the butter Colt .45 revolver back on the butter cowgirl. By this time, it wwwasn't so much a hand as a butter mitten.

Harold jumped down and ran out the other door, avoiding people as he made his wwway out of the fairgrounds. He took a bus home. WWWhen he got there, he swallowed medicine that wwwould make him poop out his green Matchbox 1973 AMC Gremlin wwwith a wwworking sunroof. As he sat rocking on the toilet, looking at his empty Matchbox car collection display case, Harold swore that he wwwould never date again.

But he wwwas definitely having eggs for breakfast.

MAC AND CHEESE

"Don't be such a dork, April," I said. "Take a drag."

"Jane," responded April. "You're my devil."

If peer pressure were an event, I was training for the Summer 1979 Olympic Gold. Smoking pot was a well-practiced hobby of mine. In fact, there was a fine line between hobby and habit. But as most girls my age will tell you, you want to moderate your high-itude when there are cute boys around. We were at the Wall. It was where we spent every summer night. The group was made up of twelve regulars, who were mostly girls, along with varying hangers-on, cousins, and friends staying with family for a week or two.

One of the new boys was Eddie. He had just moved in next door to my best friend, April. He was seventeen and killer cute. No disco haircut for the manly Eddie. A shock of slicked-back black hair graced his heavenly head. He smoked and strutted with the assurance and confidence that only comes with complete acceptance of one's place in life. And I wanted his place to be with me.

I knew he liked me as soon as we met. He sat on the Wall with his muscular legs dangling, swinging, and occasionally brushing my bare arms with his own. I leaned against the Wall next to him, partially to be near him and partially to support myself in my half-drunk, half-high, and full-on love splendor. April hadn't told me much about him. She didn't have to. I was at the age when a boy's cuteness was sure to land him the job during the interview.

I took stock of these visiting tourists. I couldn't imagine coming here for a family vacation. How bad did home have to be to come here voluntarily? Hicksville was in the middle of Long Island, a one-hour train ride into the city. Overall, it was working class, dreadfully dull, and devoid of adventure. Admittedly, I was biased. I lived with an adoptive family who didn't care much for me and my ways.

Later I found out that April had told Eddie a bit about me—I was sixteen, had been smoking for eight years, had enjoyed smoking for seven of those years, was still a virgin, grew up in this small town, had a tight circle of friends, and lived with my adoptive family. April also told him that if he hurt me, my friends would kill him.

Truth is that my friends wouldn't hurt a fly, let alone bash the brain of some horny, pot-smoking, Mott-the-Hoople-listening, vacationing molester. But Eddie didn't know that. He'd just come to the Wall because he'd heard he could get high and maybe get lucky. That's why we all came to the Wall. It was a rite of passage in the eight-block radius of my neighborhood. Kids had been coming to the Wall for years to take this adolescent sacrament. Even calling it "the Wall" was indicative of our desire to make our lives more dramatic and decadent than they really were.

The Wall had been built by Mr. Dietrich years ago. Mr. Dietrich had lived at 82 Wrightsborough Street all his life. He was a farmer who grew only debt. He came into some money through an inheritance from some distant relative. He sold the farm at a loss and disappeared into his house, a bitter, ailing, and wealthy male spinster at sixty-three. His house was eventually joined by other houses as his fields were bought and subdivided by developers.

The townsfolk only saw or heard from old Farmer Dietrich once a year, when he'd walk to the bank for some presumably important transaction. Maybe he was gone for months at a time. No one knew or much cared.

Dietrich's house was set back from the street. In front of the house stood a short, crudely built wall made up of old stones turned up by Dietrich's till. Dietrich had gathered the stones years ago and built a single wall that was three feet high and about thirty feet long. It served no purpose other than to forewarn all passersby that here lived a hostile and slightly irrational coot.

Dietrich had been a terrible farmer, but when he planted his Wall, he finally grew something that flourished perennially: teenagers.

When it got dark, we knew instinctively to collect at the Wall. It acted as a silent beacon for our restless souls. It was where our evening plans were made and where our evenings ended. Drinks were poured, cigarettes smoked, pot inhaled, kisses traded, dreams shared, music played, and lives planned. In short, it was the coolest spot in the world.

When things got dull, we constantly dared each other to sneak up to the dark house behind us and peer into the front window. Whoever discovered Dietrich's decaying body— doubtless in the kitchen on the floor with a broken bottle of rye in his withered hand—would become a Wall legend for the rest of his or her life. No one had been brave enough or relished that kind of fame, however. We feared we would peak at sixteen and the rest of our lives would be a depressing downhill sprint.

Eddie's leg, still dangling from the Wall, brushed up against my bare shoulder again. I hadn't decided yet whether he would be the First One. It was an important decision. Since last Tuesday, it was all I could think about.

That morning I had woken from a sleepover at my friend Suzie's house, and we had a long talk about boys. Suzie told me she was going out with Billy Dylan. Billy lived down the street from Frankie Mulligan, a boy on whom I'd had a crush since second grade.

At the beginning of the summer, Frankie had promised to go out with me but assured me he wasn't interested in sex and wanted to wait. Listening to Suzie's graphic details,

I decided then and there that I wanted to try sex. And be really good at it. It was as if I'd sat down at the school lunch room day after day, and the whole table was eating mac and cheese. And I'd never had mac and cheese. I'd heard about it. My friends were always talking about how good it was, how comforting and easy it was. Now I wanted to try it. And I wanted to try the instant kind—devoid of nutrition, probably forgettable, and not as good as homemade.

So I was at the Wall, smoking a cigarette, debating with myself as to whether this Wall visitor, this Eddie, would be my first mac and cheese. I dragged deeply on my cigarette while the minutes loudly clicked by in my head. By ten o'clock, quite a crowd had gathered. Some of the older kids were making plans to train it into Manhattan and hit some nightspots.

Suddenly, a police car turned down the street. We all ducked behind the Wall, which was, after all, the purpose and prime benefit of the structure. The neighboring houses were far enough away that we never bothered them with our noise. Dietrich's neighbors knew our parents and either decided to look the other way, possibly remembering when they were our age hanging out at the Wall, or simply couldn't make us out through the haze of smoke and long hair that encapsulated us.

Eye level with the gravel behind the Wall, I heard some giggling as we waited for the police car to drive by. Somebody whimpered as a lit cigarette burned their hand. A long shadow, silhouetted by the cop car's lights, stretched across the ground. It was the figure of someone still sitting on the Wall. I slowly looked up, my body pressed flat to the ground, and saw Eddie's back, high and oblivious, on the Wall.

"Eddie," I whispered. No response. I whispered his name several more times, wondering if that was really his name.

Okay, I thought, no mac and cheese for Eddie, thank you very much. What if we were enjoying some spirited bonking, and he was just as clueless as to where he was and what he was doing? I couldn't let my first mac and cheese be with some oblivious-to-the-cops Wall sitter. No way.

Beside me, April reached up and grabbed the back of Eddie's shirt, pulling him off the Wall like a ventriloquist putting away his dummy. The rest of the night was difficult to forget. As we all hunkered down behind the Wall, a light flickered on behind us and shone down on all of us. The light came from Dietrich's porch. To say we were utterly shocked and surprised would be an understatement.

We were trapped between that unexpected light and the Wall. The air suddenly felt very hot and sticky. I imagined the authorities on the other side setting up a well-organized SWAT team, and felt like a teenage deer caught in Dietrich's porch light. It occurred to me that the police had been consulting with Dietrich for years, conspiratorially advising him to keep his porch light off in order to better monitor us, record our action; and they doubtless suggested that he should avoid movement in the house, and limit public appearances to once a year so as to avoid suspicion and lull these marauding kids into a false sense of security.

The cops had been waiting years for the moment when Operation Bag-the-Wall-Stoners would commence, and we would all be caught in a carefully constructed sting. We would be put behind bars, our parents and guardians humiliated, parole denied, our young futures ruined. Forget mac and cheese. No high school graduation or college for me. No marrying Shaun Cassidy and having three kids and living in London, as they did in the PBS movie I'd seen the previous week. No, instead I'd be one of those short-haired prison ladies who dress only in gray, wear no makeup, and shuffle along with an empty tray to the cafeteria for the rest of my life.

Admittedly, I was a bit of a worrier when I was high. Maybe the situation was exaggerated in my head? I took stock of my surroundings as objectively as I could. A police car was driving toward us in a slow and deliberate manner. Old Farmer Dietrich's porch light had come on for the first time since pterodactyls had flown overhead. Eddie was lying next to me. I took a good look at him. He was concealing a badge pinned under his shirt.

Shit! And a gun in his holster. Double-shit!

"He's a narc!" I yelled. "Eddie's a goddamn narc!"

All my friends ran for their lives, scattering in every direction. Their headlong rush attracted the attention of the police car, which sped off in pursuit. I looked past Eddie to those of us still behind the Wall, hoping to elude the police by staying put.

"It's a fake, you moron," Eddie yelled to me.

"What?"

Dietrich's porch light turned off.

"It's a fake," whispered Eddie. "I'm not a narc."

"Then what the hell is that?" I whispered, pointing toward his badge.

"Keep quiet," said Eddie. "It's embarrassing."

"This whole night is embarrassing," I said.

A quiet minute passed. "It's a Lone Ranger badge and gun," said Eddie finally.

One of the others laughed and the rest of them stood, checked to make sure the coast was clear, and ran off.

"Like the TV show?" I asked.

"Just leave me alone," said Eddie. He stood up and sulked homeward.

I sat up alone and brushed gravel off my arms. So this mystery boy was really just a nerd with a thing for pot and the Lone Ranger? He went out to get high wearing a fake Texas badge and toy pistol? I breathed a sigh of relief.

The evening had been highly educational. For starters, I was definitely not interested in being Eddie's kemosabe. Nor did I ever wish to hear him utter, "Hi-ho, Silver!" in any context. And for finishers, I was banned from the Wall for the rest of the summer. It was the social end of my teenage years.

Mrs. Clancy, who lived down the street from me, had been born again. Again. Apparently, the first time she'd been born again, it didn't take. She was fifty-seven and looked fairly sexless with her short brown bob, high-collar starched shirts, beige trousers, and mannish features. She had grown up in this town. In fact, aside from her unexplained absences the past few years, she had lived here longer than anyone else. She might have been one of the prototype Wall members when she was a teenager.

Rumor had it that she had sown quite the wild oats in her day. Unbelievably, at least to me, she had been credited with setting fire to the old public school. On my first day there, I had been told that I had Old Lady Clancy to thank for the shiny new school. Even the auditorium was nicknamed Clancy Hall. This all seemed quite odd when I considered the genderless frump who shuffled along the sidewalk with her privately owned shopping cart, on her way to save thirty cents on a dozen cans of cat food across town.

Then, a few years ago, Mrs. Clancy disappeared for six months. Rumors sprang up like weeds. When she returned, religion had overcome her in a wave of piety and self-righteousness, crashing upon the shores of her rabble-rousing. Maybe she saw the weeping face of the Virgin Mary in her cat's hairballs. All I knew was that one morning she started dressing in a way that made the Catholic school dress code look positively alluring. She'd walk around town blessing people. Sometimes, while standing in line at the checkout, she'd start preaching the Good Word. I'd stand there and pray for an announcement about a cleanup in aisle five just to drown her out.

The kids on the block were generally indifferent to Mrs.

Clancy. She was simply the rigid and zealous kook who lived down the street. At best, her fanaticism was a drop of holy water in our neighborhood's sunshine. We didn't give Mrs. Clancy much thought.

A year or two later, I saw her smoking and wearing lipstick. She tried to hide it from me as she walked past my house. Unbeknownst to her, two of my passions were smoking and lipstick, so I absolutely noticed.

It turned out that Mrs. Clancy had landed a man. Mr. Clancy, as we thought of him, was gregarious, a bit younger than she, and a little on the plump side, and he had a weird sense of humor. But generally, he was an agreeable sort. No one knew where they'd met. All we knew was that one day we woke up and there was a Mr. Clancy in our neighborhood. He, of course, had another name. I believe she took his name when they married, but we, as did the whole neighborhood, continued to address her as Mrs. Clancy, and he, naturally, as Mr. Clancy. After all, she had squatter's rights on the name in our memories.

About three years ago, religion clobbered poor Mrs. Clancy over the head again. Maybe this time she had worked out the bugs in the system. She reverted back to the buttoned-up sweaters, long prim skirts, Frankenstein-like orthopedic shoes, thick glasses, and man-hair. In fact, she looked more like a man than most men. Mr. Clancy disappeared from the picture. We all assumed either they'd divorced or she'd buried him in the backyard. Right after that, she started disappearing again every six months or so.

April's mom, in order to earn a little spending money, offered her services as a house cleaner. There was no shame in it, and everyone agreed she was quite industrious. Mrs. Clancy was one of the women in our neighborhood who regularly took advantage of her hygienic help. This seemed odd, considering Mrs. Clancy was either home all day or not at all, but we came to the conclusion that she was taking care of the godliness while April's mom worked on the cleanliness.

If someone had told me that Mrs. Clancy was going to be my savior that summer, I would have told them to go take a swim in Jersey.

Being banned from the Wall put me in a desperate panic. My parents were both out of the house. They had adopted me when I was an infant, after my real parents had died in a car accident. My adoptive father was a lawyer. My adoptive mom stayed at home and took care of herself, her house, her husband, and me. In that order. But I tried not to think about that as I smoked my second cigarette of the morning, enjoying my Lucky Charms, watching *H.R. Pufnstuf*, and trying to come up with some way to get back into the good graces of the Wall-folk. No plan came to mind. Pufnstuf always made my mind wander.

I decided to walk over to April's house. April was very pretty, very skinny, and very smart. It was enough to make you hate her, except she was also very nice and the only friend who hadn't abandoned me.

"You'll never believe what I overheard my mom telling my dad," said April. "She's cleaning Old Lady Clancy's house and found a huge stash of clit lit!" she continued, barely able to contain herself. Our pubescent eyes lit up at the prospect of the pornographic paperbacks. The pot we had just smoked helped, too. This was the equivalent of being in prison and hearing about a hidden carton of cigarettes. Clit lit was used as barter and fetched quite a handsome price on our black market. It also did wonders for our standing in the teenage community.

I had heard a rumor on the Wall a few weeks earlier, before I had been most injudiciously thrown out of the club, about a shopping bag full of heavy breathers. These were considered gold among our age set. These slight, poorly worded, dog-eared pornographic paperbacks—with titles like *Swedish*

Odyssey 1975, Mindy and Mona: Cocktail Waitresses A-Go-Go, and *The Trouble with Conjoined Twin Nymphomaniacs,* all written by the same author with the trashy pseudonym "Gina Putanesca"—had gotten us through many an afternoon's dry patch.

I can't say I understood everything that was going on in these strange, bouncy, sexual adventures. But this window into a forbidden adult world seemed a harmless pastime. I knew it was all bullshit, but at sixteen, cheap, provocative, forbidden entertainment was fascinating and, quite frankly, the only game in town.

"Jesus," I remarked. "Old Lady Clancy? I can't believe it."

"Obviously, they belonged to her pervert husband," April said.

There was a silent hum of agreement between us.

"It all makes sense. I mean, wouldn't you be reading with one hand if you were married to that repressed old battle-ax?" continued April.

"Coming home day after day, thinking that this lady is going to snap out of her perpetual Sermon on the Mount and instead getting a lecture on the wicked horrors of sex," I added.

We stood in April's kitchen and felt sorry for Mrs. Clancy. And Mr. Clancy, wherever he was.

"How do we get at these books?" I asked, giving voice to what was dancing eagerly across both our minds. It was decided that April would steal her mother's copy of Mrs. Clancy's key, make a duplicate at the hardware store, and return the original to her mother's collection.

April executed this plan undetected, and with military precision.

The next day, after we watched Mrs. Clancy shuffle off with her shopping cart to buy her week's groceries and do God's Will in aisle three, April and I crept stealthily through her backyard.

"This has to be double-quick," I reminded April. She nod-ded in an equally nervous fashion. The back door opened easily, and we stepped into Mrs. Clancy's sunroom.

"How do we know no one else is home?" I asked April, kicking myself for not thinking of this before we broke and entered.

"Because no one is. When was the last time she had a vis-itor?" said April. She could always be counted on to drown out my panic with cold reason. It was great to have her around when I was high.

We proceeded further into the house. The den and adjoin-ing living room were exactly as we had imagined. The décor represented the many Catholic lives of Mrs. Clancy. Portraits of Jesus and Mary flanked a lava lamp. Posters of bullfight-ers outlined a small, candled shrine to St. Francis de Assisi. Mr. Clancy wasn't represented in the house. In fact, aside from the books we were about to filch, you'd never know he'd lived here at all. As we crept up the stairs, I realized we were about to steal one of the precious few possessions he had left in this house.

Mrs. Clancy's bedroom was positively austere. A monk's room, by comparison, would look deliriously wild and wooly. The somber room was decorated with dark, monastic furni-ture, bookended by his-and-her closets.

April opened the closet. It was empty and probably had once held Mr. Clancy's suits and assorted weekend and holiday clothes. Two small boxes were stacked on a shelf. "Bingo," she said, lowering the boxes carefully to the floor. I decided to have a poke around Mrs. Clancy's side of things. The top drawer of her nightstand contained a Bible. It sat there alone, looking pious and smug as if wondering why anyone but her mistress was exposing it to daylight. I opened the bottom drawer. "They're not here," whispered April. "This is old tax shit." She closed the box and carefully ma-neuvered her way back into his closet.

Mrs. Clancy's bottom drawer contained a box of tissues, an autographed wallet photo of Jesus, an atomizer bottle labeled Holy Water, a nightgown, a clit lit with a bookmark, and the biggest, shimmering red vibrator I had ever seen.

"My God," I uttered, picking up the dog-eared clit lit. "*The Farmer in the Belle.*"

"What in the name of Monty Hall is that?" inquired April incredulously, pointing at a monstrously ribbed red vibrator. It looked like a fire hydrant taking a nap.

"That, my dear, is an officially sanctioned, living and breathing vibrator," I said.

"That thing moves?"

We didn't really have time to find out. We were on a tight schedule. The Great Fire Hydrant seemed to have transfixed April, much as it had Mrs. Clancy. The old lady was getting more interesting by the inch. I opened her closet door, and hidden behind the depressing collection of black and brown robe-like dresses sat twelve large shopping bags brimming with paperbacks. I tapped April on the shoulder. She was kneeling in front of the nightstand ready to light candles and pray at the altar of the Holy Vibrator Shrine. I foresaw years of therapy in her future.

"Let's go. Found 'em."

We decided to take only what we could carry—about twenty paperbacks each. It didn't make a dent in Mrs. Clancy's huge inventory. We straightened the bed quilt and closed all the doors and drawers. We crept out of the house and raced across the street, giggling louder with each step.

"There had to be a thousand of them in there," said April as we reached her backyard.

"Maybe she belongs to one of those book clubs," I conjectured, breathing heavily. Then I noticed that April's purse was bulging. "Don't even tell me," I said.

"Oh, shit," said April. She opened her purse to reveal the

Vibrating Fire Hydrant. "I must have taken it without realizing," she said, still transfixed by the object.

"Please tell me you're not planning on using that thing. Seems like you'd need to take some kind of class first."

"Like a pilot's license?"

"April, you have to throw that away. Promise me."

"Promise," said April reluctantly.

We agreed to split our booty down the middle. April said goodbye, dreamily, and I went inside, stashing my half of the books away in our garage under the artificial Christmas tree. It was June, so they would be safe there. My mother cleaned my room a few times a week, so I had learned never to keep any contraband there. As I put the books away, a piece of paper flitted out of one of the books, twirling in the air before landing near my foot. I picked it up. It was a ticket stub.

Teatro dell' Opera
La Forza del Destino
Giuseppe Verdi
13 Giugno 1978
Roma, Italia

On the back was handwritten, *Spozo, 13-25-47.*

I pocketed it as a good luck souvenir from the afternoon's adventures, then went for a walk. I thought about Mrs. Clancy and how I had been very wrong and very right about her—one of my first insights into the complexities of adult life. I was capable of being quite devious, I realized. It was the perfect crime. I now had some goods with which to barter my way back in with the Wall-folk. If Mrs. Clancy had been hiding these books from Mr. Clancy, she clearly couldn't report that they were missing. Or, if he was still around, she might suspect Mr. Clancy had taken them and was reading them himself, which might rekindle their relationship in the bedroom. I might have saved their marriage!

"Jane, get in."

I spun around and stared in horror. A familiar car pulled

up beside me with April's mom in the driver's seat. April sat sheepishly in the backseat. I quietly got in next to April. The car pulled away.

"We're so busted," April whispered.

We drove to April's house. My mother's car was in the driveway. This was not good news. "How did my mother find out?" I whispered to April. My mother had set aside the entire day for a hair appointment. And she would never give up her hair appointment.

"I called her at the salon," answered April's mom, glancing at us sternly in the rearview mirror. "I told her I'd pick you up." I couldn't speak aloud in the presence of April's mom without fear that my words might be used against me in a court of law.

To April, I quietly mouthed, "How bad?"

April pointed to the front passenger seat.

I glanced over. There, riding shotgun, was Mrs. Clancy's giant flaming red vibrator, partially wrapped in a blue-and-white towel. April's mom had sat it upright and strapped it in place with the seat belt. It shone patriotically in the midday sun.

We pulled into April's driveway, got out of the car, and started toward the house. April's mom tapped us on the shoulder and pointed us around to the back of the house. April and I held hands like convicts about to be sentenced. I knew that April had not ratted me out. She was as cool-headed as could be. On the other hand, I never should have let her back into the world with that faraway look in her eyes. She was trapped in some strange, euphoric vibrator haze. It was addling her brain, preventing any rational thought or precaution.

As we walked along the side of the house, I smelled something burning. April looked at me, then at her mom, who was walking calmly behind us. I ruled out the possibility that her house was on fire. We weren't *that* lucky. April and I rounded the corner to find my mother standing over the grill, burning one of our paperbacks. They had found April's stash.

"Missy," my mother cried out, calling me by my kindergarten nickname. She threw another clit lit into the fire and marched toward me. Things were not looking good. She took me by the arm and spoke quietly into my ear. "This was your doing, right?" she asked as she pointed at the stack of books. I stared in silence. "You had a hand in this, I can tell," she stated matter of factly. The burning books made small wisps of gray smoke that drifted over the sunny, midday roofs. April stared at the fire as if she were an Eskimo watching her igloo melt.

I nodded and suddenly felt ashamed.

"Are there more, young lady?" asked my mother.

April looked at me, and I stared right back at her. I knew I couldn't give up my half of the stash. "No," I said calmly.

I would share my stash with April later. I couldn't access them now, because my mom would be keeping a very close eye on me.

Things were bad but they could have been worse. At least my mother didn't tell my father about the Great Clit Lit Robbery. My chance at repatriation with the Wall community was over. It was no fun to be a teenage castaway. A week after I had been ostracized from the Wall, and five days after the conclusion of the Great Clit Lit Debacle, my parents felt it necessary to saddle me with one of their lectures. "Jane, we just don't want you to end up like your cousin."

Whenever my parents brought up my errant cousin Anna, battle stations were generally at full alert.

"Anna's fine," I noted.

I had been adopted as an infant, but my parents still treated me as if they were holding the purchase receipt and might decide at any moment to return me.

"She was sent to a convent," my mother corrected me.

I knew I should end the trajectory of this conversation by changing the subject, but I couldn't let go of my fear. "Are you going to give me up like Anna's parents did?"

My parents, the clean-cut suburbanites, flustered easily. "We're just so worried about you."

"If you've been good parents, you shouldn't have to worry!"

Okay, I went a bit far. But at this point, the tense silence in the air made it impossible to take it back.

"Young lady…."

I stormed off before they could finish. I left the house intending to explore, hoping things would simmer down in the few hours I was away. In my little suburb, exploring meant the mall. I wandered around by myself, window-shopping the smaller stores, waiting for my life to begin, waiting for my adopted parents to simmer down. I wanted my life to explode with passion and excitement. I wanted adventure and hijinks. And just as I was thinking of hijinks, I found myself in front of the new Tobacconist Shoppe. I had heard rumors that the back of the store operated as a head shop. Well, this was too much mystery for me to resist. I had to know.

I innocently made my way into the store. A few respectable-looking customers milled about, inspecting silver lighters and mahogany pipes. No one made furtive glances to the back of the store, so I assumed that they were either shopping for legitimate tobacco purchases and weren't interested in getting high, or were paranoid of narcs.

I screwed up my courage and made a beeline to the back. Past the shelves of foreign tobacco paraphernalia, I was confronted by an enormous Grateful Dead beaded curtain and Indian sitar music. Glass cases displayed bongs of every shape and size, and a revolving pillar presented rolling paper samples. Groovy tie-dye lighters were arranged beside paisley bandanas and hemp blankets. Vials of patchouli oil mingled with multi-colored incense sticks under Robert Crumb posters. Wood and jade Buddhas observed the proceedings from meditative poses. I thought I had died and gone to Stoner World.

"Can I help you?" asked a familiar voice.

I turned around and there stood Eddie.

"Eddie, what are you doing here?"

"I don't really work here. I just thought it was funny to find you here."

There didn't seem to be anyone else in the back but Eddie and me. He was wearing a Bob Marley T-shirt and shorts. A rolled bandana had been pressed into service as a headband to keep his long hair from covering his face.

"So you fancy yourself the Lone Ranger?" I asked with a kidding lilt.

"More like the Stoned Ranger," he said and laughed. "Weed."

My notion of Eddie began to take on a different feeling. Perhaps I had been wrong about him.

"So," he asked, "what brings you here?"

"Just looking."

"No one ever comes back here to just look. You're either lost or buying."

"Actually, I'm kinda screwed," I said, immediately regretting both the intimacy of my confession and the word choice describing my circumstance.

"Really?" said Eddie, moving his hand along the counter where the majority of the bong inventory was kept.

"You know, it's sort of because of you. But not really. My parents busted me. They threatened to send me off to a convent!"

Eddie's eyes widened. "A convent?"

"Parents. Am I right?"

He moved in closer, looking around conspiratorially. Our common paranoia bonded us in the back of the head shop.

"Can you keep a secret?" he said.

"I live for secrets."

"Follow me," he said and walked out of the store.

I followed him, expecting to be led into a giant underground lair where the world's drug traffic flowed. Instead, Eddie walked to the food court and ordered two Cokes, and we sat down. The food court was on the second level of the mall, overlooking the bustling ground floor.

"This is where you want to tell me a secret?"

"No better place. No one is really listening. No one expects anything really important to be said here," said Eddie.

"Really important?"

"I've been watching you," he said, making complete eye contact. Something about his manner shifted, as if he'd suddenly become more mature. I'm sure he saw me blushing.

"So, this is how you ask a girl out? I mean, I like that you...."

He laughed. "No, please listen. I've been watching you. I think I can trust you. I *need* to trust you." He was so serious in his delivery. So earnest. The goofy stoner was gone.

"Am I in trouble?" I said. There was something about his demeanor that told me maybe the jig was up.

"You might be in trouble. That's why I followed you to the mall."

"You're stalking me?" I said.

"That night on the Wall? You were right about me. I'm undercover." He motioned under the table and revealed his badge. "It's not Lone Ranger kid stuff."

"Oh my God," I said. "I got a narc following me." I was thrilled and petrified. This was turning out to be quite a juicy afternoon.

"Jane," said Eddie, "you have to help me. I know you have part of the adult literature collection that belonged to Mrs. Clancy."

"That's what this is about? That's why I'm in trouble?"

"You're in trouble because he's going to figure it out like I did and he's going to come after you, looking for them."

"Who's coming after me?" I said.

"Dietrich."

"Old Farmer Dietrich?"

"I went to the Wall that night because we had a strong suspicion he was back from Italy," said Eddie. "That's why I was sitting on the Wall. To signal the cops that he was home." I took a long sip of my Coke. This was all too much. "Didn't you ever notice that Mrs. Clancy's absences coincided with Dietrich's?"

"Never thought about it." I opened my purse and took out the opera ticket I had discovered within the pages of Mrs. Clancy's book. "Is this what you're looking for?"

"You catch on quick," said Eddie, inspecting the ticket.

"What is this?" I was enjoying being Nancy Drew.

"Dietrich and Mrs. Clancy have been going to Italy together and arranging for drug deals. All the info on where the drugs are stored and the corresponding account numbers are coded in bookmarks in her adult books."

"Holy crap!"

"Will you help me?" said Eddie. It was the question of a lifetime.

"More than I want mac and cheese," I said.

Eddie walked me back home, and I turned over all the books.

The next few days bore much fruit. The feds came and arrested Mrs. Clancy and Dietrich in broad daylight in front of all the neighbors. They even had a TV crew there to capture the whole thing. My parents were so proud of me for helping out. For now, the threat of convent life was held at bay.

My summer was saved. The feds left Dietrich's house alone. The kids returned in even greater numbers to the Wall as word spread of the town drug dealers. They gathered, as if to a campfire, to tell stories about Dietrich's double life. Each night the stories got more and more grand. And I became a Wall legend for single-handedly turning in a couple of international criminals who happened to be a pain in our collective ass.

Before Eddie went back to his real life, I gave him a hug. I tilted my head up for a kiss. He smiled at me and reminded me that I was only sixteen and he was twenty-four. He told me to look him up in a few years. I might. In the meantime, I might wait until college before trying mac and cheese.

THE SPOT ON AUNT GOOGIE'S HEAD

Like Officer Powell said, we know you're heavily medicated. That's all right. We'll come back and ask you the same questions tomorrow. Standard procedure for NYPD. But for now, we need to find out what happened.

I just wanted love and companionship. All right, I would have been happy with getting to first base. But who was I fooling? I don't think you can understand a word I'm saying. Is it all just mumbling and moaning? I don't think my mouth works.

What was that? Nurse, can you take that breathing thing away so we can hear him?

Want to know my profound truth? Clearing away the oxygen line may help. Or maybe smothering me with the pillow is a better treatment. Are you allowed to do that?

Buddy, you're at the county hospital in a full body cast. You got a whole lot of people wanting to press charges. We need to find out what happened.

Ramp up the morphine dosage and I'll tell you.

You're mumbling again.

I will try to enunciate. I'm usually a very articulate person. Also, can you please put on your mask and gloves? I don't want to catch whatever you have. Can you blame me?

Why don't you start at the beginning? Officer Powell and I will wait. Nurse, can you crank up the morphine?

Thanks. That's better. Now, could you please make sure to keep your gloves on? I'm not a germophobe or anything, but the worst place to be is in the hospital. It's a giant petri dish.

So, you want to know what happened. Probably helpful then to know a bit about me. Once, in grade school, I couldn't pronounce a particular word. It was too complicated, so I looked it up in the giant classroom dictionary, which was thicker than my face. I found the word broken down phonetically—small chunks typeset in moron language for me. That's how I think of myself now. I'm emotionally phonetic. And women are the literati. That's a twenty-five-cent way of explaining my five-cent road to the hospital. When I get nervous, I tend to ramble on and on. It's like a nervous tic. Can't imagine why I'd be nervous now.

Can't make heads or tails.

The worst thing to do, though, is to try and stop me. Then I ramble even more. But the morphine is making me see things very clearly. How refreshing: like a mental bidet.

Yes, it was all about a woman. You got me. Isn't that what it always comes down to? Ester Mantzakis. I'd admired her from afar when I'd temped at her accounting office for a few months. When I finally met her, my thoughts were:

1. She's stunning. She's intelligent. She's funny.

2. Didn't they stop making Esters? Didn't they also cease production on all Eleanors, Hazels, and Gertrudes? Something about a recall.

3. Why would she go out with me? Didn't I just note her intelligence?

I've been single for as long as I can remember. So, to avoid the whole "No Dating in the Workplace" rule, I quit my job and asked her out. Her reaction:

1. She seemed to think I was kidding.

2. After a few awkward moments, she said she found my request oddly touching.

3. No restraining order was issued, which was a happy surprise.

Am I revealing too much here? That's just my nature. I've

been told by a revolving door of therapists that I have this intense need to be liked and will try anything to get approval. I'm sure it's in my chart somewhere. Ironically, when I experience Stage Three Anxiety, I get wildly inappropriate and politically incorrect. It's a bit of a birth defect, really. I was born without a self-editor.

Okay, back to the thirty-year-old Greek goddess. Did I mention that Ester was intensely Greek? Her favorite perfume was baklava. She had a huge, tight-knit family that made the Kennedys look like a tiny, disjointed clan.

I picked her up at her parents' house for our first date. I had to remind myself not to say the usual dumb things, like asking if she wanted to play Naked Crisco Twister. I was intent on not screwing this one up. Her parents, Nick and Eleni Mantzakis, met me at the door and were very traditional. I could tell from their weak smiles:

1. I was not who they imagined their daughter should be dating.

2. I should have been born Greek. Or at least taller.

3. This was a terrible, terrible idea. Not only was Ester way out of my league, but her parents were out of my league. I didn't even know there was a potential in-law league, but apparently I was being sent down to the minors.

Ester came down the stairs, looking beautiful. I let her shake my hand even though I distinctly did not see her wash her hands beforehand. She was worth it.

For our first date, we just took a walk in the park. Nothing special. Except it was everything special. She made me feel so comfortable, and I found her so charming. I even made her laugh. It was all hand-holding, googly eyes, and nervous smiles, followed by my secret and rigorous hand sanitizer application. To the outside world, we looked as if we'd just stepped out of a tampon commercial.

Ester caught me washing my hands one too many times

and asked if I was obsessive compulsive. I told her it was a recent thing. I had only experienced it since I was three months old. She smiled and whispered in my ear. She said it was okay. She told me she was just getting off antidepressants. That was quite a disclosure for our first date, and I took it as a good sign.

So far, she hadn't seen the real me. I decided to give her a peek, like a trailer for an overblown summer action blockbuster, starring me. I told her that I had seen a commercial for her drug. "They have the announcer at the end talking a mile a minute. One of them says, 'Take one tablet daily by mouth.' And I thought, 'Of course by mouth: what am I going to do, cram it in my ear? Or…Whoa!' So I immediately went online, praying that I'd picked the good HMO plan, the one that allows prescription drugs to be taken daily by mouth. Do you know how sad it is that I did a little happy dance because my health care provider allows me to take pharmaceuticals orally? Because you know that somewhere out there, there's a plan that costs $4.99 less a month but only covers drugs to be administered in the downstairs region. And I don't even want to know what orifice is used for generic brands."

Please try and focus, pal. You're blathering. Can't make you out.

First dates can always be measured by their capacity for giving birth to a second date. I'm happy to report that the gestation of our first outing culminated in the successful delivery of said offspring.

I think the first date went so well because of one specific moment. There were some small shops on the outskirts of the park and we ducked into an antique store. The old lady behind the counter, knowing suckers when she saw them, commented that we must be shopping for our wedding anniversary, because we looked like such a nice married couple. Both Ester and I blushed and our eyes met.

In that moment, I think Ester decided a second date

wouldn't be the worst idea. Terrible judgment on her part.

However, I always fail to pay close attention on my first dates. I never listen to what they want to do on a second date. I'm just so happy that there will *be* a second date. When I spoke to Ester a few days after our first date, she said something about a family obligation for our second and that I should wear a suit. I thought we were going to a wedding. My immediate thoughts were:

1. Holy crap! I have a second date with the beautiful Ester Mantzakis!

2. She's going to want to discuss our wedding plans at this wedding, which is the natural and normal thing to do.

3. She's going to catch the bouquet, take one look at me, and run off with the clarinet player.

4. I hope I don't get stuck at the kids table after Ester abandons me.

When I picked up Ester for our second date, her parents, formally dressed in somber tones, opened the door and glared at me even more ferociously than they had on the first date. They told me Ester was still getting ready. I panicked right away. Nick and Eleni stood together like a small assassination squad. They asked me to sit down in their living room. I was twenty-eight, but it suddenly felt like prom night.

We sat in silence in their very formal living room. The wood-paneled room was adorned with candles and framed black-and-white photos of family from the old country. There were a number of open flames near wood. I kept hoping we wouldn't have to stop, drop, and roll. The awkward silence kept growing. Where was Ester? That's when her parents informed me we were going to a funeral.

1. Do you know what it sounded like you just said?

2. Well, hopefully it's someone you know, and you're not just attending for the free snacks. I mean, no one enjoys

pigs-in-a-blanket more than me, but even I know where to draw the line.

3. Panic. Utter panic. Choking-on-my-own-tongue panic.

4. Keep it together. Ester is there for you on the other side of this day.

5. No, panic feels right. I'm going to go with panic at this moment.

We sat in a death cone of silence. Sir, Stage Two Anxiety, ready and waiting, sir!

The Mantzakis told me a little about who would be attending. They advised me not to make eye contact with Uncle Constantine, as he generally hated non-Greeks. Great. I was a non-Greek. It was my most salient feature. Maybe if I changed my name to Ouzo?

More silence. More glances at the stairs where Ester still hadn't made an appearance. I had showered seven times already to make sure I wasn't malodorous for the date. I decided to break the silence.

1. I have to say that the shower is the best. It's like I experience all my ages in there. It's a soggy *This is your Life*.

2. First, I'm a kid again, pretending to be Waterboy, you know, shooting water from my fingertips to save the world.

3. Then, I'm an adult Jacques Cousteau and start narrating with my best French accent. "The mysteries of the legendary Capistrano Waterfalls will be explored today by me and my trusty crew chief, Soapy."

4. Then, of course, I save being a horny teenager for last. And that's always the part of the show when the shower curtain opens for an unexpected cameo.

5. By my Mom.

6. And I always have the same look on my face. I can't really describe it. Well, actually, Mrs. Mantzakis, it's a lot like the look on your face right now.

Ester's mom gave her husband a look that implied

something about a car battery, jumper cables, and my testicles. She went to see what was keeping her daughter.

While I waited for Ester to finish getting ready, Ester's dad went to his bar to make himself a drink. "You want a Rickety Dog? It's my own creation," he said proudly, trying to smooth out the tension. "It's vodka, raspberry syrup, and Tabasco sauce."

1. That's not a drink.

2. That's what you have left over in the fridge on Monday morning.

3. How about I make you a Flea-Bitten Varmint? It's Cheez Whiz, bong water, and Lemon Pledge.

Ester came downstairs and lit up the room with her smile. Without much debate, Ester's parents left the room, implying that Ester was now my keeper. Tag, you're it. They decided to drive to the funeral service separately.

Ester and I stood in her living room, and she kept apologizing over and over. She said this wasn't her idea of a second date, but her Aunt Googie had just died and she had been very close to her aunt. Aunt Googie was always happiest when Ester had a boyfriend. It only seemed proper to invite me. I'm sorry, she kept saying. Boy, would she be sorry.

What was that? Sorry? Sorry isn't going to cut it, pal. Nurse, this guy isn't lucid. Should we come back later? Hello? Buddy?

Next thing I knew, Ester brought me to a Greek Orthodox Church on the other side of town. It was located next to a butcher shop. I thought the slaughtered pigs were the lucky ones. Ester and I entered the ornate church. I was hoping to quietly scoot into the back row of pews with Ester. Unfortunately, as soon as we arrived, I was surrounded by a sea of Greek mourners. They all kissed and pinched and hugged, and I kept searching for a Purell dispenser. With all the tears, blubbering, and sweat under the wool coats, the church was a bacteria factory.

The mourners led us down the aisle, intending to seat us in

one of the front pews reserved for immediate family. Ester pointed out some of her family, including her grandparents, her sister, and her Uncle Constantine. There were way too many chaperones on this date. As Ester and I walked down the aisle in a move that would have pleased the old lady in the antique store, I glanced past the mourners toward the front of the church. The mourners were all facing the open casket of eighty-three-year-old Aunt Googie. Photos taken throughout her life were displayed on a nearby table.

1. I wanted to be there for Ester and respect her desires to properly honor her Aunt Googie.

2. The mourners were placing their hands on my shoulders, shaking my hand and giving me their best comfort face that said, "I feel your pain." And I thought, *Who are you people? I'm on a date here!*

3. Math has never been a strong subject for me, but I quickly deduced that I was not family. On the "Knew Aunt Googie Well" industry-standard scale:

4. Ester scored a solid ten.

5. I barely registered a 0.1, and that's only because I could see her framed black-and-white photographs by her coffin.

6. That brought our collective average to a five.

7. An average five score does not entitle the bearers to a front row seat to the show.

I pulled Ester into a pew in the statistical middle of the church. You can't argue with math in times like these.

The service started. I tried wiping my hands and cheek with whatever napkin or soft paper I could find. I had never been to a Greek funeral but was hoping it would be a quick one. After some prayers, Ester got up to deliver part of the eulogy. I listened to my date regale everyone with a touching story of her Aunt Googie. A tear meandered down her cheek.

1. It was at this point that I realized that Ester was a deeply wonderful person.

2. Was there an app that could quickly convert me to Greek so her family would stop scowling at me?

3. A towelette! A towelette! My kingdom for a little, moist towelette!

4. It was at this point that I also realized I wasn't getting to first base that night.

When Ester's eulogy was over, the priest and Archbishop said some final words, then everyone stood up solemnly and formed a line down the center of the aisle. Holding Ester's hand, I couldn't have been standing more than twenty yards from the open casket. Everyone shuffled Googieward one at a time, as if it were Friday night at an ATM.

I asked Ester what was going on, twitching slowly into Stage Two-and-a-Half Anxiety.

Ester replied sweetly that they were all saying their personal goodbyes to Aunt Googie one at a time. I told her I would wait for her in the parking lot. She smiled and held my hand tighter, thinking I had been kidding to cheer her up.

A small choir started singing a solemn ballad as we marched forward in line. "What is the socially correct thing here?" I asked Ester. "I'd never actually met Googie, so I can't really say goodbye to someone I never said hello to, can I? I mean, isn't there some Rule Book of Etiquette we could consult here?"

Before she could respond, we overheard Uncle Constantine behind us talking on his cell phone via a remote ear piece. Ester whispered to me that she hated that her Uncle Constantine was always on his cell phone. It was probably his ex-wife on the other end, she said.

"Yeah," I replied, "but what a great time in the history of mankind to be crazy. I mean, thank God for cell phones. No one bats an eye if they see you talking to yourself."

Turns out Ester was a feminist. She was upset that I said "mankind" and not "personkind" or "man-and-woman-kind." I told her that if she was serious about her endeavor to practice feminism, she should legally change her last name to "Persontzakis."

I said this, you understand, out loud.

As you can imagine, this went over slightly less well than if I had showed up dressed as the Grim Reaper on stilts. The surrounding congregation stared small ice picks into the back of my neck. I may not be invited back to Aunt Googie's next funeral.

And, really, I was just trying to distract myself because everyone, and I mean everyone, was leaning over, one by one, and solemnly kissing Aunt Googie on the forehead. By the looks of her photos on the table, she was getting more action now than when she was alive. How could I press the ejection button on this? My eyes darted around the church, searching frantically for a sign that depicted a priest with his hands held slightly apart that read, "You Must Have Been This Close to the Deceased to Enjoy This Ride."

It was during this part of the date that I started to question our relationship. I mean, it was only—what?—a second date? Suddenly, I didn't care how cute Ester was. I had not bargained on having to kiss a dead body. But then Ester looked at me with those big hazel eyes. And I thought, "Okay, I can wear the big boy Underoos in this situation."

I glanced over to the front of the line, which, like the Mediterranean tide at Santorini, was quickly flowing closer. We took a few steps closer to this twisted hellscape of a kissing booth. I couldn't get the sight of Aunt Googie's forehead out of my field of vision. It was like a postage stamp being licked by the whole village before being affixed and mailed. Now, I'm no germophobe, but I started scoping the joint, looking for any cases of medical maladies. I don't play a doctor on TV, but it was my sincere diagnosis that the room was full of diseased, infectious lepers.

Noticing that I was slowly turning into a post-iceberg Titanic in a suit, Ester attempted to distract me, if only to prevent any further embarrassment. She asked me if I had gotten another job since I quit the temp assignment. I told her that I was now self-employed. She stared at me nervously, clearly regretting that she had brought the subject up.

1. I explained that I used to have a goatee. My old girlfriend liked how it looked but complained that it felt bristly when we kissed.

2. I came up with a solution—I shaved off the goatee and developed a substitute: a goatee toupee.

3. The Goapee.

Crap, we were getting closer to the deceased! I asked Ester in a panic if we could go to the back of the line. She turned with a look of great disappointment, as if we'd camped out all night for these tickets. I told her it wasn't Beyoncé up there doing a meet and greet. It's Aunt Googie! Clearly, we were not on the same page. She looked ahead hopefully to the front of the line, as if there were scalpers with better tickets yelling, "I got two for Googie. Get 'em while they're hot. Googie, second row, on the aisle!"

No go. Only five people in front of us.

Ester's family started to notice that the only non-Greek was behaving like a retreating Turk. To deflect the negative attention being bestowed on us by the entire congregation, Ester pointed out the architecture and history of the church. Her sweetness kept me from running away. The expression on Ester's face, however, made it clear that there wouldn't be a third date. But for now, she had made this extremely anxious bed and was obligated to lie in it.

I pushed on, endeavoring to keep my mind off Aunt Googie. Uncle Constantine got off the phone and tapped me on the shoulder. "Are you even Christian?" he asked scornfully, in a tone that would have made the collective testicles of the *Goodfellas* cast shrink up in their body cavities.

I told him that a few years before, for a girl I'd been crazy about, I'd converted. I'd had to pick a patron saint.

1. I found this Yellow Pages of Saints. Wow. I thought I'd had some awful days. Saint Gerstaine got drawn and quartered after having molten lead siphoned into his ass. After which, he summoned the strength to hand out leaflets that spoke out against the church. After the whole ass-molten-lead episode! I call in sick when a repeat of *Big Bang Theory* is pre-empted.

2. I picked a saint, stood before the church committee, and stated in a proud voice, "I have chosen as my patron, Saint Bobo." Yes, Bobo. Look it up, he's real. I like 50s rock, and he sounded like a doo-wop lyric. Could you imagine being called Bobo? Back in the Middle Ages? Where they would behead you just to fight boredom? Bobo, Patron Saint of Snack Cakes, with his assistant, Little Debbie. New Hostess Bobos: chocolatey goodness on the outside, creamy eternal salvation inside.

3. I may not be invited back to any religion.

I concluded my story near Aunt Googie's casket, extending my arms in a flourish designed to give the end of my story an exciting crescendo. Instead, I smacked the priest in the face, which caused the entire congregation to gasp in unison. The Great Priest Sucker Punch—as I'm sure it is referred to at Ester's family reunions—also resulted in the priest spilling holy water on the floor near Aunt Googie's casket. The priest waved the incident off as an inconsequential accident, and everyone breathed a sigh of relief. Ester, however, looked discouraged and disappointed. The priest approached me, whispering, "Please, my son, in the name of St. Augustus, this is a holy place."

Ester grabbed my hand and led me to Aunt Googie. My mind was clamoring for excuses to delay the inevitable, and I suddenly felt the need to speak a few words on behalf of all those who had never known old Googie. Rushing frantically to the podium, I flipped on the microphone, the pilgrimage to Aunt Googie momentarily waylaid.

Everyone stood agog, waiting to hear what the outsider had to say. Ester just shook her head. That's when my mind went blank. I couldn't think of anything to say. I put my brain on autopilot, grasping the podium tightly with both hands, as if this were Mr. Toad's Wild Ride. Impulsively, I started to sing Queen's "Another One Bites the Dust."

The congregation stood in utter silence, as if God had hit the pause button on the Church remote. Clearly, they weren't big fans of Freddie Mercury. Uncle Constantine rushed the stage like a coked-out roadie, briskly escorting me back to the line and telling me to pipe down. Actually, he spoke in Greek and his words were later translated as a threat to stick an olive fork into my right kidney. Now, I'd heard plenty about Uncle Constantine from Ester and her parents. He'd been divorced twice and paid two alimonies.

"No problem, Bra. I'll keep it down, Bra," I said.

Uncle Constantine demanded to know who Bra was.

"You are Bra," I answered.

"I'm Bra?" asked Uncle Constantine, turning redder.

"Of course," I said in my most amiable fashion. "Because you separate and support."

He scowled, looming toward me menacingly, but Ester intervened. She pleaded with me to keep it together before I was kicked out. She didn't want to be humiliated in front of her family.

I understood, but Aunt Googie loomed ever-large in my future. "Wait," I told her. "There's a pharmacy next door! They have alcoholic wipes made specifically for foreheads! Maybe I could...."

But it was too late. Like a mosh pit, the surge of the crowd pushed me forward toward Googie's ever-waiting forehead, which grew larger than those featured on Mount Rushmore.

I inspected Aunt Googie. Lying in the casket, having been kissed by the entire population of Astoria, Queens, as well as Athens, Sparta, and Crete, Aunt Googie was looking aggressively loved. There was this giant spot on her forehead where everyone had kissed her, where her death makeup had worn off, revealing actual Aunt Googie skin! And despite everyone watching me, there was no way I was kissing actual forehead that was in the process of Googification. So I slyly covered the spot with the palm of my right hand. I would kiss the back of my hand just as I had done when I was thirteen to practice making out.

Then I got an even better idea. I started to discreetly backfill the bald spot on Aunt Googie's forehead with the adjacent makeup. It was like spackling drywall. I went in for a respectful kiss on the freshly paved forehead when I accidentally slipped on the puddle of holy water and kissed Aunt Googie square on the mouth. And because my slip was a complete surprise to me, this was a senior-prom-last-dance-last-chance-for-romance-open-mouth kiss. Aunt Googie may have been proudly Greek, but that kiss was shamefully French.

The entire congregation watched with horror as I made out with Aunt Googie. The place erupted with so much activity and terror that if a rat had been present to observe the goings-on, he would have done well to take careful notes on the proper way to abandon a sinking ship. Ester started crying as the priest quickly ushered everyone out of the church. The archbishop seized Aunt Googie's casket and wheeled it away from me as if he were a caterer who had served bad salmon.

I spied Uncle Constantine and two of his larger relatives rushing at me in a menacing fashion. I slipped out through the back of the church and raced down the alleyway. I recalled a butcher shop next to the church—it would provide safe shelter until Hurricane Constantine blew over. Cuts of meat hung in the butcher shop window in front of me. The shop, the hanging meat, would save my life—it was Bovine Intervention.

I reached the door, but it was locked. The shop was closed.

Nurse, hook him back up to the breathing thing. He's just making weird noises now. We'll come back tomorrow when he's making more sense.

Let's just say Uncle Constantine and his goons helped me achieve a vocal range previously undisplayed by humans. At least they had the courtesy to call an ambulance afterward.

But here's the thing. As I lay in the gutter, bleeding and broken, I finally realized I had been wrong.

I had gotten to first base that night.

EQUINITY

"I'm sorry I strayed, Darlin'," said Ed. "I've been a horse's ass. It won't ever happen again."

They rode together through the twisted path of the verdant mountainside, as if they had never been apart, as if they still belonged together. But Ed was feeling guilty about his betrayal, despite her ready forgiveness. He could tell by the way she moved, the look on her face, the sorrowed distance in her eyes, that she was crushed.

"Maybe I should tell you everything," said Ed, reversing a decision they'd made three minutes before never to discuss Ed's infidelity again. Darlin' remained silent, her mood clearly still gloomy. Ed interpreted this as acceptance. "Well, you know I think you're absolutely beautiful," started Ed, "but even so, I always had a thing for, how do I put it? Horse-faced women. Not that you're a horse-faced woman at all. No, ma'am. But ever since I was a little boy, I wanted to try myself one of them horsey-faced women.

"It's like I had blinders on. Something about them. I guess if I went to a head doctor, he could explain it all to me. But I soon realized there just weren't any women out there with the specific qualities I was looking for. So I got myself one of them computers and internets, and tried to find someone on one of them dating services. No such luck.

"Then I met you, Darlin', and life was all oats and honey. But one day I was on the computer and I came across this dating site called Stallions and Mares, and I figured this might be just about perfect for me. I signed up, and within two weeks, had a blind date with this woman named Harriet.

"Now, I want you to know that I felt real bad about what I was doing, but the prospect of dating a woman with a horse-face was just too irresistible for me to pass up. Harriet asked me to meet her at her horse farm. She was a whole lot horsier than even I had fantasized. She had the Holy Trinity of horse-faced features: a disproportionally huge chin, a long, drawn-out nose, and a mouth full of oversized teeth. Goddamn, if she didn't pull my trigger.

"We said hello and she took me into her barn, 'cause she still had work to do. I asked her if she'd ever done this before. She didn't reply, but I swear I saw her foot scrape the ground four times. This woman was getting me hot. I thought this might turn out to be a real stable romance.

"Then we went into her house across the field. The whole time, I'm admiring her gait. I asked Harriet about herself, but she only wanted to talk about her horses. In her parlor, I saw framed pictures of horses and some rodeo guy.

"'That's my husband,' said Harriet.

"'You're married?' I asked. I couldn't believe it. There were other men in the world attracted to horse-faced women? Instead of answering me, she gave me a look that would have made the Grand National Rodeo Pageant Queen blush. She led me back outside, asking me to wait by the fence outside the riding arena. She came back with a fine-looking mare which she led into the arena. She was wearing a long glove on her right arm that went up to her shoulder. I thought this was all part of her seduction, you know, showing me she knew her way around horses. I have to say I was riveted.

"She shot me another one of her intense looks and got down to business with that horse. She got behind the mare, pulled something out of her pocket, and, how do I say this delicately? Proceeded to stick it inside the horse's woo-hoo. Within a few minutes, she had her hand, then her whole arm in there. What the hell was I watching? I wondered. But then, I realized Harriet was artificially inseminating the mare.

I wondered if I'd have to hold Harriet's hand later, and I couldn't tell if the prospect turned me on or off. A disturbing moment later, I found the whole thing offensive. No way I was going to mount her, side saddle or any other way.

"I told her the date was over. She said, 'What date? I advertised my mare on the horse farm message board, Stallions and Mares.' You see, that was her game—lure desiring men to her farm, tease them, and then coldly sell her farm animal wares. I already had a horse back home and was looking for a fling with a horse-faced woman, and she was a married woman looking for someone to buy her horse. That felt like a good time to consider the relationship over. I had no interest in animal husbandry.

"Again, Darlin', I'm so sorry and it won't ever happen again. I've learned my lesson," said Ed.

Darlin' and Ed reached the top of the mountain. The morning view was glorious. The scattered clouds broke up shafts of purple-red light that gilded the mountain tops. A flock of birds circled past.

"You ain't learned your lesson yet," thought Darlin', "not by a damn sight."

She reared up on her hind legs and threw Ed off her saddle. He lost his grip and tumbled to the ground. With a wild neigh, she kicked him off the cliff. Her last view of Ed was of a small cowboy with a horse-faced-woman fetish faintly yelling, "Whoooooaaaaaa," as he disappeared into the rocky chasm below.

Darlin' headed back down the mountainside, wondering how long it would take her to find Harriet's farm. That Harriet sounded like fun.

CASA DE LOS GATOS

"This is no way to start a marriage," Rex said under his breath, pecking at the pumpkin seeds in his right hand while he drove with the left.

"Well, we're six months in," said Avis. Her auburn hair whipped wildly in the wind. "All right, I surrender. Put the top up. I can't stand this."

"But you just…"

"I know. Now I want it up," yelled Avis over the wind.

The ragtop of their convertible sealed them into the exaggerated silence. Rex thought about bringing up the conversation she had abandoned an hour earlier, but he decided against it. If they weren't discussing her recently deceased mother, they were arguing about the wedding—how much the wedding had cost, the extravagance of it, the obscene surplus of food, how it had all been too much. In their six months of marriage, and in their six months of dating before that, Rex had developed a winning strategy to let sleeping dogs lie. And ultimately, it wasn't Avis's fault that he had a measly entry-level job or that her family was exceedingly wealthy. He rolled down the window and spit out several pumpkin seed shells.

"What is it?" said Rex, knowing her silence never boded well.

"Your job was to arrange for the honeymoon," she said quietly. "Not even to pay. Just arrange."

"Honeymoon?"

Avis's mother had made sure there was no honeymoon. She'd dragged out her illness, refusing to see a doctor while

Avis stayed at her side. It wasn't until four months after they were married that Rex insisted that an actual doctor visit her mother. By then, it had been too late.

Avis was in one of her moods. He had agreed to this trip, just weeks after her mother died, in the hope that she would lighten up and turn back into the funny, easygoing woman he had fallen in love with. But that was the smiling Avis from a year ago. He didn't even recognize this Avis.

The route started to get congested, lined with billboards and tourist traps. Rex began to feel very claustrophobic. He saw a sign up ahead for their exit and downshifted the Corvette, one of many gifts from Avis's dad. It would have been one thing if Rex had liked cars, but Avis's family hadn't bothered to get to know him. They'd just bestowed gift after gift that held no real meaning for Rex. And they always acted imperious the following day, as if the gifts were just small, shiny down payments on his soul.

To initiate the lifetime of requests and implied servitude to their family, Avis's father had strongly suggested Rex make reservations for the honeymoon suite in the sprawling Orlando hotel where Avis's parents had spent their honeymoon—a suggestion Rex deliberately ignored. He found, instead, a two-star hotel room outside Orlando and waited until the second day of their drive from Connecticut to Orlando before he broke the news to Avis. It had not gone over well.

Rex pulled off the exit.

"Are we really still going through with this?" said Avis.

"Didn't we just take our vows six months ago?"

"Not the marriage, you idiot. The hotel. Are we really staying there?"

Rex continued down the road, passing Orlando, not sure if she was kidding. "Idiot?"

"Yes," said Avis in a confident manner. "At least you're not a moron."

"Gee, thanks."

"A moron is incapable of learning anything. But an idiot can be taught. Trained, if you like." She smiled at him, flirting for the first time in what seemed an eternity.

"Well, lucky me," he said, "I'm an idiot on Moron Island. Things are looking up."

"I knew you'd see it my way."

"You really have a way of selling your ideas." Rex smiled and breathed deeply. He wanted to start over. New attitude. Commence the marriage properly. "Want to know what I'm thinking?" he said.

"See? You're thinking. That proves you'll be running Moron Island in no time."

Rex was not someone given to impulses, but he wanted to be the man that she deserved. God knows she kept lording over him how many men wanted her, and he was determined to be the guy that all her old boyfriends envied. Not the guy who'd been a virgin before he'd met Avis.

"This is getting funnier by the minute," said Rex. "No, what I'm thinking is we abandon our plans and drive down to Key West." Rex wanted to be adventurous. Perhaps that would spark some spontaneity and fun from his bride.

"Seriously?"

"The heck with your family and their traditions. The heck with our own traditions. Key West."

A slow smile came to her face, crinkling her nose and making her freckles coalesce into a mini galaxy. She had never disappointed her father but this was a new chapter in her life. "I love this. Let's be adventurous. We're doing this," said Avis.

"I'm sorry, we're all booked," said the hotel registration clerk at the seventh hotel they tried.

By the third hotel, they didn't bother taking out their luggage before checking for vacancies. Avis called her father's secretary to see if there was anything she could do. So far, nothing.

Outside, Key West was bustling with honeymooners, tourists, college students on break, families with crying children, and local expats who had given up on the rest of the country. The music blaring from the open bars was familiar and foreign at the same time. The Key West inhabitants all executed the same tribal dance under a blazing sun and the sweet ocean spray that swept up from the Atlantic and all points Cuban.

Other than the wedding, Rex realized, he and Avis hadn't endured much to test them as a team. And as far as the wedding was concerned, there had been a clear division of labor—Rex was to plan the honeymoon, while Avis's family took care of everything else. Avis merely pointed at things with a ravenous finger, sporting a two-karat vintage engagement ring she had picked out.

At first, Rex thought the lack of a hotel room and temporary homelessness might bring them closer, make Avis feel connected to him. The two of them against the world and all that pop song sentiment. Instead, she elevated her complaints to DEFCON 3 and focused all her frustration on Rex.

"How did I ever let you talk me into this?" said Avis, getting back into the car to search for yet another hotel.

"I'm so sorry, honey," said Rex. "There's got to be a place we can stay."

"You'd think so."

"Maybe if we try looking outside all the hubbub," he suggested.

"The whole reason we came here is to be in the middle of the hubbub, Bub."

Rex already missed the Avis he knew. Or was this really her? Maybe his friends had been right and they should have traveled together before getting married. Or lived together first. But Rex had wanted to keep their relationship old-fashioned. He and Avis had gone from casually dating to whatever this was. One emergency at a time, he told himself. Why had he even suggested Key West? He hated the overgrown college atmosphere of the town. He revved the Corvette's engine and took the first road out of the main strip. A few blocks away, the heat seemed less intense, the noise less corrosive. They passed shaded green and yellow houses nestled in palm-filled lots with large blue swimming pools. Rex followed dusty roads through the neighborhood, feeling very much at home. This suburb felt authentic, not manufactured and calculated into some eternal Key West spring break.

"Where the hell are you taking us?" said Avis, cell phone to her ear, waiting for her father's secretary to save the day with deluxe five-star accommodations.

"Relax," said Rex. "Remember, I'm an idiot, not a…"

A chicken crossed the road in front of them. Rex cut the wheel hard to the right to avoid the bird, kicking up gravel and road dust. Suddenly, the road threw an intersection at him and he took a violent left.

"What the flaming hell?" screamed Avis.

He was breathing hard. He slowed down and shot a look in the rearview mirror. "The rooster," said Rex. "Did you see that goddamn rooster?"

"A chicken?" said Avis. "Seriously?"

"I think it was a rooster," said Rex.

"There are chickens everywhere here. You drove us into Hee-Haw!" yelled Avis. "Except there was no rooster on the road, Colonel Sanders."

Rex knew better than to argue with her. He caught his breath and relaxed his shoulders. A few minutes later, they were driving down a dirt road surrounded by miles of farmland. There were no houses in sight, and certainly no hotels.

"You're saying it was a hen?" asked Rex, trying to make light of the situation.

"Idiot."

They drove for three more miles in silence, looking for a turnoff or some way to get back to the main road. Rex pulled over to the side of the road. He heard a low grumbling sound outside and put the top down.

"What are you doing now?" said Avis. She glanced at her phone. "Great, no cell coverage. Nice job, baby."

"You don't hear that?" he asked.

"Hear what?"

"That rumbling. It's like a purring."

"That's the car," she said in a tone that conveyed both annoyance and condescension.

Rex drove ahead slowly, and the purring got louder. He sped up, following the low, vibrating noise. Then he saw it. Rex screeched the brakes and came to a dead stop.

"Rex!"

"Avis, did I tell you I would take care of you?" He nodded to his left. "Our luck is about to change."

The old wooden sign stood ten feet above the road, fastened to a rusting metal pole. Tall vegetation had been winning a war of attrition with the road, and thick, fibrous vines encircled the pole. Painted on the sign in sun-faded colors was a large rooster in full flourish. Over the rooster, in simple red block letters, were the words:

Casa de los Gatos
Bed and Breakfast
Always Open

They drove toward the B&B, slowing down to avoid colliding with a thick thorny bush that encircled the property. It stood about two feet tall, with yellow-green foliage at the base and red leaves on top. As the car drew closer, the bush appeared to open up like a gate. It let them in and closed behind them. Then the bush started shimmering and changing shape.

"Is it moving in the wind?" Rex muttered to himself.

"That's not a bush. Those are roosters," said Avis, her gaze transfixed by the pageant around her. "Freakin' roosters."

The "bush" consisted of three concentric rings of roosters, standing tightly shoulder to shoulder, closing ranks around the perimeter of the property, their heads jerking from side to side.

"I don't know about you but I'm suddenly in the mood for cornflakes," said Rex, trying to break the tension.

"Is this what chickens do? I mean, is this a thing?" said Avis.

"I always see them stacked up in the supermarket on little Styrofoam trays," said Rex. "Maybe they're practicing."

He stopped the car a few feet from the roosters and put it into park. He opened his door. The moment his foot hit the gravel driveway, the roosters shifted away from the car, as if they were one unit moving in unison at some unspoken command. Then, suddenly, they scattered toward a barn behind the house, their exodus eerily silent. He got back into the car and they drove to the house.

"Those chickens better not come anywhere near me," said Avis. "I'm here on vacation, not to work at a game farm."

The house was a two-story modest affair with a simple porch and sunbaked metal roof. Behind the house was the rooster barn and beyond that, dense woods. Rex could hear a distant cat meowing, but other than that, there were no signs of life, except for the rooster tracks that led to the barn. Rex retrieved their luggage from the trunk as Avis applied lipstick with her compact mirror.

The front door to the house creaked open, and a young man with curly red hair approached them. He smiled and Rex thought that there was something familiar about the way he walked. The man reached the car and, smiling broadly, reached for their luggage.

"Oh, hi," said Rex. "We were just…"

The man walked back to the house with their luggage, the front door closing behind him.

"Well, I guess we just met the bell captain," said Avis. "We better go in and have a gander at the concierge."

The foyer of the house was decorated in 1920s art deco. The house smelled clean but retained a faint musty odor. Avis grimaced, clearly unhappy to be taking part in this particular adventure. Her adventures usually required hotels with more professional staff and more luxurious smells.

"Welcome," said an elderly plump woman sitting behind an old oak desk. "What a happy surprise! We weren't expecting guests today." She wore a simple housecoat, and tiny glasses pinched the bridge of her nose. Her graying red hair was pulled tight behind her head.

"Sorry we didn't call ahead," began Rex.

"Do you have a room?" asked Avis.

"Of course, we have rooms available," said the old woman. "Have a seat. I'm Madame Julia."

Rex and Avis sat in overstuffed, upholstered chairs and introduced themselves. Rex looked around, but didn't see the bellhop or their luggage. He could still hear the distant meow of a cat, perhaps two.

"So," said Rex, "Casa de los Gatos. Interesting name."

"Honey, I'm sure…" started Avis.

"Oh, yes," said Madame Julia. "Make no mistake. Back in the day, this fine establishment was a house of ill-repute in the 1920s, a bordello." She leaned in, conspiratorially. "You know, a whorehouse."

"We get it," said Avis. "Cat house. Jesus."

"When we bought it," continued Madame Julia, "my husband—God rest his soul—and I, we loved the idea of converting this into a place where people could actually get some sleeping done in the beds." She let out a loud laugh.

"Charming," said Avis, shooting Rex a glance.

"And you're Madame Julia," said Rex.

"Part of the charm. In fact, each of our thirteen rooms is

named after the girls who worked here. You'll be staying in the Cherri Room," she said, handing them the keys.

"Thanks," said Rex. "And our luggage?"

"Already getting cozy in the Cherri Room, John," said Madame Julia.

"My name is Rex."

"Honey, she's calling you John because…"

"All the men here are Johns," said Madame Julia. She let out her loud laugh again.

The Cherri Room was small and held only a full-size bed on a rusting wire frame, a small wooden dresser, and a cracked window with a frayed orange curtain. The walls were painted a chipping mint green. The bathroom must have been down the hall, Rex surmised. The only thing remotely new in the room was their luggage.

Avis crossed to the bedroom window. "Charming," she muttered. "At least we have a full view of the chicken barn."

Rex wrestled the key out of the lock and closed the door behind him. "It's just for one night. Then we can go find something else."

"Is this one of those stories we'll be telling our grandchildren?"

Rex moved toward the bed. "Close the window and come here."

Avis looked at him oddly. "You have got to be kidding me. Are you going to leave money on the dresser when you're done?"

"Haven't you ever—"

"No, I haven't. Besides, I'm feeling slightly faint. Can you go see if there is any ice and water?"

"Sure," said Rex. He closed the door behind him and walked down the hall. Madame Julia was right; every room had a name like Satin, Blondie, or Midnight. For variety, a sign on one of the doors simply read Tits. Rex thought of the old joke—*Did you hear the one about the blind prostitute? You really had to hand it to her.* Or maybe Madame Julia was making this whole thing up.

The bathroom was tiny but functional, with a small bathtub and no shower. Rex held his travel mug up to the faucet. As soon as the water came on, he heard that strange purring sound again. The purring got louder and turned into the rumbling sound he had heard on the road. It echoed throughout the room, bouncing off the ceramic tiles and increasing in volume by the second. He dropped the mug into the sink and put his hands to his ears to block out the sound. Finally, he turned off the water and the rumble stopped.

Breathing hard, Rex picked up the mug and looked at himself in the mirror. Three slight parallel lines of blood had appeared across his cheek. He investigated these red tracks tenderly. They stung like cat scratches. Grabbing some tissues, he dabbed at them. Returning to his room, he tried the door, but it was locked. He searched for his key but discovered he'd left it inside with Avis. He knocked on the door. "Avis?"

No answer came from within. Rex ran downstairs to look for Madame Julia. There was no one at the front desk. Dashing outside, he saw that it was already sundown. How long had they been here? he wondered, bewildered.

"In need of help, are you?" said Madame Julia from behind the front desk.

Rex swung around, disoriented. He held the tissue to his cheek. It still stung.

"Yes, my wife, I think she fell asleep, and I locked myself out. Would you have an extra key?"

"Of course, my dear. Enjoying your stay here so far? Everything to your liking? You'll want to tend to those scratches before infection sets in." She didn't move. She just stared at him.

"Everything's fine. Thanks. I just need to check on my wife."

"It's not the fanciest place," said Madame Julia, still as a statue. "Funds are low, so we make do with what we got. Your wife is worth a pretty penny, though, isn't she?"

"Pardon?"

Madame Julia unfroze and reached into the desk. "Here's your key."

"Thanks," said Rex. "Would you have any hydrogen peroxide? I'm not quite sure how it happened."

"How what happened, dearie? Are you okay?"

"My face," said Rex.

"Your face looks very fine to me," said Madame Julia. "Reminds me of my poor departed husband. Have a look for yourself." She moved aside to reveal a small mirror on the wall that Rex hadn't noticed before. The cat scratches were gone, along with the pain.

"I really need to rest. Good night," said Rex, backing away from her.

Madame Julia watched him with an unblinking gaze. "Good night, John," she said.

Avis was sleeping fitfully, thrashing violently every few minutes from one side of the bed to the other. Rex watched her as he undressed, wondering where he should sleep. The wire bed frame groaned from her movement, making rusty metallic squeals. A chorus of cat meows wafted in from the open window and joined the metallic screeches of the bed. Rex looked outside, but it was completely dark. The cats sang in unison from somewhere in the field on the peripheries of the property.

His cheek started to burn again, and a look in the mirror confirmed that the triple scratches were back, and they were bleeding again. He gently touched them, and as he did, there was a scraping sound on the other side of the door.

Avis continued to toss about erratically; usually, though, she was a calm sleeper. He peered out the window; the meowing had dissipated. No, not dissipated, he realized, just coming from a new direction. The cat meows were now coming from outside his door. The scratching sounds outside his door intensified as well. The caterwauling made the scratches on his cheek burn. Unable to stand the noise a moment longer, he opened the door.

The hallway was empty. The noise had stopped, supplanted by a gentle rain and distant thunder. Rex got dressed and closed the window. He looked back lovingly at Avis, though she was clearly in the midst of a horrible nightmare. She hated to be woken up once asleep, so he left her there.

There were no other guests to be found. He sat under an awning by the pool and saw from his vantage point that there were no other cars in the parking lot. The pool, a built-in rectangle, was clearly well maintained. The smell of chlorine hovered over it and underwater lights sent a rippling invitation to Rex to come in for a midnight swim.

He thought of having a quick dip, despite his lack of bathing attire. There was no one around. He hadn't been skinny-dipping since he was eighteen. He removed his shoes and clothes, tossing them into a pile by the lounger. He took a step toward the pool when something caught his eye. His pile of clothes began to move, the purring sounds began again, and a cat crawled out from under his shirt. It stopped and looked up at him. He smiled at the cat, a long-haired breed with burnt orange fur and a black stripe across its face. The pile writhed and a second cat came out, sat on its haunches, and looked at him. This one was a short-haired black cat with green eyes.

"Just how many of you are there?" said Rex.

In response, the two cats leapt up at the same time, each landing on Rex's shoulders. The force and surprise of the cats' jumps caused Rex to lurch backwards and trip on the leg of the lounger. Sitting in the lounger, he laughed—the two cats crawled down across his chest and landed in his lap, each cat forming a yin-and-yang as they settled against each other with a deep purring sound. Rex petted them and felt oddly comforted.

His clothes pile began to wriggle again and, one by one, ten additional cats came out and approached him, each one different in color, fur type, and markings. The purring got louder and louder. Each cat rubbed against Rex, butting its head against him, until he was quite overwhelmed by felines. They swarmed his head. The rhythmic purring enveloped him; it was all he could hear, and the cats were all he could see. He was lulled to sleep almost immediately.

Rex had a vivid dream. He was still at Casa de los Gatos, but it was 1923 and the brothel was in full swing. Jazz played on the gramophone and a gentle breeze blew across the back porch where he sat in a wicker chair. Madame Julia walked in with cool glasses of lemonade on a tray and handed him one. He drank it, and it was the most miraculous thing he had ever tasted.

A beautiful woman in her twenties with thick burnt-orange hair and dressed in a flowing black-striped silky robe came through the doors, took his hand, and led him upstairs. As they walked silently down the hallway, he could hear the sounds of sweaty love from the other rooms. They stopped at a door marked *Cherri*.

The woman smiled and licked the back of her hand. She opened the door and asked him to enter. The room was white and decorated with white wicker furniture. The bed was crisply made and rested in a shiny brass frame. The woman closed the door behind her and began to take off her robe. She kissed him deeply, and he tasted fish. Rex grabbed a corner of the bed covers and pulled them back, revealing the rotting corpse of Avis. She was horribly contorted, her purple neck and tongue grotesquely swollen. Her skin, the color of old cheese, glistened in the dim light.

Rex awoke from his nightmare with a start. He tried to scream but only a muffled, choking noise emerged from his throat. He was floating facedown in the pool, he realized. Coughing and spluttering, he dragged himself out of the pool and onto the cool, rough concrete. His clothes lay in a neat pile, and there wasn't a cat to be found. Exhausted, he closed his eyes and fell asleep on the wet concrete, dreaming that he was a tiny mouse lying on a cat's tongue.

He woke up on the hot concrete and looked up at the bright sky. He got up and stretched, expecting to be sore and stiff, but he had never felt better. The scratches on his cheek were gone and the warm sun had made a cozy bed of the concrete. It was then he realized that he was completely naked. Rex quickly got dressed and went to his room. The door was locked, so he knocked, hoping he wouldn't have to ask Madame Julia for a third key. He heard movement on the other side of the door.

"Rex?" said Avis weakly.

"I'm locked out," said Rex.

He heard her exhale irritably, followed by shuffling noises as she made her way to the door. She opened the door and immediately turned to go back to bed.

"Oh, honey," said Rex. "What's the matter?"

"I've never been this sick," she said, crawling into bed and covering herself with the sheets. "My back is killing me. I can't breathe. My throat's closing up."

"Let's get you to a doctor," said Rex, having no idea how he was going to accomplish this feat.

"A doctor? It was all I could do to let you in. I'm here for the day. Need to sleep." She winced in pain.

"Can I ask you something stupid? I mean, I should know this since I'm your husband and all."

"What?"

"Are you allergic to cats?"

"It's a good thing you didn't become a doctor. That's a terrible diagnosis," said Avis. "No, I'm not allergic to cats. I had one when I was a little girl."

"I'll see if they have any medicine here," said Rex turning to leave.

"Rex," said Avis faintly, "hold me."

He lay next to her and held her in his arms until she drifted off into another fitful sleep. He quietly left, remembering to take the key with him. Madame Julia was outside, feeding the roosters seeds out of a metal bucket. He explained Avis's ailments.

"It sounds like a severe cat allergy," said Madame Julia, smiling.

"Coupled with the uncomfortable mattress," added Rex. Madame Julia glanced at him, her smile gone. "Sorry, she's just very sensitive."

"I'll see what I have in the medicine cabinet," said Madame Julia.

"I'm so sorry to be such a burden. I feel like we're the worst guests in the world."

"Nonsense, I find your company very comforting. Now, there are the occasional stray cats here, so you be sure to keep her window closed and away from any breezes that could be carrying dander."

"Oh, shit," said Rex. He had left Avis's window open, thinking the fresh air would do her good. He ran to their room and opened the door to find her in the middle of a seizure. She lay on her back, her arms and legs flailing violently. He dove into the bed and held her tight. Her flailing stopped, but she was shivering. He held her tighter, whispering in her ear how much he loved her. Slowly, Avis calmed and went back to sleep. A cat with long burnt-orange fur jumped out of the corner of the room, leapt on the bed, then bounced out the window. He closed her window and quietly left the room.

"Madame Julia!" shouted Rex as he ran downstairs. The front desk being vacant, he ran outside and into the barn. Madame Julia sat on a hay bale, petting one of the roosters.

141

"Avis has gotten worse," Rex panted. "We need to figure out how to get her to a doctor."

"You won't get a doctor to come out here," said Madame Julia. "How bad is it?"

"She says she wasn't allergic to cats but now she's having seizures. Is there a hospital we could…."

"Seizures. She can't be moved. No phones here. Tell you what, my young man," said Madame Julia, while she stroked the rooster on her lap. "You stay here one more day while I tend to poor Avis. I'm a pretty good nurse, you know." The rooster stared at Rex helplessly. "I've got just the fix she needs. Nothing like good old-fashioned country medicine."

"I don't know," said Rex.

"*You* seem to be flourishing here," she said, with a guttural laugh.

"My wife is dying," said Rex. He ran out of the barn, determined to do something. If Avis couldn't be moved, he'd find the local hospital and bring a doctor to her. He raced to the parking lot on the other side of the house, but his car was gone. He felt thousands of eyes watching him and saw that the perimeter fence of roosters had once again surrounded the property. As he walked toward the triple ring of roosters, they gathered more tightly, fortifying their wall.

"What the hell is happening?" he muttered.

Rex ran back into the house, where he found Madame Julia crouched on her desk with a rooster in her grip, her teeth on its outstretched neck. She turned her head as Rex entered the foyer, and he watched her bite off the bird's head. Blood sprayed across the walls. Madame Julia caught Rex's gaze; she blinked, and her eyes became cat eyes. She opened her mouth, still ripe with the redness of the rooster, and let out an ungodly meow. The rooster lay limp in her paw.

Twelve cats came running into the foyer and surrounded Rex. Madame Julia-Cat watched from the perch of her desk as she licked blood from her paws. The cats circled Rex menacingly. A terrible purring and rumbling began, and Rex, with his hands to his ears, jumped over the cats and ran upstairs. He was more than halfway down the hall, near his room, when he glanced over his shoulder and saw Cherri-Cat chasing him. She leapt on him, sinking her claws into his chest as he reeled backward into his room. The door crashed closed behind them.

Five months later, Rex walked into the local Key West post office wearing a cowboy hat. He handed the woman behind the counter a slip. She went into the back and fetched him an envelope. He scrawled his name on a form. She noticed he wasn't wearing a wedding ring and smiled flirtatiously at him. He smiled back. He went out to his car and opened the envelope. It was from Avis's family's attorney. A handwritten note expressed his sorrow at Avis's passing and acknowledged that the vast majority of her wealth and estate had been transferred to Rex. The attorney ended the note with an attempt at humor. He said that while Rex's signature was chicken scratch, it was legally binding.

Rex drove back to Casa de los Gatos, where he gave Madame Julia the power of attorney form, along with all the associated account numbers and passwords. She nodded and told him to get back in line. He walked out to the property boundary and took off his hat, revealing a shock of curly red hair. The ring of roosters moved aside and gave him room. As they did so, Rex shrank in size and shape to take his place among them. Rex and the rest of the roosters all turned their heads in unison toward the driveway, waiting for the next guest at Casa de los Gatos.

THE CASE OF THE DISARMING DAME

I was on my fourth Guinness when the phone rang. After I finished an assignment, which meant after the client's last check cleared, I always had four beers and ducked for four days. So I was at home when I answered the phone. In hindsight, I should have let it ring.

The dame's name was Penny Plunkett. She said her boyfriend was headed for the pine box derby, and only I could help her. She pleaded with me to take the case, her voice like a wool scarf wrapping around my head on a cold day. She wanted to know if we could meet at my office. Then she let loose with the tears.

Outside, the rain pounded hard against my windows. It was the kind of rain where you expected to see an ark floating down Broad Street.

They say that if you look hard under every rock in this city, you're gonna find a story of brotherly love. But that's not the Philadelphia I know. Most of the time, the city's as hard and twisted as yesterday's pretzel. And if you're gonna make it in this racket, you better have onions of stone. You better be the kind of Joe that doesn't mind punching a guy until his face looks like a South Philly veal parm, the kind of guy that wants to save this dame on the phone from having to go to her boyfriend's funeral.

Well, that was me. Squint Lonigan, private detective. But even the toughest cactus can develop a soft spot for crying dames. I told her I'd meet her in half an hour.

I got the name Squint on account I was too proud to wear glasses, even if it meant I couldn't flash a heater. In this town, though, you didn't always have to fire a gun, just make the dumb mug think you're gonna fire one.

"Mr. Lonigan," said Penny Plunkett as she stood in my office doorway. I practically swallowed my cigarette when I saw her. She had a face that would make a priest forget about altar boys. And legs so long, the only thing stopping them from going on forever was my dirty wooden floor. Outside, I was all aces. That's what you learn in this business. A cool exterior always cashes the check at the end of the day. I torched another smoke.

"Private investigator at your service," I said, inviting her to plant it.

"I prefer Dick," she said, looking up at me with her gorgeous baby blues, the kind that made me want to slap the first guy who disagreed with me that men are just God's first draft, but that He got it right with dames.

"I prefer women who do," I said. Then I realized what she meant. "You pay my fee, you can slap my ass and call me Betty," I said, torching her smoke. It felt good to be close to her. "So suppose you tell me all about it."

"Yes. My boyfriend. He's in mortal danger."

"I'll need more than that to go on."

She sat back and drew a long one from her pack of Virginia Slims. The smoke wafted over her head like a halo. She seemed like a lost soul. A few minutes went by as she took another drag of her cigarette. Finally, she spilled.

"My boyfriend is Seamus McDougal. You've heard of him? He was in all the papers. He just won a full scholarship to go play soccer and study in Dublin. He's the best soccer player in the country right now. And he's being recruited for the American team for the World Cup. I can't allow that to happen."

"Sounds like Mr. All-American can take care of himself."

"But he can't," she said. That same scared voice that I heard on the phone was suddenly in the room with us. "The American coach is crazy. He'll do anything to get Seamus to join his team. I want to hire you to protect Seamus until he leaves for Dublin next week. I have money, and I'll double your regular fee. Only, nothing happens to Seamus. He can't be allowed to come in contact with that team or the coach. He must go to Dublin, and he must never learn I hired you."

"You fell hard for this guy, didn't you?"

"With all my heart," she said. She was back to being her perky self.

"What do you do?" I asked.

"Teach at Princeton University."

"What department?"

"Public policy," she said. "Particularly post-partum."

"This dame has been brought to you by the letter P," I said out loud.

"Pardon?" said Perky Post-Partum Public Policy Princeton Professor Penny Plunkett.

"Never mind. I need the name of that coach and when and where you and Beckham will be in town making with the red paint."

After calling for an appointment, I rabbited over to Coach Lombard's office, located in the old Eastern State Penitentiary where they now charged yokels a fin for a tour. The coach had sectioned off half of the jail for his World Cup training center. A guy hears all kinds of things about Coach Lombard. Mostly, that he was connected. Everyone knew his brother was next in line to be governor. I had never met the coach myself. I did most of my running while being chased. I walked into the coach's office without knocking.

"Ah, Mr. Lonigan, have a seat," he said in a gruff voice that sounded like a lawnmower in need of a tune-up.

What I noticed first about the coach was not his expensively appointed office, his thousand-dollar suit, or his scarred, harsh face framed by a Frankenstein haircut. No. What I noticed first about the coach, the little detail I picked up on, was that he had no arms.

"Old war wound," he said, noticing my gaze directed at his neatly pinned, and empty, jacket sleeves.

"Same war that they wrote *A Farewell to Arms* about?" I said.

"What can I do for you?"

"You ever hear of a soccer player goes by the name of Seamus McDougal?"

"Everyone's heard of Mr. McDougal, Squint. The most promising soccer player this country has produced in a long while."

I torched a smoke and asked the coach if he wanted one. A second later, I felt dumber than a sack of wet mice.

"And you want him on your team," I said, trying not to think about this man eating his corn flakes in the morning with his feet.

"Wouldn't you?"

"What I mean, Coach Lombard, is you wouldn't think of threatening him to join your team against his will, would you?" I met his intense stare. The coach had me by fifty pounds, but I figured if things got rough, I could handle a guy who wasn't going to be winning any Macarena contests.

The coach stood up. He pushed a pedal by his window and the drapes closed. He pushed another pedal and the lights turned brighter. "His girlfriend get to you? Let me tell you something about little Miss Plunkett. She's got her own reasons for holding on to Seamus. You're looking for trouble in all the wrong places, Squint."

"Story of my life." I stood up and blew smoke in his face. "Where's the rest of the team? I'd like to talk to them."

"This conversation is over, Mr. Lonigan."

I was nose to nose with this guy. "I'd hate to have to slap you around," I said, "governor's brother or not."

Before I could move, the coach gave me a hard knee to the old cheese steak and onions. The onions took the brunt of it. I went down quicker than Pavarotti on a Winter Olympics luge.

When I came to, I was in my office, wondering how a man with no arms could lug a 180-pound private detective up three flights of stairs. I didn't have too much time to think about it. The clock said it was seven-thirty p.m., and Seamus and Penny were meeting at an Irish bar at eight.

I needed to call in a big favor. I needed someone quick, someone who could dress up as an Irish folk singer and who was good with his mitts in case we got into a mix. But he had to dress up like a broad so no one would think we were there to mix. That meant one guy.

I called Fruity Molloy. Back in Shakespeare's time, Fruity would have been the star of merry old England. He was slender and had a high voice. Water cooler word was that he served himself from both sides of the salad bar. I had helped him out of a tight spot once and he owed me big.

No one at the bar looked twice at me and Fruity singing folk songs. They either bought it that Fruity was an Irish broad singing harmony with me on "Danny Boy," or they didn't want to catch a glimpse of the drag queen's lucky charms. Either way, I didn't care. I was getting paid more than I had in a long time.

We were into our second set when Seamus and Penny showed up. I was worried that something had already happened to him, and I wanted him alive so I could keep on collecting. Nothing happened in the bar. The only thing that got killed were a couple of folk songs. At around eleven p.m., Seamus escorted Penny out the door.

Fruity and I stayed a few blocks behind Seamus and Penny. The lovebirds looked like they were arguing about something as they walked home. Fruity lagged behind. He said he wasn't used to walking in heels. Somehow, I didn't think that was

the reason. Probably had his panties in a scared bunch. I told
Fruity he didn't have to go along for the stakeout. He kissed
me goodnight on the lips and got into his car. I reminded
myself to rearrange my schedule the next day so I could kill
him.

Suddenly, a black Caddy pulled up and two mugs pulled
Seamus into the car. Penny was left behind, among the dust
and noise of the screeching wheels. I bolted up the street.
"You all right, kid?" I asked.

She fainted in my arms, and I had a good mind to kiss
her right then and there. And I mean a good kiss—the kind
that you remember giving when you're old and in the P.I.
rest home; the kind that you hope she remembers and leaves
soccer boy for.

Who was I kidding? I slid her into the backseat of my car
and raced off, hoping to catch up with the black Caddy. I had
a hunch where they were going.

As I sped down the street, I glanced in the rearview mirror.
Angel-puss was still out. I thought about my history with
women. *Lucky* wasn't exactly a word that came to mind. I
once went with this dame who was an extreme vegetarian,
the kind who'll stick a cord of hemp in your eye if you even
say "burger." She told me that not only was it murder to
eat meat, but it was murder to eat vegetables that had been
plucked from their vines. I asked, "What the hell do you call
a hazelnut that fell from a tree? A suicide? Would you eat a
suicidal nut? Because you're turning me into one."

The black Caddy pulled up to Eastern State Penitentiary. I
put a call into Captain Mendoza. Philly's finest would be here
shortly. I also put a call into Fruity Molloy and asked him for
another favor. I grabbed the heater from the glove box, even
though it had no bullets and I couldn't aim to save my life. I
left the sleeping dame locked in the backseat of my car and
broke into the old jail. Coach Lombard's office was empty. I
heard shouting and walked slowly toward the ruckus, feeling

my way down the dark hallway. I found the source of the noise in the main shower room.

Prison showers aren't known for their Norman Rockwell scenes, but what I saw was something that a thousand maniacs couldn't have dreamed up in a thousand years. Seamus was tied to a chair, his head shaved; the coach stood over him. A doctor in scrubs was testing the blade of a hacksaw. The entire American World Cup soccer team was in attendance, encircling Seamus. But that wasn't the odd part.

Each and every player had been similarly shaved, and they were all, to each man, without arms. It looked as if they were about to make Seamus a team member with or without his okay. I barged in, my gun held out. "All right, hands up." Maybe I could have picked a better command.

They all spun around, each looking more nervous than a hemophiliac in a razor factory. All except the coach. He just stood there smiling wildly like a fat guy who's won a truckload of Ho-Hos. I circled around so I could get between all of them and Seamus. "Looks like you boys ain't taking home the Gold in the Patty Cake contest. Come on, Seamus, I'm getting you out of here."

The team moved to the exit where I hoped they'd run off. Run right into a net, if Captain Mendoza had taken my call seriously. The coach stood his ground. "Nobody goes nowhere," he demanded in that lawnmower voice of his. "The dick's shooting blanks. Ain't you, Squint?"

The team stopped in their tracks and circled back around the coach. They weren't buying what I was selling. "You try me, Lombard," I said, pointing the heater at one of the players. "You trained these boys hard, I can see that. It'd be a shame if something was to happen to one of them."

"I want to join the team, Lonigan," Seamus said.

Standing behind him now, I could see that his hands had been tied not to restrain him but to prepare him for his double amputation. A hypodermic needle with anesthesia was parked on a nearby table. It didn't make any sense. "Kid, before you ask Dr. Frankenstein here to lop off your arms, maybe you could ask him to take your head out of your ass," I said.

The coach stepped in. "Think about the fear, Lonigan. America has never won a Cup. Think of the fear on the other teams' faces when they see us get on the field. You want to talk about commitment? You want to talk about desire? You want to talk about intensity?"

"Let me ask you—what color is the sky in your world?" I said.

"Every one of these boys, including Mr. Seamus McDougal, is here of his own free will. Isn't that right, boys?"

They all nodded. Maybe I was wrong. Maybe in the land of the no-armed men, the guy dancing to "YMCA" is crazy. I turned to Seamus.

"Are you sure about this, kid? What about the doll? Doesn't she mean anything to you?"

"She doesn't understand," he said sadly.

"She understands, all right," came a voice from the doorway. It was Fruity Molloy, holding a piece of paper in one hand and Penny Plunkett in the other. It's always a bad night when I end up in a shower room with a bunch of guys and Fruity Molloy ends up holding the dame.

"Thanks, Molloy," I said. "What do you got for me?"

"Copy of a letter from the Plunkett family lawyer. It's from her parents saying that if she marries a guy with no arms, she's out of the family fortune."

"Bastards," said the dame. I suppose she meant all of us.

"Goddamn armists," said Seamus bitterly. I was beginning to like this kid. "One of Penny's distant cousins loses his arms in World War I and gets shunned by his town, and I have to pay the price."

Fruity let Penny go and she ran away. Dames like that always run away alone. I noticed everyone except Fruity was watching the caboose leave the station. I'd find her tomorrow and settle up.

"So that's why she wanted you followed. She didn't want you joining the team so she could keep the family dough," I said.

"Now if you'll excuse us?" said the coach.

I pocketed the heater and faced the team. "Sorry about all this. What do you guys do instead of shaking hands goodbye?" They violently butted their heads together. I turned to Fruity. Now I owed him one. "Come on, Molloy."

Sometimes, in this City of Fraternal Love, it pays to leave without saying goodbye.

FORGIVING YOKO

(Thick folder found in the bottom of my late father's memory box.)
A letter dated October 18, 2005

Dear Mr. H. Golden:

After retrieving all relevant files from your wife's office, I am sending you the attached items found in Petrina's file cabinet that do not seem to be related to work (I have obviously not opened them since I presume they are confidential). I apologize for this inconvenience, but yours was the only forwarding address she left us. If you speak to her, give her my best.

Sincerely,

Betty Rodriguez

Vice President, Global Timber Development, Inc.

Petrina Golden's private journal entry dated September 5, 2005, first page missing:

...direct result on my life.

I never agreed with your politics but as a woman, I had always looked up to you, Yoko. That feeling later turned to great disdain. No, wait, that's rather mild, actually. There were times I really hated you for what you did. I know part of it was my ignorance. You're from a culture foreign to me. But back then, you were my worst-case scenario. And the worst part about it was that I didn't even know you. No one did.

Except John, of course.

That was a long time ago. You know, it seems like yesterday because I can still feel the abandonment and absolute frustrating confusion. My eyes sometimes well up when I realize the anguish I experienced. At the family breaking up, of my parents breaking up....

Note from Ben to Petrina, no date:

I'd love to talk with you some more. Dinner?

Continuation of Petrina Golden's private journal entry dated September 5, 2005:

...Of course I don't blame you for my folks divorcing. I mean, was it a coincidence that the group broke up when my family did? My mother didn't approve of your lifestyle, which is probably what attracted me to you at the beginning. I went to live with my father since my mother had a black belt in lowering my self-esteem.

What was going through your mind at the time? Didn't you know he was married and had a family? That he was happy? What priority do you put on those things? Over your own feelings?

Why are we drawn to others regardless of consequence? Is it the way we feel when we're around them? Seems childish. But that's what we all are: lost children.

I was at a conference for responsible Third World timber management (in Cleveland of all places!). They had split up the rather large audience into several fifty-person groups to discuss modernization of African lumber factories. I was one of the few Caucasian women there. And blonde to boot! Some pompous moderator was feeling very full of himself that night. He went on and on. Just as I was about to stand up and respond to his incorrect assumptions, someone else stood up, a few rows ahead of me. I could only see the back of him: a tall, assured black man. I knew from his shoulders that he had to be handsome. He proceeded to tell off the speaker using not only the same points I was going to make, but the same language, the same words! When this man was done, I quietly said, "Amen."

He turned around, saw me, and smiled. Those penetrating eyes, the ones that took me deep into his soul and said we were of the same mind. An immediate visceral connection. It was overwhelming. I panicked and left the room at once. The first meeting. Was it like that for you?

Flash drive containing an email file from Ben Stafford to Petrina Golden dated June 3, 2003, Re: The Dancer's Body:

I know this is awfully forward of me but when we spoke yesterday, there seemed to be a sea of unexpressed thoughts and unasked questions. There is this line that people aren't supposed to cross this soon, even if invited. But as we discovered yesterday, you and I are creative people by nature, and the worst thing you can do to creative people is deny them the ability to express themselves.

So here goes. I'm stepping over the line. Just like that. Here's a small collection of what went unsaid by me yesterday:

I love you.

I could listen to your laugh, watch you smile, stare at your beautiful, expressive hands, and just fall into your eyes forever. You are the most interesting person I've ever met. There is a luminescence about you that I find difficult to describe. The way you carry yourself indicates a presence, a beguiling aura that is so feminine. That magnetic emotion you emit makes everyone's heart turn toward you when you walk into a room. I've noticed.

Physically, you are incredible. You possess a dancer's body, which is the sexiest kind of body there is. You claim not to be a dancer but the way you move or sit or stand, the way you hold yourself, is always done in such an expressive, angular, curvy way that implies the promise of something exciting. There is more drama and suspense in watching you wait in line than in a hundred plays. That is you.

You're also thoughtful and funny. I adore hearing you talk. You are essentially a good person who feels pain at the plight of others, and you believe, I know, that the world is fundamentally a great place and its people are all deserving of kindness.

I love you. Mind, body, and soul. You are a complete woman to me. You share the other half of this amulet. We are destined to be together. Think of the odds, the overwhelming chance that in this planet's history of humans, we two should end up living here at the same time, on the same continent, and that we should find each other. Then add the chances that we would evolve out of small talk into an understanding of who we really are for each other.

I won't place you on a pedestal. I know it's awfully lonely up there. You are not perfect, nor am I. But we are perfect for each other. Our circumstances bear much thought, however.

How's that for crossing the line? If I have offended you, or if you'd like to send me away, I understand.

Email from Petrina Golden to Ben Stafford dated July 8, 2003, Re: That Beautiful Song!:

I love hearing your voice. It is so masculine, so primal. Shivers! Thank you for sending me that gorgeous song. Music is so important to me. Thanks for picking up on that. And thank you for the song we're in.

Email from Ben Stafford to Petrina Golden dated July 10, 2003, Re: That Beautiful Song!:

We're not in a song. Songs end.

Email from Petrina Golden to Ben Stafford dated August 8, 2003, Re: Oceans and Rituals:

Got to work yesterday and there was a message from you on my voicemail. You listen to me and give me what I need. You are not dependent on me, but rather we are like two timbers holding up an enchanted treehouse in the forest. Separate but together.

So you want to know where I was yesterday. All right, here

goes. But, sweetheart, promise me that if you think I'm a kook, you'll tell me right away. I'm serious about that.

When my father died three years ago, I was his only child, his only family. I already told you that my folks divorced, and I haven't heard from my mother since. Being an only child is a horrible thing when you outlive your parents. I had promised my father that I would remain strong but I needed him to provide me with courage. He loved the ocean. He should have been a sailor. After he was cremated, the ashes were given to me in a cold, gray ceramic container. I couldn't bear to look at it.

Because I come from a cancer family, I made a pact with God that I would take care of myself, and that, in return, He would let me live to the age of ninety-six. I don't know where that number came from but it still feels right. I was forty when my father died. So I had a local craftsman make me fifty-six delicate glass bottles with an exquisite purple-orange shimmer. Then I had a chemist friend divide my father's ashes equally among the bottles. I'll never forget my father's remains being rationed out on a chemical balance like a drug. I know it sounds bizarre but neither of these people asked any questions. They just knew.

So now, every year on the anniversary of my father's death (which was yesterday), I rent a boat and take it out to the Atlantic with one of these glass bottles in my pocket. When no one's around, I say goodbye to a piece of my father and throw the bottle into the currents. This way, we'll both be gone at the same time. Isn't that the craziest thing you've ever heard of? And the loveliest?

Thought you should know what you're getting yourself into.

Letter dated August 9, 2003 from Ben Stafford to Petrina Golden:

How is it that we know each other? We met, talked, stared with anticipation, and shared that delicious silence: telling each other everything with our eyes, the shape of our mouths, and the sighs we let out. Distant voices from other rooms tried pushing in but our mutual gaze locked everything out but us.

We know this is wrong, that you are married and I am engaged. Those are the earthly, hard, cold facts. But this is love. Not some windswept epic love or high school hormone thing. This is a once-in-a-lifetime event, a herald to adventure. How can we not go forth and investigate? People talk and they always will. They are the watchers. We are the doers, the lovers. Every art needs a critic but it doesn't stop the art.

Those are my thoughts on you, on us. I love you.

Email from Petrina Golden to Ben Stafford dated September 27, 2003, Re: The Time for African Skies:

That phone call today! Ben! I could talk to you all day. Thanks for sharing so much with me. It was so special. You are right; I did feel alone when we hung up. I realize that three weeks with no communication is a blip, but it's also a lifetime.

I looked it up. South Africa is six hours ahead. So here are the final touches to the plan. At five p.m. my time, and eleven p.m. your time, we'll look up at the same liquid sky, the same brie moon together, my darling. That is the time for our African skies. I want you to breathe in that whole savannah sky and know that we will be under it together soon. For now, know that we are both gazing upon the same stars, being bathed in the same moonlight.

As you fly from Oregon over me, you will eclipse slowly to my time zone, and then you'll be ahead of me in Mandela time. That is you perfectly. You are my yesterday, my today, my tomorrow.

Until we can speak again.

Email from Ben Stafford to Petrina Golden dated September 29, 2003, Re: The Airport!:

Angel woman! Flight delayed by more than nine hours! But I'm in your time zone, albeit in Miami. We are looking at the same sun, and all I desire is your warmth beside me. As I'm sure you have guessed by the time you get this email, I devised an inspired plan with my windfall of time. I grabbed a quick flight up to New York, rented a car, stopped by a florist, walked into your office, and did the whole thing in reverse just in time to catch my flight to Johannesburg! So you see, it was I who left you those roses and the compass. I'll bet you wish you were in your office today! All these spontaneous things poured out of me because of you. Why the compass? For when you get lost.

This may be the last time we communicate for a while. Feels like I'm going to war and you're at the train station kissing me goodbye. When I get back, we must talk about this situation. We both know that. Until then, smile that secret smile for me. And for yourself.

First-class posted 9" x 13" envelope labeled, "Ben" and postmarked October 7, 2003, from Johannesburg, ZA:

THE COMPASSED MOON
Let this compass point you
to me
When you lose your way.
Hold it gleaming in the air, feather-light
Locating rapture in your day
And your secret arms around me at night,
Your fingers meshed at the small of my back
Like a lovely needlepoint
Binding you close to me.

Let this compass point you
to yourself
The left-sided/right-sided you.
Deepest sorrow and loss

Upset by dizzying heights and
Soaring strands of private music.
Partner to all,
You are the Mother and the World is your son.
Daughter of the past, making peace with the dead.
In the crowded, shimmering night sky,
Ever radiant in the singular moonlight.

Let this compass point others
to you
Your love of the crescent moon
Is a beacon for others.
A wine tasted eagerly but not savored and grasped,
In the same instant a woman and a little girl.
Flowers that bloom in every shape throughout the year
Are all you;
To be admired and, yes, gathered.

When the business ventures bitter,
When the artist's desperate journey seems in peril,
When the furious seas find your ship's bow,
Let this compass direct you to your heart's sweet venture;
To North which is love and safe harbor
And to True North
Which is me.

*Email from Petrina Golden to Ben Stafford dated October 11, 2003,
Re: Reborn in the City:*

I'm writing to you in an empty house again. Harry, too, is
traveling on business, but it's only for a few days. I made the
beds in the kids' rooms. They're away at college but I like to
keep things in order when I can. Before you, my whole life
was in order. I say that to thank you.

I tried to take a walk around New York City, hoping that
the busy streets and noise would raise my spirits. The lonely

crowd syndrome is a tough one to beat. I was waiting to cross the street when my knees went weak. I grabbed onto the light pole for dear life. There I was, clinging to this cold metal pole, as the crowd hurriedly walked across the street, leaving me behind. I screamed out for you, calling your name for the first time. The rush of the city absorbed your name with no response, but saying it aloud calmed me.

Africa must be amazing. The cradle of civilization—it's where we all started. I don't even know if you'll get this email. At least you'll have a stack of these things when you return in ten days. But who's counting? You've opened up so much in me. I see things differently, brighter. I feel like a woman again, a feeling I hadn't even known I had lost. And I am revealed with you. I've never been so naked with anyone. I'm like one of my models when I paint but with everything exposed—my past, my thoughts, my soul. And here's this man who looks at me and approves and wants more, warts and all. I haven't managed to scare you off yet. Or bore you to death. I still don't quite believe you are real.

I can't accept that we are doing this still. Married women of twenty-three years aren't supposed to act in this fashion. I thought I had grown up, but it turns out I'm still a kid, learning about my new adult life, my complete life with you.

You know what I love about you? I can go out there and be a hard-as-nails businesswoman in a tough, male-dominated world, pursue my work, my dreams, and my art, and you simply let me. You encourage me. You aren't intimidated by all that. You don't punish or hate me for it. And at the end of the day, I can crawl into your lap and be your little baby doll. I love you for that.

Yes, we will talk about Harry and Becky when you return, but not like this. In person, as we agreed. I do love him, you know. It pains you to hear that, I know.

I'm starting to cry again. Promised myself I'd limit that to only four times a day.

Take care of yourself and know that you are loved.

Letter from Ben Stafford to Petrina Golden dated October 16, 2003:

Petrina. Just saying your name reassures me that you are real. I hope you are well. As you know, we have not been able to set up telephone or data transmissions here. The Third World really is a different universe. I feel very isolated. The rest of the team here, including the senator, are working night and day to work out a solution so we can get these lumber factories at full production in an environmentally safe fashion. I am exhausted but am doing everything I can to stay busy.

You are the light that keeps me going. Everywhere I look—the great flat plains, the soaring mountains, the vegetarian food, and the kind faces of the villagers we meet—you are with me. The Africans are a remarkable people. They are constantly laughing, touching, and trying to connect with others. Very sensual, very tactile people.

You would love it here. I keep looking up at our African skies every night and my heart lifts with the moon birds above. The team here has noticed, without too much detective work or insight, that something's going on with me unrelated to Becky. I hope you don't mind but I told the senator and two of my business partners about us. They are in full support. The senator even wrote a speech using our relationship as an analogy (without our names, of course!) and faxed it to Washington.

The strangeness of this life cannot be measured; how do we go from leading ordinary lives to having our story discussed on the Senate floor?

Since I've gone this far, I might as well tell you that I have thought about getting out of this engagement since I met you. These are terrible things we consider, you and I. Many will be hurt. We are selfish and childish. But how can we deny each other a lifetime of rapture and deep love? Many things to talk about. Regardless of the outcome, I will have no regrets about having known you. I will always love you.

Give yourself the biggest hug from me and know that this will all work out.

Continuation of Petrina Golden's private journal entry dated September 5, 2005:

Harry and I met in college. His parents had died when he was young, and he was on his own. We have always felt, and still do, so comfortable around each other. We give each other what we need. We have grown together and are truly married. However, he is still the same young man I married with no hope of growing up or changing. He doesn't support my work or my painting. He has even said that he prefers me at home. Often, I just feel tolerated.

This comfort is blinding. I lost myself in his warm embraces and reassuring talks. I was so many things—mom, wife, neighbor, PTA member, businesswoman. I got lost, and I didn't even know it.

It has taken me years to realize that Harry and I have stayed together because he was in need of a mother and I desperately needed a father. That was our love. That has always been the basis of our relationship. And it isn't a bad basis. Until I woke up. Until Ben woke me up.

E-mail from Ben Stafford to Petrina Golden dated December 20, 2003, Re: Becky:

I've been engaged to her since before I even met her. Our parents were always close, since their days in Jamaica. It was a foregone conclusion that their children would marry, making their bond official. Becky and I were born within three weeks of each other, so tell me this wasn't planned! I have pictures of us at four, five, and six years old dressed up as a bride and groom for Halloween.

At first we didn't realize we were pledged to each other

and played normally as children do. The teenage years were tough because the two governing tides in a teenager's life—rebelling against one's parents and hormonal drives toward the opposite sex—were completely opposed with us. We wanted to separate to upset our parents, but we were drawn to each other sexually. We always listened to our parents in the end. Sometimes right away, sometimes after twenty years. But they always won. I didn't have it in me to break off the engagement and now the wedding is four months away. Then, like a cosmic poker game, the heavens looked down and said, "I'll see you one Becky and raise you one Petrina." Bless you. I can't wait until you come out here.

Copy of letter dated March 12, 2004, from Petrina Golden to Ben Stafford:

Couldn't bear to send this to you so impersonally via email, but then couldn't bear to tell you over the phone either. My children, my husband. They mean too much. I haven't slept lately and feel so paranoid. They must all know. I'm not a religious woman but find myself thinking about sin a lot. What are we doing?

We knew this wasn't going to be possible. Why did I wave my arms about when I am not in need of rescue? This has remained unexpressed for too long. The more I want to be with you, the guiltier I become. Too many lives to ruin. Who am I to be that memory for my children?

Ben, I'll never forget you, and I'll carry you around in my secret pocket always. Thank you for showing me that I am someone to be loved, that I am a woman. And for the riches you have bestowed on my soul. I love you. Have a good life and know that I am watching over you.

Continuation of Petrina Golden's private journal entry dated September 5, 2005:

What is it like when you realize you are breaking up a

family? What justification makes you carry out plans like that? Love has a price tag, and, romantic or not, it comes at a handsome cost.

I told Ben no.

The most wrenching decision of my life. I took everything that was personal and unrevealed about me, everything pure, untouched, and intact from my heart, and placed it away in the attic of my mind. I returned to life as usual. The crying took nine days to stop.

I lost weight and threw myself into my work. Periodically, I found myself out of breath, gasping for life as if I were underwater. Ben never left my mind. I gave it a year to forget him but he stayed with me. To his credit, he remained out of touch.

I was sadder at the end of that year than I had ever been. A great blandness settled into me. Nothing excited or saddened me. I was on too even a keel and lacked the capacity to experience any emotion.

On the first year anniversary, to the very day, of my goodbye letter, Ben emailed me. But it was too late. Two weeks prior, my heart literally exploded.

Email from Ben Stafford to Petrina Golden dated March 12, 2005, Re: Hello:

I know there is an ongoing embargo, but I thought I'd break rank and say hello. How are you, Petrina? I hope you have found joy in your life. As you can see by this communication, I've learned not to always follow orders.

I've divorced Becky, been cut off from my parents' will— the whole nine yards. I've moved away from their side of the country and am now living in Maryland. I've not fallen into the temptation of driving the six hours to see you.

I was wrecked by you, and yet you have sustained me throughout this turbulent year. I tried to rationalize that it was over between us, and I felt our journey together had reached its natural conclusion, that we had given each other the energy we needed to proceed with our lives.

I was foolishly wrong and we have wasted a year!

I love you still and that remains undiminished. What am I to do? We are still meant for each other. I know you disagree, and I will understand if you choose not to respond. Just tearing my heart out as I write this. Goodbye.

Continuation of Petrina Golden's private journal entry dated September 5, 2005:

Hypertrophic cardiomyopathy. It crushed me and sent me reeling to the emergency room in the middle of the night. Harry was away on business, and so again I was terribly alone and near death. Ironic that cancer had always claimed my family, but even with all the health food and daily exercise, it was my heart that gave out on me.

The wall between my left and right ventricles became enlarged and was preventing blood from getting into the left ventricle. I have felt this way emotionally since I said goodbye to Ben, and now the doctors have confirmed it with their tests. To add further to the lunacy and pain, the doctor tells me that this is hereditary from my father's side. My father, who was supposed to give me courage and strength, has passed on this suffering, this anguish to me.

They operated, inserting little gizmos, and snipped here and there, trying to give my heart a second chance. No promises were made. I could still go at any minute, or I could live until the ripe old age of ninety-six. I stayed, alone, in the hospital for two days before my kids heard and were able to visit. Harry came a week later. He has always feared death, and this new reality scared him. He had always been a provider, never a caregiver. But what happens when your caregiver is the one in need of you? Harry chose to ignore the answer and brought me flowers instead.

Floral card attached to three pressed "Get Well" mylar balloons:

Called your office and heard the news. I'll be there today.

Continuation of Petrina Golden's private journal entry dated September 5, 2005:

Two weeks after my surgery, I woke up in the same hospital bed. It felt as if I'd been there for months. Every day it was the same view, the same scenery. Except this morning, Ben was standing in the doorway with tears in his eyes.

Please, God. No IV drips, no pills. Just give me this man, and I'll be well. As we were meant to be.

I carefully explained my condition. I was being released in a week, but I would have to exercise religiously and eat a careful diet. And even with all that, I could check out at any minute. I was damaged goods. He leaned in and told me he loved me. He wanted me. He told me tenderly that any time together was a gift, a small miracle. It was my turn to cry.

After all that has happened, my father did bring me joy by bringing me Ben. Bless the two men in my life. I checked into the hospital as Harry's wife, but left with Ben. The children did not take it well, but they were old enough to eventually grasp the situation. A few months later, they told me they were tired of having a downcast mom and were glad that I had gone in search of my heart.

Harry said he wasn't surprised, but I could tell he was devastated. I have come to realize that even in marriage, we have no control over anybody's lives but our own. I cannot be a crutch to anyone. Ultimately, Harry has to find his own happiness. I will look in on him from time to time, but he has his own life to live and it stopped including me many years ago.

Ben and I are beyond happy. People look at us and beam as if they're at a Fourth of July fireworks show. There are always those who whisper disapprovingly behind our backs, but we listen neither to praise nor to criticism. We have each other and that is good food to live on.

So to get back to my point before all this meandering, I

have always blamed you for many things. You ceased being a role model for me. I didn't understand you. You exemplified everything wrong about love.

But I forgive you, Yoko. I know now and understand. And I'm glad you had your lifetime with your man. He was everything to you and he was worth all the misery that relationship caused. That misery is now a memory, and you will share eternity with him. You and he were one. I know now, and I forgive you.

FUN WITH THE KNOTT SISTERS

"Calm down, cherry. You don't look too sure about this. Done it a thousand times," Steverino said to Rudy as they stealthily pursued the blue ragtop Mustang down the lonely state route. Rudy, riding shotgun, had a strange, nervous look about him, which comforted Steverino. Rudy was a freshman pledge at Steverino's old fraternity, and another in a long string of customers.

"Don't worry, we'll get you laid tonight. Never fails with Steverino at the wheel," said Steverino, easing up on the gas. It was getting dark and he didn't want to get too close to their prey. A quarter-mile would do just fine.

"You don't talk much, do you?" asked Steverino.

Rudy, shifting slightly in his seat, gave Steverino a quick glance before returning his gaze to the car ahead. Rudy's dirty-blond hair was neatly combed and his complexion, thankfully, was clearing up.

Steverino, in his late thirties but still sporting the requisite facial hair and fashion of a frat boy, ran a lucrative night business that was quickly outpacing his cemetery grounds management day job. Fresh virgin pledges from his alma mater college fraternity were placed under his care for one week at a thousand dollars a pop. He taught them how to pick up chicks on Monday. On Friday, they took their final exams: getting laid.

The driver of the car ahead, a beautiful brunette in her twenties, roared along the two-lane highway, oblivious to the

169

fact that she was being followed. On either side of the road lay miles of cornfields. Steverino figured it would be a while before she got home. He would be patient. It always paid in the end.

Every night that week, Steverino had taken Rudy to the usual low-rent bar to meet women. It was a point of pride with Steverino that he never resorted to prostitutes to meet his customers' needs. Women who patronized these bars left with his boys of their own free will.

Steverino and Rudy had spotted the brunette on Monday night and immediately approached her. Rudy stood behind Steverino, as instructed, observing, watching carefully. The brunette, drinking alone, waved them off politely, clearly un-interested. But Steverino was nothing if not persistent. She had been at the bar every night and by Wednesday, they had coaxed her name out of her glossy red-lipped mouth: Gina Knott.

Despite giving them her name, Gina had seemed increas-ingly dismissive each night that she had been approached by Steverino. Rudy was fascinated by her but never said a word. In fact, he kept his distance, content to drink in her beauty from afar. Despite her continual brush-offs, Steverino re-mained very much in the game. Each night, however, just before going to sleep in his shabby one-room apartment, he felt that there was something strange about Gina Knott. He just couldn't quite put his finger on it.

Finally, on Thursday, just under the wire, Gina Knott turned her head in Steverino and Rudy's direction as she was leaving the bar. She gave them a brief glance, the slightest trace of a smile on her beautiful mouth.

Sitting at the bar, Steverino said, "See that look, cherry? It means she wants you."

Rudy felt that her look conveyed a sense of pity more than anything else, which made Rudy smile too.

"So what do you think of Ms. Gina Knott, cherry?" asked Steverino, his mouth full of chewing tobacco. Rudy didn't comment. He just continued staring out at the passing cornfields. "Pretty sweet that she's leading us right to her house, ain't it? Then we casually knock on her door. I'm not saying we force our way in if she don't take kindly to us, though shit, you know, I've had to do that before. But it's all good." Steverino suddenly thought again about the indefinable otherness of Gina Knott. "She'll be fine," said Steverino, muttered to himself. "I mean, at first, I thought she was a little...?"

"Creepy?" said Rudy. It was the first thing he had said all night.

"Well, if by creepy, you mean hot, then, yeah. No, I meant something about her mouth. Well, it don't matter now. She'll be fine."

Gina Knott's car turned off the highway and started up the twisting gravel road that led to her ranch house.

Steverino laughed, loving the sensation of surreptitiously following someone. He was so caught up in this joy that he never noticed the truck—about a quarter-mile behind—that had followed him from the bar to the Knott ranch.

Steverino was dreaming, disoriented, foggy. He felt as if he were waking from a deep sleep, his mind enveloped in what felt like a thick, burlap sack. His breathing was labored, and his heart raced. He remembered turning his headlights off as they made their way up the gravel drive. They saw the light in the bathroom go on and watched as Gina Knott undressed. Surely she knew they were watching her. This was clearly her signal that she was ready for them.

Steverino and Rudy exultantly broke down the door and ran upstairs to catch her. When they flung open the bathroom door, however, she was nowhere to be found. In the bedroom they were confronted by a startling sight: five Gina Knotts, each with differently colored hair, standing there, waiting for them. Behind Steverino and Rudy, two more Knott sisters, who had followed the two in their truck, blocked their escape.

Steverino didn't remember what happened next. He did recall shaking hands with one of the Knott sisters. And she wouldn't let go. Wouldn't let go. Wouldn't...

Steverino woke again a few minutes later, as the blonde Knott sister pulled the bag off his head. He was tied to a chair in the middle of a huge living room. The curtains were drawn and the only source of light was a roaring fire behind him. The living room was decorated in a rustic style, with bulky log furniture and Indian blankets. The Knott sisters, seven in all, stood in a circle around him wearing loose-fitting black robes.

"Whaddafukzhapnin?" Steverino slurred. His head felt heavy and he was having trouble focusing. Slouching to the right, he saw Rudy tied to a chair in the far corner of the room. Rudy returned his stare with the same fascination he had exhibited for the passing cornfields during their drive.

Gina Knott, distinguishable from her sisters only by the color of her hair, waved innocently at Steverino and smiled. Steverino instinctively smiled and tried to wave back through the ropes that bound him. It was then that he realized something was horribly wrong. *Wait a minute. Wait a goddamn minute.* With his left hand, he felt for his right hand. It wasn't there. He felt the broken bone and tubing and meat of the stump.

"Whaddafuk..."

Five of the Knott sisters each produced a severed finger— Steverino recognized his frat ring on one of them—and brought them to their waiting mouths. Their gazes fixed upon him, they began sucking upon his severed fingers. The other two Knott sisters, sans Steverino fingers, walked behind him and took hold of his left hand. He saw them pick up a pair of serious lopping shears, the kind professionals used to clear old brush.

Steverino's mind suddenly focused. He screamed in equal parts terror and pain as the anesthesia finally wore off. The two Knott sisters dropped the loppers and let go of his hand as the others dropped his fingers to the floor. The Knott sisters held hands and, closing their eyes, formed a circle. They began to hum and sway in harmony with Steverino's shrieks. His screams echoed off the wooden walls and bounced back and forth, creating an indescribable choir of panic and horror.

The Knott sisters seemed to drink in his fear, swaying to the power of his cries and growing increasingly aroused. After twenty minutes, Steverino started to pass out. Gina Knott yanked him up by the hair and slapped his face. When his eyes focused blearily on her, she leaned in closer. "We're not done with you yet, cherry," she hissed.

Then, to Steverino's horror, her face ripped apart to reveal seven snakes, each equipped with enormous deadly fangs. The seven snakes, as he watched, transfixed, then merged into one giant snake that lunged at his neck, sank its fangs into his flesh, and just as quickly withdrew. Steverino screamed again and again and the seven Knott sisters drank in his fear until they were done with him.

Then they slit his throat.

Rudy sat calmly in his chair as the Knott sisters encircled him, hands clasped. He looked at them curiously. Unbeknownst to the freshman, the Knott sisters were succubae from another dimension, and they relished nothing more than the delicate energy that accompanied Earthlings' fear of death.

"This one isn't scared," said the redhead.

"How can he not feel fear?" asked the brunette.

"Is he one of their slow ones?" asked the strawberry blonde.

"It doesn't matter," Gina insisted. "They're all the same in the end."

At once, the heads of the seven Knott sisters each burst open to reveal seven snakes, each hissing and snapping at Rudy's bound body. Rudy let out a soft, satisfied groan as his clothes ripped apart, his body growing exponentially in size. He was transformed into a purple-scaled, six-legged beast with a blue-furred head, from which emerged an enormous snout. His mouth, lined with eight rows of razor-sharp teeth, snapped open, seized the snake-headed sisters, and swallowed their heads whole. The Knott sisters' bodies, having reverted back to their reptilian state, wriggled and writhed on the floor. He sucked them down, tasting the years of delicious fear distilled in each one of them.

Content with the night's repast and back in human form, Rudy slid behind the wheel of Steverino's car and proceeded down the highway. He didn't notice the two-seater Miata slowly following him into the dark night, its driver smiling to herself.

THE COBBLER CHERRY

The passenger, a distinguished gentleman who had thus far vigorously enjoyed his fifty-three postnatal years, awoke in a small, unfamiliar room to the rumbling of muffled thunder from above. The porthole informed him that he was at sea, quite likely as a passenger aboard a cruise ship. He attempted with great effort to recall why he was traversing a body of water, but his head pounded with such brutality that he abandoned all hope of intersecting with a sufficient conclusion. Wiping the perspiration from his brow, he opened his eyes and vaguely recalled his recent dream, in which he had been dying of a self-inflicted gunshot to the brain. His head, now slightly more alert, continued to throb as if a thousand little dancing robots had mistaken his cranium for a stage.

The morning sunlight beaming in the porthole suggested that the rumbling thunder was not due to inclement weather, but rather to someone snoring in the cabin above. It sounded as though the poor fellow was in vigorous training for some new Olympic snoring event and, determined to bring home the golden medallion, had thrown himself into the compulsories with great zeal and enthusiasm. The passenger held his head tightly, hoping to squeeze it into some semblance of lucidity, but it was of little use. The horrific snoring from above was an incessant distraction and brought to mind a wounded yak in heat, in the process of extracting its trapped paw from a pool of tar. Standing on his bunk, beneath the cabin's ceiling vent, he rapped on the ceiling with his knuckles and cleared his throat, ready to aim his vocal projections up through the ductwork.

"Pardon," he exclaimed loudly in a froggy voice. He cleared his throat, his head pulsating with pain. "I say, are you quite all right up there?" The person in the cabin above responded with even more enthusiastic snoring, having moved on from the compulsories to the finals. "Now, really," said the passenger, resolved to wake this human outboard motor. He banged with more force on the ceiling. "A bit rude, going on as if this ship were your own private yacht!"

This was followed by the sound of a large gulp of air being sucked in very quickly. "Huh? What? Eh?" came the muffled voice of the snorer awaking to consciousness.

"Ah, my dear fellow, your wind tunnel experiments have attained resolution and we can count you among the living. Excellent. Good morning. Sorry about all the banging!" the passenger called through the vent..

The snorer took in another gulp of air. "Who…? What…? Where are you? What's happened?"

"Yes, all reasonable and cogent questions. I found myself asking the very same when I awoke just minutes ago."

"Are you a ghost?" the man upstairs asked, his voice echoing through the vent.

"Well, I imagine I look a fright, if that's what you imply. No, no. I am merely a fellow passenger, albeit on a lower deck. As circumstance and fate have dictated, I am beneath you. And it appears that we are on a ship of some size." There was no response so the passenger continued with a nagging question. "Tell me, you don't happen to be a telemarketer, do you?"

"Eh?" came the response from above.

"Right. Oddish question. This telemarketer, you see, has been calling me at home with alarming frequency, insisting that I join some technofunk web-streaming club. Driving me crazy, is what he's doing. At least I think it's a he. Distorted voice, I believe. Still. Hell of a snore you've got there, by the way. I'm sure you've been told. Really first rate."

"Who are you?" repeated the man from upstairs.

"Yes, who am I?" The passenger thought it a relevant question. He found it difficult maneuvering through the jungle of his thoughts while all conscious ruminations were blanketed with pain. Who, in fact, was he? Suddenly, a thought darted through the underbrush, and he grabbed hold of it, wincing as the little dancing robots came back for an encore.

He was a judge. Yes, a judge. But what kind of judge? A court judge, perhaps? Maybe a federal court judge in the who's-it-what's-it District. His mind was full of holes.

"You still there?" asked the man from upstairs.

"Just," said the passenger.

"Me, too," he replied. "Here until I find her."

"Yes, let's talk of you. Nothing on my end but fog and confusion. You wouldn't happen to have two aspirin the size of deck chair cushions, would you? No? Well. How goes it over there? Who's this mysterious *her* you refer to? Love is involved, I presume?"

There was a groan from above. "You mentioned my snoring before. I used to be a quiet sleeper but recently started snoring. It got so bad, my lover left me. I followed her onto this ship as a stowaway. I probably shouldn't be telling this to a stranger but you seem trustworthy," he said.

"A more excellent judge of character there has never been. Please, continue. I find your woeful tale soothing to my headache."

"When we dock, I hope to find a cure for this cursed snoring." A distant metal clang sounded from above. "Wait! I hear a steward coming. I must hide."

"My heart is moved by your tragic tale. But honestly… hide? With that foghorn of a snore? My dear fellow, surely they must know of your whereabouts from Atlantis to the International Space Station by now. And besides…" The passenger's diatribe was stopped short when he noticed the tag on his left big toe. He sat down on his bed, took off the toe tag, and examined it carefully. It said his name was Servo. He didn't remember being in a morgue. And he certainly didn't remember being released from one.

Servo lifted his head, his headache having subsided sufficiently to allow functionality within normal operating practices. He decided to start his day properly. His disorientation would be soothed by a brisk wash and a shave, followed by the donning of his favorite silk tie and matching waistcoat. He was pondering the fate of his upstairs neighbor when he suddenly became aware of the contents of his cabin. Strange, oversized metal shoes lined the wall, next to a sock monkey who stared at him through button-eyes. Servo shrieked involuntarily and scuttled back under the sheets, yanking the pillow over his head and coming to the doleful conclusion that it would take more than a bit of water, soap, and Japanese silk to overcome this peculiar feeling of apprehension.

After an hour-long personal pep talk, Servo screwed up his courage to the sticking place and pulled himself together. He realized that it would be rude to spend all day huddled in bed, particularly since his headache could now be filed under "manageable." He got dressed and walked out onto the observation deck.

Servo noted that it was, indeed, a massive cruise ship he was on, one apparently devoid of all other passengers and crew. The salty sea air, however, felt quite invigorating, and he was pleased to observe that his cabin was located on one of the higher decks. He took note of the gleam of sunlight on the polished wooden deck and mentally commended the crew for their attention to detail. Rushing waves lapped alongside the great ship as it sailed in the middle of an ocean with nothing in sight from any direction. Servo gripped the rail firmly.

Knowing just what to do in these sorts of situations, he went in search of the ship's bar for a drink that would muffle the little dancing robots that persisted in stomping on his head. Holding on to the rails, he smartly executed a hand-over-hand sideways shuffle that led him to the other end of the ship. A faint buzz sounded over the deck speakers. He swore it sounded like that telemarketer, taunting him to join the technofunk web-streaming club. He discovered the bar on the deck below his own. It was impressively stocked, and he shook himself a stiffish martini. He said a little prayer, wondering if there was a patron saint of Headaches-Caused-by-Little-Dancing-Robots and gratefully brought the glass to his lips.

"Hello," said a gentle feminine voice.

"Upon the soul of Saint Crispin," he exclaimed aloud, sloshing his drink. A beautiful Japanese woman had taken the seat next to him. "Sorry. Didn't see you there." He offered his hand. "Servo's the name, apparently. You rather snuck up on me, didn't you?"

"I am Sakura," the woman replied, her voice delicate and gentle.

"Funny thing being on a ship with no passengers or crew," said Servo. He picked up his glass. "Care for a restorative?" She shook her head. "Have you happened upon anyone else?" he asked as he mixed another drink.

"Only you," she said.

"My deepest apologies for that. Tell me, dear girl, are we sailing to Japan?"

"Not Japan," she said.

He took a sip of his drink and admired its bracing qualities. Then, with all the focus he could bring to bear, he took a good look at the woman sitting next to him. Wearing traditional Japanese robes, she was in her twenties, sweet of face, and fine of features. "And what brings you here, my dear lady?" he asked.

She sighed and looked away. "I am a sock monkey seamstress," she said. "There's not a lot of money in it."

"Live stitch by stitch and all that?"

"When I don't work my second job," she said.

"I rather like the sock monkey you placed in my cabin," he said. "Gave me a bit of a start, though."

She looked deeply into his eyes. "I am so sorry," she said in a hushed tone.

"Think nothing of it," he said, finishing his drink. "I say, is something troubling you?"

Sakura continued to gaze apologetically into his eyes. "You have to understand that Simon Cherry and I were in love. He was a handsome cobbler from my village. He is known simply as Cobbler Cherry. Our country had entered a robot for the World Dancing Robot Olympics, and he had designed an ingenious robot shoe. His dancing robot shoe was judged to be perfect by all who perceived it."

"Sounds like you rather picked yourself a peach in this Cherry fellow," said Servo.

"But a rival cobbler, who called himself Jolly Roger, was jealous of Cobbler Cherry. He tried to poison Simon before the competition. Thankfully, the poison did not kill him, but it left him with a horrible side effect, a terrible habit, which drained all the joy from our happy union. I was forced to break off our relationship," she admitted tearfully.

Before Servo could inquire as to the nature of this troublesome habit and properly offer her a fatherly comfort, she ran away crying. Moved by this display of emotion, Servo yearned for companionship. The sea had calmed, and he strolled the ship in search of a friendly ear. He came upon a stairway and descended yet another level. Without warning, his head pulsated with sharp pains, as if a rock tumbler had been installed within his skull. Falling to his knees, he felt a strange movement within his ear canals, as if small spheres were trying to escape his cranium. Were they fragments of his brain? he wondered frantically. He couldn't afford to literally lose his marbles at this particular juncture.

The faint buzzing from the ship's speakers increased in

volume, and he placed his hands over his ears until the pain subsided. At that moment, he recalled again the message on his voicemail, the telemarketer's distorted voice. Then the voice became a multiplicity of distorted voices, all pertaining to killer dancing robots. *We will rip out your who's-it and what's-it,* they seemed to say.

Just as he had given up hope of finding any peace, Servo came to the dining room. He didn't imagine that a meal would be served in a ship devoid as it was of wait staff. However, optimist that he was, he sat at one of the elegant tables and closed his eyes, trying to make some sense of recent events. When he opened his eyes, a young man had seated himself across the table.

"Evening. Roger's the name," said the young man. His black hair was slicked back, and his eyes were set apart just an inch or so too far for Servo's taste. He was a shifty-eyed sort, the kind Servo usually associated with pedophiles or lawyers who advertised on billboards.

"Upon the soul of Saint Crispin," said Servo, "people certainly do pop in, don't they? Roger, is it? Jolly good. Servo's the name."

"Yes, I know."

"Sorry?" asked Servo, puzzled. "Have we met? I must admit, you look familiar but I can't quite place it. Perhaps you're a member at my club?"

"And which club is that?" asked Roger.

"The, uh… Well, there you have me. It's the Something-Something Club. You'll have to excuse me. My memory's a bit off its feed today."

"Think nothing of it."

Servo found a small bar along the wall and mixed himself and Roger a drink. "Would you happen to know where we're headed?" asked Servo as he sat back down.

"As long as it's far from home, I'm okay with it."

"And what do you do, sir?"

"I'm a hypnotist."

"Really?"

"Oh yes. My specialty is curing people of snoring," said Roger.

Servo leapt out of his seat, spilling his second drink of the day. "Why, this is extraordinary!" he exclaimed to the man, whose name he had already forgotten.

"Why?" asked Roger.

"Because there's a snoring...something-something." Servo cursed himself for his inability to recall much of anything it seemed. "You're not hypnotizing me now, are you?"

"What answer would suffice?"

Servo looked into the man's eyes and had an epiphany. "What did you say your name was?"

"Roger."

Lucid thought graced Servo's head for the first time all day. He recalled, in a flash of insight, that he himself was a dancing robot competition judge. "Now hold on there. You're Jolly Roger. I remember now. You're the cobbler who tried to bribe me into favoring your dancing robot shoe design," said Servo, connecting the dots in a crackerjack fashion.

"All true," said Roger without a hint of shame.

"And it was you who placed those metal dancing robot shoes in my cabin."

"Now there you have me baffled. That wasn't me," said Roger. "I was invited on this cruise by a Japanese woman named Sakura with the promise that I would finally receive what I was owed."

"I see," said Servo, nodding his head, still feeling befuddled.

"But tell me," said Roger, "you were alluding a moment ago to the extraordinary coincidence of someone snoring?"

"The fellow in the cabin above mine is a hellacious snorer. A helicopter of a sleeper. Why did you try to bribe me?"

"What?" said Roger. "The shoes. He's trying to curry favor with you again."

"Eh?"

"What's his cabin number?"

"The helicopter? Well, I'm 408 so I would imagine it's 508. But about..."

The conversation would have continued pleasantly were it not for the fact that Roger immediately fled the dining room toward the stairwell.

Servo, finding himself again alone, decided to return to his cabin to dress for a morning of sunbathing. Perhaps some fresh air and relaxation would assuage the dancing robots. As he proceeded down the hall toward his cabin, the ship's speakers again bellowed white noise. The telemarketers were calling him with alarming frequency and tenacity, insisting that he join their interminable technofunk web-streaming club.

Hearing a scream, Servo bolted down the hallway, passing Roger, who was lounging in a deck chair in the morning sun. Servo came upon Sakura, clutching a large, bloody knife and sobbing inconsolably. This was all too much for Servo at so early an hour. It was one thing to have disturbing dreams of telemarketers and robots, spotty memory loss, and vague memories of a dancing robot competition, let alone finding oneself sailing on a crewless ship and being forced to shake one's own martini, but it was an altogether different barrel of monkeys to come upon an unattended sobbing Japanese woman wielding a bloody knife.

He approached her cautiously, as he typically did in these kinds of situations. "My dear girl."

"Again, I am so sorry," Sakura wailed, between sobs and hiccups.

"Think nothing of it. What has happened?"

She drew herself closer to him. "I insist you accept my apology," she said tearfully.

"And yet, under the circumstances, I would humbly suggest our topic of conversation focus on a certain bloody, serrated metal object. I respectfully draw your attention to Exhibit A in your hand."

"Accept my apology!" she demanded, brandishing the knife inches from his nose.

Servo, knowing when to accept direction from those of the distressed, knife-wielding persuasion, rapidly acquiesced. "Very well. I forgive you. You are hereby given a pardon in perpetuity and need apologize no further."

"Thank you," Sakura said, dropping the knife.

"Just one question, if I may," Servo said tentatively, nodding toward the bloody knife.

Sakura drew a deep breath and explained. "Months ago, you rebuffed Roger's bribe for the dancing robot competition shoe designs, and instead you selected Cobbler Cherry's designs. Roger sought his revenge, not just on Cobbler Cherry, but on you. He gave your name and phone number to an aggressive technofunk web-streaming club telemarketer."

"Pardon?"

"In addition, Roger left threatening robot messages on your answering machine. He knew these daily sorties would eventually undo you."

"But, my dear, how could you possibly know any of this?"

"There is not a lot of money to be had as a sock monkey seamstress," she said quietly. "I sell technofunk web-streaming club memberships on the side to support myself. I was the telemarketer. I am so sorry."

Servo, in a final moment of clarity, realized that his dream wasn't a dream after all. He had been driven crazy by the telemarketers and the answering machine messages, and, in a display of the ultimate "do not call" request, had personally escorted a bullet through his brain. He left Sakura and ran back to his room, diving under his bedcovers.

"Ahem," insisted a wooly voice. Servo peeked out from his covers. The sock monkey began to speak. "Sir, I insist you pull yourself together."

"Easy for you to say," said Servo.

"You must understand that Sakura thought her telemarketing calls were innocent," the sock monkey said, its head happily bobbing from side to side. "When she discovered how her calls were affecting you, she invited Roger on this cruise ship so you could exact your revenge."

Servo attempted to process this information without causing further mental injury. He sat up in bed. "I don't understand," he said.

The sock monkey cleared its throat and continued. "Sakura hadn't counted on Cobbler Cherry following her onto the cruise ship as a stowaway."

"You mean the snoring fellow above?"

"When Roger found out that Cobbler Cherry was on board, he sought out his cabin and administered a deadly overdose of snoring medication. Cobbler Cherry tragically expired this morning."

"Upon the soul of Saint Crispin!" exclaimed Servo. "How ghastly."

"After discovering this tragic event, Sakura arranged a meeting with Roger, who was under the false impression that he was due some dancing robot prize money. Instead, he discovered the singular misfortune of finding himself standing in the exact space and time being occupied by Sakura's knife. Death was, for him, unfortunately, astonishingly slow and painful."

Servo, ever the judge, saw the flaw in the sock monkey's story. "But I have just seen Roger. He was lounging on the deck as plain as the sun in the sky."

The sock monkey looked at him with pity.

"Cobbler Cherry is dead. Roger is dead. You killed yourself weeks ago. Sakura died in a car crash, which resulted from extreme sleep deprivation after leaving Cobbler Cherry's bed." The ship's speakers finally became clear and a great horn sounded. The ship was docking. The sock monkey hopped up and opened the door for Servo. "Come on then. We're here."

"It's been the strangest morning. So glad to be rid of this day," said Servo.

All four passengers and a very lively sock monkey marched off the ship to be greeted by Saint Crispin, the Patron Saint of Shoemakers, and a multitude of dancing robots, each of them pounding their shod feet in anticipation of the new arrivals.

BRAIN TAKES A SICK DAY

PLAN B

Life was absurd. Sue Jumper dragged along with the eight a.m. traffic in her new 1997 Ford Windstar minivan, sipping coffee from a Winnie-the-Pooh-shaped travel mug her kids had gotten her when she turned forty. The coffee, traffic, and morning weather were the same: thick, hot, and begging to get better. The Princeton Junction station was two miles ahead, but the suburban crawl of cars left her with the conviction that it would take years to get there.

Her kids had left, and it was just Sue and her husband in that empty colonial. After twelve years of marriage, she had found out about his affair through the goddamn gossiping book club. When confronted, he'd admitted to the affair but insisted he'd broken it off, that there was nothing more between him and the Slurpee girl at the 7-Eleven. He'd also agreed to marriage counseling. That was four months ago.

Sue sucked coffee from Pooh's insulated body and forced her mind in a different direction. This was *her* day, *her* chance at finding a new beginning. She was determined not to spend it wallowing in her woes, but Pooh's caffeinated innards offered little solace. She had been a CEO once. Two children ago. Seventeen years ago. A lifetime ago. She'd reentered the work force with a lesser-paying job with fewer responsibilities and hours. Everything about it was less, she reflected. Today, she felt, was the day for more. She had kept dozens of contacts, names, and numbers in a little black book. It was, she now realized, the secret Plan B should her marriage fail.

The parking lot was full, so she parked on a nearby street and walked the three blocks to the train station. She readied her monthly pass like a seasoned professional, then bought her usual *Wall Street Journal* and asked herself what other little rituals she used to perform as CEO. Making her way through the morning crowds, she found the food kiosk. "Coffee black and a blueberry muffin," she asked in her the-CEO-is-back-in-town-and-she-ain't-taking-no-prisoners voice.

The man behind the counter, his eyes glued to his Arabic newspaper, said, "Sorry, sold the last one a minute ago. All I have left is a jelly donut."

So much for take no prisoners. Sue walked away with her coffee, paper, jelly donut, smart suit, and sad life. Leaning against the barrier, she sipped the hot coffee and swallowed her bitter past. She had sacrificed everything for him. No more. She felt a sudden urge to buy a lottery ticket and, making her way back against the morning foot traffic, bought one from a vendor. Inadvertently reaching into her wallet with jelly-sticky fingers, she handed the ticket seller an unread handwritten note, along with the two singles required for purchase. She had used her children's birthdays as her lottery numbers, Sue realized. What a predictable suburbanite I have become, she thought.

Perplexed, the seller unfolded the note, which was from Sue's husband—written that morning and stuffed into her wallet while she slept. The note informed Sue that he was leaving her. Being a busy and efficient sort of vendor during rush hour, the seller tossed the note in the garbage.

11:00 a.m.

Sue was early for an important meeting across town, so she decided to walk. The traffic had been diverted around Forty-Sixth Street due to a car accident with a taxicab, and her route was strangely deserted. Her footsteps echoed between the tall buildings like the ticking of a clock. Where were Infotelcom's offices anyway? she wondered, her hair blowing wildly in the wind. She felt suddenly wild, as if she had an excess of exuberant, angry energy. She began to run into the wind, a Rottweiler-German Shepherd mix loping silently behind her.

Hearing the heavy pant behind her, Sue glanced over her shoulder and spotted the collarless mutt, running silently. Later, it would seem to her that she had always lived in the suburbs. Suburbs meant leashed dogs, which in turn meant dogs with collars and tags. She had never known dogs that didn't jangle when they walked. It was as if a naked toddler surprised his parents, who were accustomed to the plastic crinkle of diapers. Sue ducked into the revolving door of the Infotelcom building. The dog followed her in.

1:00 p.m.

In the emergency ward of the university hospital two blocks from her office, Sue Jumper was having her stomach pumped. She had been in the middle of negotiations with Infotelcom, when the pain ripped through her abdomen and caused her to drop to her knees in agony.

"You appear to have food poisoning from a randy jelly donut," the doctor proclaimed, skimming through her chart.

3:00 p.m.

The hospital orderlies placed Sue in a two-bed hospital room. After a brief nap, she woke to a room full of visitors, who had come to visit the man in the next bed. She asked the nurse to call her husband. Then she began to fret about the Infotelcom deal being derailed but felt certain someone from her office could keep things on track.

Later, after her fellow patient's guests had left, Sue introduced herself. His name was Craig Hoffman, the CEO of Futures DeltaCom, a competitor of Sue's company. He'd been admitted for minor chest pains that turned out to be gas. Their conversation revealed three things to Sue: first, he was single; second, he was handsome and very funny; third, he was looking for an executive vice president that could succeed to CEO when he retired. Craig was planning on retiring early to take up gardening, he told her. Sue ruminated over this information as he slept.

The nurse, drawing the curtain around Sue's bed, said gently, "You can go home in a few hours. We tried calling your husband at the number you gave us, but there was no answer. Is there anyone else we could call?"

Sue thanked the nurse but said, sadly, no. Her kids were away at college. She'd try her husband later. When the nurse returned a few hours later, she drew back the curtains and Sue noticed that Craig was awake.

"Can I go home now?" Sue asked the nurse.

"I am afraid we cannot release you without someone to drive you home," the nurse replied.

"I can give her a lift," Craig interjected. "My driver will take you anywhere you'd like."

"I'd like to find a place to sit and have a drink," said Sue, "with the nurse's permission."

"You should go home to bed," the nurse said with a frown.

Craig looked at Sue and she reciprocated, and there in the sterile quiet they planned a date.

7:00 p.m.

Sue and Craig made a good team. This was silently but mutually agreed upon as they waited at the bar for a table at Chez Watt, the avant-garde dinner theatre. Sue sipped her fourth Long Island Iced Tea and quietly developed a crush on the man. Thoughts of her husband, however, were very much at the forefront of her mind. He'd never visited her at the hospital; he hadn't even bothered to call. Now she was with a man who was going to set her career into high gear and who was, in addition, adorable.

7:30 p.m.

They were seated at a table adjacent to the floor-level stage, discussing the contract for her new position at Craig's firm while he tenderly held her hand. Her professional life seemed secure. Thoughts of her husband, however, were never far from Sue's mind. Then, glancing across the packed room, she saw her husband kissing a brunette from his office.

7:53 p.m.

All hell broke loose.

TELEPATHETIC

Judith Maisley was slightly telepathic. She didn't possess the type of powers that the FBI consulted when they were stumped on a case. Her telepathy was of a domestic, not-good-for-much variety. A piece of mail would arrive, and she could see all the people who had handled it en route to her house. Her husband would buy something and give her the receipt. She could determine, from the scrap of paper, the gender of the cashier, if they lived with their parents, if they had gone to junior college, and if he or she was still a virgin. She never revealed her secret gift to anyone and had a sneaking suspicion that if she did, her visions might prove to be wrong.

At eight a.m., Judith hung up the phone, convinced that Brain's decision to call in sick was going to have unsavory consequences. She called the temp agency to find a replacement, but when he arrived, Judith received the distinct impression the world was indeed against her. The boy couldn't have been more than twelve years old and had the red-haired, dim-witted smile of an Opie-savant.

Bob Steen, the CEO of Infotelcom, approached Judith in a hurry. "Where's Brain Ripple?"

"He called in sick today. First time in three years, I think."

"He's completely irresponsible," Bob snapped. "Call Human Resources and have them fire him immediately. They've figured out a way of breaking the news so he won't sue us for anything."

Human Resources left Brain a message on his answering machine, telling him that this was his last day. Fifteen minutes later, Judith, musing over recent events, told Bob Steen that Brain had cleaned up his office the day before.

"He's jumping ship!" Bob exclaimed. "Maybe to Future Tel-Link, or Communication plus Telcom Futures. Well, they can't have him. Call Human Resources for a counteroffer. Ripple gets a promotion to Northeast manager and a 25% increase in salary. No, make it 45%." Proud of himself, Bob Steen went off to tackle some other crisis.

Opie couldn't open Brain's file cabinet, so Judith called a locksmith—they needed access to Brain's files for a meeting later that afternoon with Sue Jumper. In the meantime, she sent Opie to the mailroom to keep him out of trouble. The locksmith arrived within twenty minutes, disgruntled that he had been called away from his scheduled work at Chez Watt fixing kitchen cabinet locks.

Watching him work, Judith thought how efficient office matters would be if the locksmith could place all seventy-two filing cabinets under a master lock system. With the corporate money Infotelcom threw his way, the locksmith could not refuse. Chez Watt's cabinets could wait for another day.

Meanwhile, in the mailroom, Opie was in charge of only one thing and he got it stupefyingly wrong. Infotelcom was waiting for a fax that contained a major part of the agreement it needed to win the $1.2 billion infrastructure project that had been bid in Mulvania. Opie received the incoming fax, then he sent it upstairs via the outgoing fax machine, since he had been told not to leave the mailroom. Tragically, the outgoing fax machine was, in actuality, a paper shredder. In a panic, Opie fled the building.

11:15 a.m.

Judith's day was proceeding with her usual frenzied rush. Being an executive secretary for Bob Steen was exhausting, and this day more than most. The Japanese were expected to partner with Infotelcom in a merger bid with Silicon East, Inc., and many protocols needed to be followed.

Judith had arrived by six that morning; by eleven, she had already performed what seemed like a full day of work. She had arranged lunch for their Japanese guests with the company's corporate caterer, Chef Henri Patelle. Bob Steen reviewed the menu with the chef to ensure it was appropriate, noting in the process that a distinct aroma of raw fish enveloped Patelle's person. Judith, her memo pad balanced on one knee, scribbled furiously as Steen dictated last-minute instructions for the afternoon's events. The shrill ringing of the phone interrupted them, and, rising to his feet, Bob took the call, taking off his glasses and dropping them onto his desk. Never quite happy being idle, Judith decided to clean Steen's glasses of fingerprints and dropped her memo pad unnoticed to the floor. "Mr. Steen," Judith said weakly, then louder, "Bob!"

"Excuse me a moment," said Steen into the phone. "Yes, Judith, what is it?"

"Bob, tell the Japanese not to meet you here in your office. Go out today," Judith said, with an uncharacteristic tremor in her voice.

"What the hell are you talking about? We've been through all that with the protocol group and we're meeting here."

"Just go out today," Judith insisted. "Please."

"I'll call you right back," Bob said into the phone before hanging up. "Mind telling me what's gotten into you?"

"A dog is going to bite you on the elevator," Judith said quietly. "You will lose your right index finger and there will be lots of blood, ruining your suit. The meeting will be cancelled and the Japanese will be highly offended. I'm afraid that is all I can see."

"Oh, Judy, you're a riot. I needed that light relief, especially today."

Bob gave her a hug, but Judith still saw images of the microsurgery team trying to reattach his right index finger, and the dry cleaners trying to remove the bloodstains from his suit. At that moment, the Japanese arrived, and Steen, still chuckling, released Judith and crossed to the elevator to greet his guests. Judith was on hold for an ambulance when she heard Chef Patelle's scream from the elevator.

12:20 p.m.

Judith Maisley, still feeling jittery over the events in the elevator, had just been served her salad. As a reward for muzzling the dog, Infotelcom had booked her a lunch reservation at Marta's.

"Excuse me, miss, but there seems to have been some type of mix-up here. You see, I'm—"

"Interrupting my lunch," said Judith, looking up from her mixed greens and buttermilk dressing.

Fred Evans had been coming to Marta's for hurried lunches and dinners since his divorce twelve years earlier. What was the point of being president, chairman, and CEO of Future Tel-Link if you couldn't rely on your usual table at Marta's? he fumed. He practically owned the restaurant on tip money alone. And now this stranger, this woman, who was not president, chairman, and CEO of Future Tel-Link was going to take his table? "This is my table, and you are eating my salad," said Evans through clenched teeth. His stress management training flew out the window, along with the succulent aroma of prime rib.

"You have wonderful taste. The salad's delicious," answered Judith, determined not to let yet another executive suit ruin her day. "Infotelcom, my company, got me this table. You can have it when I'm through if you'd like. Or better yet, go bother one of the waiters."

"I know Infotelcom and you're as good as fired," yelled Fred Evans, throwing down his business card as if he were challenging Judith to throw down a higher-ranking card of her own.

Picking up his card, Judith read it, rubbing it between her fingers. Looking up at the red-faced CEO, she smiled. "You're right. It is your table. Excuse me." And with that, she took her salad and sat herself at the bar. She didn't have the heart to tell Fred Evans that he was going to get fired the following day.

Evans savored his lunch slowly, only to miss his flight to Mulvania, for a bid opening for a multi-million dollar project. By the time he had booked a seat on the next flight out, his company was on the hook for much more than they could financially handle.

Judith went back to work with a dilemma. Having touched the competitor's business card, she was now in possession of insider information on the upcoming negotiations meeting. It was time, she decided, to get this telepathy thing working for her once and for all. She slyly revealed a little of what she knew, doling out the information like soup to the hungry. She made vice president inside of one week.

BAFO

Outside the conference room, Rodney Kemp paced the hall, cigarette smoke trailing behind him as if he were skywriting. The clock read one-thirty p.m., but time ticked by excruciatingly slowly. At forty-five, he had managed to categorize his problems into those that were either short- or long-term. If he was lucky, and he usually was, he had only one of those kinds of problems. Today, he had both in spades. He had had yet another fight with his wife that morning over her damn job, which was a long-term problem—due to the potential for paying long-term alimony. Inside the conference room, behind the walnut-paneled door, was his short-term problem. He needed a Best And Final Offer and he needed it now.

Communication Plus Telcom Futures had been the low bidder on the $300 million Mulvanian contract that his company, Future Tel-Link, had worked for two years to win. Kemp was made vice president with the clear understanding that he needed to win this job to justify his existence. He had been hired because he used to date the secretary who sat on the Board of the Tokyo Exchange, the group handling the procurement and financing administration for Mulvania. No one knew of Kemp's tryst with the secretary, and he had felt it was a good foot in the door. But now Futures had come in with a lower bid, and Kemp could hardly complain that the Tokyo Exchange secretary had given him bad information.

The good news was that Futures' international insurance coverage was under question, and they had one hour to resolve the issue, or the contract would be awarded to one of the other three bidders with the best offer. Sue Jumper was supposed to fax him some critical figures so he could make the call on how much profit to cut from the budget, the only way he figured he could win the bid It was, however, a tricky business—cut too much profit, he'd be fired; don't cut enough, lose the bid, and he'd get fired. Ten minutes to go. Where the hell was Fred Evans?

2:12 p.m.

Kemp needed Evans to make some hard decisions. Tokyo wanted Kemp to sign their contract "as is." If he did, the job was theirs. However, Kemp had some questions regarding liability and insurance. He stood before them all, forty people staring at him, waiting for a decision in a badly lit, stuffy room. If he said no, the next lowest bidder would certainly win the job.

Kemp turned to his client. "All right, I accept your terms and conditions, and as an authorized representative of my firm, I'm ready to sign the contract." But the negotiation wasn't over. The Japanese contingent asked if he could reduce the number of management hours by twenty percent. The wolves in the room drooled at the prospect of Kemp's refusal.

"That will be acceptable," said Kemp.

With that, Kemp signed the contract and two things happened. First, he effectively priced himself out of his job since his hours had been eliminated. This led to his being fired, which, in turn, led to Sue Jumper's being promoted to senior manager. By then, of course, she had already fallen in love and quit. Secondly, Future Tel-Link's insurance company tripled the premium to absorb the risk for which the company had signed. Fred Evans was fired the next day. Company stock plummeted, which caused Infotelcom's stock to skyrocket. This boon to Infotelcom caused yet another promotion for Brain to vice president of marketing.

THE ALL-DANCING, ALL-KILLING MULVANIANS

Sven and Olaf, sitting at a café by the United Nations, roughly gulping their double café mocha skim nutmeg frappuccino lattes, were secret lovers. The two were in a quandary over the state of affairs: personal, domestic, and abroad. To the casual observer, the men—both in their mid-thirties, large and muscular yet graceful and agile—were old friends reminiscing about a distant village, a forgotten debt. On closer inspection, it became apparent that much more was on their minds.

They were from Mulvania, a slip of a country in the Baltics, nestled in a mountain region so small it was uncharted. However, under certain political and military conditions, the mountain and its adjacent river provided the perfect geography for war, battles, mercenaries, and midnight contraband runs. Sven, general of the army, and Olaf, his captain, were greatly feared by their fellow Mulvanians. Vlad the Impaler would have been envious of their reputations on the field of battle. Together, they had liberated their people from their oppressive neighbors, the menacing Borons. A statue of the two men now resided in the center of Thalma-Laguine, the capital of Mulvania.

Mulvania, however, found the cost of peace prohibitive. Without war, they found, there was no profit. The country's dependence on American foreign aid encouraged the Mulvanian parliament to start a number of wars on various fronts, in order to revitalize their economy. Dismayed by the notion of perpetual war, Olaf formulated a plan to drive a different kind of income for Mulvania, a country that prided itself on its deep-rooted traditions, which included mythic tales of enchantment told to the tunes of local composers. So, under Olaf's direction, Mulvania formed an international dance troupe.

Olaf was their director, choreographer, and star. Sven, begrudgingly, was the second lead, sometimes playing the female lead. And so it was that the mighty general-at-war, in peacetime, assumed the role of second lead, sometimes a swan princess, to his captain. Their quandary, however, was as follows: Olaf had persuaded his parliament to finance the international tour on the ground that they would actually be gathering intelligence on the countries through which they traveled, a stratagem designed to strengthen Mulvania's position during the next war. It was all done with a wink and a smile. However, Olaf's love of theatre, of dance and expression, galvanized his dance troupe during their tour, and no intelligence was gathered. If it was discovered that the two leads were in fact lovers, it would cause a tumult of publicity in the host country; the Mulvanian Dance Troupe would rake in money at the box office, and perhaps be invited as guests on *The Tonight Show*. The true nature of their relationship would be considered a great disgrace in Mulvania. Boron would doubtless seek to capitalize on their subsequent confusion; Mulvania would crumble, becoming an obscure footnote in European history.

"Svennie," said Olaf, "we need to get out of this city. That is the only way we can recoup our dignity on this tour."

"I disagree. True, we have not gotten one review, not one mention of positive appreciation. Everyone wants to see that damn *Riverdance*. Who can compete with that?"

Olaf grabbed hold of Sven's hand, but Sven pulled away. "Sven, darling. Why are you afraid of demonstrating our affection in public? Maybe that is exactly what we need to get some asses in seats, yes?"

"I hate this city," said Sven, scornfully. The general, who had personally eviscerated nine Borons the prior Spring, rubbed some mascara from the previous night's performance out of his eye.

"Shtumpie, let's leave tomorrow. Tonight, we'll play our last performance in this city. Chicago is where we will make our name. How does that song go? 'If I'm naked there, I'm naked everywhere.' Now, about us…"

"No!" shouted Sven. He was the general again. Looking deeply into his captain's eyes, he said, "Let's see what happens. I'm not ready to give up my country, and Mulvania is surely doomed without us."

"How you speak! Mulvania will be around long after we have taken our last curtain call," Olaf declared, and he leaned over to bestow a passionate kiss on Sven's mouth. A camera flash went off.

12:15 p.m.

"Perhaps it was a Boron spy sent to discredit us! My parents will die of shame! The embarrassment!" Sven cried.

"Relax," Olaf reassured him. "It's only one picture. Probably just a tourist. Look, he's gone already."

"He is not gone!" Sven yelled. "There he is—the one with the red baseball cap. We need to grab him before he gets to the embassy, to their photo lab, their scanner, their modem! Before we are completely ruined!"

Olaf's dance partner and lover had turned back into the general he truly was. Neither parents would take the news well, but the dance troupe was sure to get marvelous publicity. "Sven," said Olaf soothingly, "America is a very forgiving country. Let's stay here awhile and finish out our tour."

"We couldn't even get our picture taken when we tried," Sven protested. "How many photographers have arrived at our performances? None. How many reviewers even showed up? None!"

"Look, Sven, focus on tonight. Winston Thurber of the *Daily Post* is coming, remember? Let us prepare."

"You go prepare for that bastard. He's canceled twice on us already. I'm going after that Boron son of a bitch with the camera." And with that, Sven took off at full speed, war in his eyes. Olaf had no choice but to try to keep up.

12:35 p.m.

By the time they arrived at the Boron Embassy, which was located under a Jewish deli, the doors were locked and the premises seemed deserted. "They are here. I can smell their kind," growled Sven.

"Only if Borons suddenly smell like pastrami and kasha," answered Olaf. "I told you it was probably a tourist."

Sven rushed up the stairs to the deli. By the time Olaf arrived, Sven had the deli owner by the neck, in a Darth Vader grip. "Tell me who is in there! How do I get into the Boron Embassy?" The old man had not had time to reach for the large ham he kept under the counter for just such emergencies; he began to cry.

Olaf seized Sven by the shoulders, whispering, "Svennie, we are not in Mulvania. Put him down, we don't belong here."

The general agreed. He dropped the old man and the two left. Once outside the store, Sven said, "After our obligations, we leave this country." Then they kissed for seventeen seconds.

12:37 p.m.

The security camera in the deli was, of course, hooked into the Boron Embassy below. The Boron counselor viewing the monitor immediately identified Sven and Olaf. He called his president with two pieces of information: first, Mulvania's army had attempted an overthrow of the Boron Embassy in the United States; and second, Sven and Olaf were lovers.

3:00 p.m.

Future Tel-Link's insurance company, Assure Insured, had been restructured to counteract the massive losses it had taken by investing much of its money and business in Mulvania. This, coupled with Future Tel-Link's handling of the recent bid, sent Assure Insured over the edge. The company filed for bankruptcy that day. In Mulvania, hundreds of workers had depended upon Assure Insured for employment. Riots broke out across the country, the stock market took a dive, and the Borons began to sharpen their knives.

3:30 p.m.

His Excellency Otto Ganglenene of Boron's ministers of war, peace, and dance troupes informed him that Mulvania was ripe for the plucking. Aid from the U.S. would dry up once it became known that their two military leaders were lovers. Any vestige of domestic morale would evaporate once the kissing video was televised. Ganglenene smiled and issued the command to invade and obliterate Mulvania. Two hours later, his orders were carried out.

The U.S. watched in astonishment—first, at the sight of the Mulvanian general kissing his captain; then, at one country swallowing up its neighbor like an amoeba. This sequence of events began a chain reaction within the various Soviet states, with political and economic turmoil crashing upon the shores of Russia, the U.S., and Europe.

4:15 p.m.

Infotelcom's CEO, Bob Steen, called the company's senior vice president, Dickens, that afternoon. Being one of three companies bidding for infrastructure work in Mulvania, it seemed likely that Infotelcom's stock would plummet after the evening broadcast. "How far into it are we?" asked Steen.

"I will confirm and get back to you," Dickens said apprehensively. He then asked his regional area manager for a status report. When it was discovered that the contractual agreement between Infotelcom and Mulvania had never been authorized or sent, the CEO breathed a sigh of relief. Thanks to Opie, the agreement sat in shreds in the mailroom.

"What happened?" Steen asked Dickens.

"Apparently," Dickens replied—not having a clue as to what had befallen the contract—"my project manager made the determination not to advance the deal. With my support, of course."

"Right," Bob replied. "Look, sorry if I'm a little grouchy, but I was almost attacked by a dog outside my office. The caterer took the bullet for me. Well, I can't thank you enough for your instincts on this one, Dickens. You'll have a spot bonus of five thousand dollars tomorrow. What's that project manager's name?"

"Ripple, sir. Brain Ripple."

"Mr. Brain Ripple is our new executive vice president in charge of international marketing. Double his salary. Good day." Steen hung up the phone.

7:30 p.m.

In the kitchen of Chez Watt, chaos reigned. Chef Henri Patelle had been hospitalized after having been bitten by a stray dog. The Mulvanians were performing that night, and Winston Thurber of the *Daily Post* would be in attendance. The front of the house was packed, and rumors were circulating that a TV news crew might stop by. The sous chef, Emile Chantoux, braced himself for the worst.

Sven and Olaf bickered as they applied their makeup. They had been rehearsing all afternoon and had heard nothing of their country's turmoil. The dance troupe had warmed up and their limber bodies tingled with anticipation. Olaf eagerly anticipated Winston Thurber's arrival. His glowing review would put them on the map and secure the rest of their tour. Sven, seething from the afternoon's events, sought an excuse to blow off steam. Performing Mulvanian folk dances seemed insufficient to the task.

Emile Chantoux, cursing and yelling, had thoroughly frightened his staff, who consisted primarily of street toughs and work release prisoners—gentlemen who did not scare easily. Emile had discovered that the cabinets containing the copper sauciers and butter warmers had been locked. When he asked after the keys, he was told that the locks were broken and only Chef Patelle knew how to open them. The locksmith, scheduled to come by that day, had cancelled. Emile, in a rising fury, fired the whole damn staff on the spot, then tried using his ten-inch chef's knife to jimmy open the cabinet doors. In the process, he ripped up a good part of his right hand and left thumb. While cooking was clearly out of the question for the evening, bleeding was an assured alternative with which to pass the time. He began to bark out orders to the staff.

Dinner was canceled, so the Mulvanian Dance Troupe took to the stage early. They found it a difficult performance, with an audience both disappointed and starving. Sven, red-faced with fury, danced like a madman, knocking into the other dancers. Olaf was also distracted, looking out for Winston Thurber's arrival. A stagehand, however, held up a sign that announced Thurber's cancellation, something about a car crash.

Emile's kitchen staff, furious at being summarily fired, stormed out of the theatre just as Sue Jumper threw an ashtray across the room at her husband. The noises startled

Sven, who went into battle mode. Olaf, enraged at Thurber's cancellation, joined Sven in pummeling the audience. Sven grabbed Craig Hoffman and flung him into the air. The furious kitchen staff, hearing the commotion, returned to join the fray. Emile watched and bled. Craig joked to Sue that they would need to return to the hospital. Sue's husband, grabbing his bruised forehead and the brunette, left the theatre, pushing past the TV news crew that were filming it all.

Several months later, Sven and Olaf were the hottest ticket in Las Vegas and the biggest thing since the white tigers had come to town. Mulvania, taken over by the Borons, ceased to exist. Sue was made CEO of Craig's firm, and Craig retired in order to pursue his gardening. Emile never regained use of his left thumb and, ironically, hitchhiked his way back to Quebec.

RIPPLE

Brain Ripple awoke with a start. His dream, like no other he had ever experienced, made him horribly aware of the life he was living. He had been shackled to his desk, suffering millions of paper cuts across his arms and face. Management, the faceless giant, hurled staplers, tape dispensers, and pens at him, while coworkers, walking past his office, were unmoved by his plight. He awoke, however, feeling buoyant and liberated. He wasn't going to work today. Not after that dream.

"Hello, Judith? This is Brain."

"What can I do for you, Brain?" asked Judith.

"Nothing. I'm just calling in sick today."

"Well, Cal Ripken breaks his lucky streak!"

"It's no big deal. I'm just feeling...what is it? Under the weather."

"I'll alert the chief, but he's not going to believe you broke your three-year record today of all days."

The meeting between Infotelcom and Silicon East had

been scheduled for that afternoon—Brain had quite forgotten. "Well," added Brain, "I'll probably be in tomorrow. Good-bye."

If any files were needed for the meeting, Judith could retrieve them. He had archived old files the day before, and his office was very tidy. Brain had never played hooky, and it felt great. He wouldn't be needed for the merger; the big boys were going to shake hands, sit down, and decide how to slice the pie.

Brain finished a leisurely breakfast, showered, shaved, and took a good look at himself in the foggy mirror. He stood six feet tall, with curly brown hair and sleepy eyes. Ten years before, while in college, he had boasted an athlete's build. But that was long ago now—when he'd still had a life. His parents had intended to name him Brian but were thwarted by a typographical error on his birth certificate. Amused, they then insisted on calling him Brain, because they thought it was cute.

Now, unmarried, living alone, having outgrown his cute name, Brain decided he needed a day to himself and scanned events of the day in the paper. He decided to spend his time in Manhatten's theater district and uptown at Museum Mile. Lunch at a German restaurant he had heard of but not tried, a Broadway matinee, and a trip to a museum exhibit would round out the day very nicely. He put on his red baseball cap and left his apartment.

8:00 a.m.

After grabbing the last blueberry muffin at the Princeton Junction train station, Brain smiled all the way to Manhattan. He couldn't remember the last weekday he'd enjoyed outside. Fluorescent lights and cubicle walls were no substitute for sunshine and the happy bustle of people. The train arrived in Penn Station at three minutes past nine.

On his way to the Museum of Modern Art to see the Rodin

exhibit, Brain encountered a stray dog. It looked like a Rott-weiler-German Shepherd mix. How strange, he thought, for a dog to be lost and alone in the middle of this crowded city. The dog, scrawny and jittery, leapt back when Brain reached out to pet it. "It's all right, boy. I just want to find out where you belong."

Holding the tattered collar, Brain searched through the bristly neck fur to get a better look at the tag. "Let's get you back to your owners, boy." A block from the Infotelcom building, however, the dog bolted, leaving Brain holding a broken collar. He pocketed the collar as a souvenir and went on his way.

10:30 a.m.

Winston Thurber, the *Daily Post* theatre critic, was on the outs with the arts and entertainment editor. As punishment, he had been assigned to review some damn Mulvanian dance troupe at some wretched dinner theatre that night. He was also to review the food. He sat in the backseat of the cab and fumed about the upcoming misery of an evening. Fortunately for him, that misery came early.

10:31 a.m.

Shelly Martin was waiting at the red light on Forty-Sixth Street, en route to visit her mother in Long Island. She hoped her mother didn't have another potential husband lined up for her to meet. She had determined that she could never fall in love again after Dimitri. The street light turned green and Brain proceeded to cross Forty-Sixth Street on his way to the theater district. Amid the morning shadows, with his tall build, sharp facial features and gray overcoat, he resembled Dimitri—which startled Shelly from her morning's musings. This encounter made her turn her thoughts to Dimitri. Being thus distracted by thoughts of sweet love, she didn't see the yellow cab carrying Winston Thurber racing for the light, and she plowed into its passenger door.

11:50 a.m.

Brain's morning was spent on Museum Mile, with lunch at the UN building, and an afternoon matinee in the theater district. While taking a tour of the UN building, Brain offered to take a picture of a Danish couple on their last day of a two-week vacation. Johan and Delma were miserable; they had been mugged, their hotel reservation had been cancelled, they had lost their money, and their luggage had been replaced by a suitcase filled with dog-grooming supplies. In an attempt to salvage what remained of their vacation, they were taking pictures of each other in front of the flags of the world with a disposable camera.

Brain offered to take a picture of the couple together. With blossoming smiles, the couple agreed. With his thoughtful gesture, he'd reassured them that New York was a friendly place after all. Johan and Delma's happiness was restored, and Brain continued on his way, happy to have been of service. None of the three realized that Brain had inadvertently walked off with their camera. While eating lunch at the UN café, Brain realized his mistake, but Johan and Delma were long gone. Turning the camera around in his hands, Brain sought an address or identity tag; in the process, he accidentally snapped a picture of himself. From the café, he caught a subway to the theatre.

The rest of Brain's day was equally uneventful. At home he discovered several messages on his machine from human resources. Apparently, he had been fired, re-hired, and promoted three times. The world was short one country, and three CEOs had either been fired or hired. He was now an executive vice president and in a different tax bracket.

Life was absurd, he concluded. Perhaps he would call in sick tomorrow.

ASTRONAUT TANG

I just hate science. Science has ruined my life. It has ruined the world. As a horticulturist, you would think I'd be enthralled by methodologies, procedures, and facts. But lately universal facts and processes don't mean much to me anymore. Come to think of it, I don't just hate science, I hate people. In fact, I find this whole damn planet detestable. I hate the entire package and all its wrappings. The flying cars, the portals that teleport you to China, the two-hundred-year lifespans—all of it has long ceased to impress this woman.

I'm in one of my dark moods, my coworkers insist. But, walking through this dirty, crowded city, how could I be otherwise? Pushing my way through the crowds, I steer clear of the barbed wire fences that serve to restrain and confine unregistered citizens. A few minutes later, beneath a towering government-owned skyscraper—formerly owned by a multi-national bank—I pass hordes of anti-sterility demonstrators, brandishing signs fashioned from old flaps of cardboard with menacing slogans written with the burnt end of a wooden stick or cork. I eye them warily through the screen of my helmet visor.

My coworkers warned me not to walk alone. Government proclamations always seem to set people off these days. I am not alone by choice. My boyfriend disappeared three months ago. Beneath my black antibacterial coat, I'm wearing the nano-vest he gave me, which makes me feel as if he were, somehow, with me. I trudge through the next checkpoint, past the dark-helmeted armed guards. The air feels thicker here, the body odor of packed people inescapable. Where's a stiff wind or a rainstorm when you need one? Finally, it's my turn, and I pass through the Pod-Gate, avoiding eye contact with the cameras and the guards. The Citi-Pod, implanted in my skull at birth, registers my information on the screen inside the Pod-Gate.

Gardener Fletcher 21. Citizen. Registered voter. Female. 29. Single. No offspring

A guard presses a button and the Pod-Gate opens, a green light illuminating its perimeter. I enter the city proper, where I am immediately confronted by more crowds. Over the course of an hour, I push my way past jostling skyscrapers to one of the larger sanctioned public squares, trying to avoid making contact with anyone else. Occasionally, a citizen in the crowd resembles my boyfriend and my heart leaps. Then, inevitably, I realize it's not him, and I feel humiliated because my funny little heart dance was performed for a complete stranger.

When I arrive at the square, a long line of people wraps around itself in a circular fashion like a coiled snake. In the center of this coil are two of the biggest Pod-Gates I have ever seen. Their green entry lights could probably be seen from outer space. One Pod-Gate is marked Decade Erasure, and the other is marked Wait for De-Link. Tens of millions of good citizens have journeyed here to walk through these gates and have our votes registered. I haven't decided yet how to cast my vote, through which Pod-Gate I intend to walk, but I have hours in line to make my decision. With a typical lack of irony, the government is making me walk toward the light.

Several people in front of me are entertaining themselves with a holographic drinking game, and those behind me are filming a live "historical" documentary. I find it difficult to concentrate with the noise and distractions around me, and with hours to wait I close my eyes and let my thoughts drift back to the first time I met my boyfriend.

My fellow Gardeners and I had attended a pro-procreation rally six months before in one of the city's rough outer boroughs. I wasn't really into the whole procreation cause, but spending my evenings alone in my home-cube seemed less and less appealing. My friends kept telling me that I would never meet a guy unless I put myself out there. I didn't know where "out there" was, but I decided a pro-procreation rally might be a good start. The rally was uneventful, but everyone seemed happier after several hours of screaming accusations against the government in public. No one got out of hand, so the government drones remained in observation mode.

Afterward, we went to Public Bar 782. A group of nanoscientists were leaving as we arrived. I locked eyes with one of them, a man with jet black hair, matted and rumpled as if he'd just removed his helmet. There was an aura of gentleness about him, and his eyes were kind. I felt an instant frisson of attraction, which was unusual—I don't typically find other scientists very appealing. I strictly adhered to the whole don't-pee-where-you-draw-water rule, but this nanoscientist seemed worth the breach in protocol. His friends called him, but he lingered while we made small talk. Our Citi-Pods exchanged all relevant contact information.

Nanoscientist Tang 53. Citizen. Registered voter. Male. 29. Single. No offspring

Our exchange lasted ninety seconds, but it changed my life. That night, I couldn't stop grinning. My friends thought I must be sick; they'd never seen that smile before.

On our first date, Nanoscientist Tang 53 seemed reserved at first but gradually opened up, as if he were one of the flowers in my lab. His reticence he blamed on the government and the secret project he claimed to be working on, about which he could tell me only three things: there was a project, it was secret, and he was working on it. Regardless, we laughed at each other's stupid jokes, flirted shamelessly, and got along marvelously, as long as I didn't ask him anything about himself. I discovered early his fear of commitment, which did little to put me off, since previous dates often had exhibited the same traits. I imagined all the Nanoscientist Tangs, in fact all scientists, had this long-term relationship phobia when they worked for the government.

We dated for three months and while we knew we couldn't be physically intimate, I had thought in this time I would know something more about him. But the fact of the matter is, I found his mysterious nature romantic and seductive. That last night, I told him I was falling in love with him. He smiled and we ordered another round of drinks. He dropped me at my home-cube and flew off in his hover pod. That was the last time I saw him.

The people in line behind me are broadcasting drone photos of themselves as heroes of humanity. I realize the world may be coming to an end, but I find myself inconsolable, not for this reason, but because my boyfriend has gone. The starry sky begins to glow in a familiar steel blue as the government Sky-Screen broadcasts its weekly report.

The news anchor, a tanned, self-satisfied journalist, stares down at us. "Citizens," he begins, "tonight you will cast your vote in what is the most important decision mankind has ever faced. As you know, several months ago scientists discovered that the size of the universe was equal to the collective length of the unraveled DNA strands of planet Earth's human population. As our population has rapidly increased, so, too, has the universe continued to expand and is in imminent danger of ripping itself apart. The government has subsequently forbidden breeding and issued mandatory sterility radiation for all its citizens. Brave scientists, implementing a daring plan to save us all, have been sent out to the edge of the universe: the Universe Mission Crew. So now, citizens, I urge you not to let the Universe Mission Crew down. Vote for Decade Erasure or Wait for De-Link!"

Well, that was fucking helpful, I thought. Do I want to wake up tomorrow with the last ten years erased? Do I really want to place my faith in a bunch of scientists and astronauts who weren't smart enough to get out of a mission they'll never come back from? And if I do vote to travel a decade back in time, will I remember what's happened since then? The scientists are sketchy on this point, as well as many others, since we've never done this before. This day, and this vote, is all anyone has talked about for months. You'd have to be dead to have missed out on the news. Maybe my boyfriend is dead, which would explain why he hasn't reached out to me.

The steel blue of the Sky-Screen begins to glow again. "Citizens, we have late-breaking news," the anchor exclaims. "We are receiving a live feed from the Universe Mission Crew, which we'll now bring to you."

No way! I thought.

"Citizens of Earth, I was one of the scientists who volunteered to go on this mission. My reasons were not noble but cowardly."

Oh my God.

"Our mission is to interrupt the link between humanity's DNA strands and the expansion of the universe so that the latter can expand at its own natural pace. Our other theoretical option is to force a contraction of the universe, and thereby reverse its expansion. This second option would cause time to temporarily reverse, effectively erasing the past five to ten years. The world will cast its vote on a course of action tonight. Now, I have some good news and bad news."

What the hell?

"The bad news is that I am the only survivor of the Universe Mission crew. My fellow scientists did not make it through the hyperdrive space jump. I am Astronaut Tang, and since there are no other Astronaut Tangs remaining, I have now no number designation. The good news is that I can complete our mission. I have reached the edge of the universe and both options remain available to us—I can de-link us from the fate of the universe, or we can go back in time. In addition, however, I have a personal message for Gardener Fletcher 211."

This can't be happening.

"I'm sorry I didn't call you back after our last date. But, as you see, I had to go and save the universe. Also, I feel I'm at a sufficiently safe distance to tell you that..."

Holy shit.

"... I want to break up with you. Citizens, I've come to the conclusion that I should make this weighty decision on behalf of all of humanity. Gardener Fletcher 211, I did not enjoy our recent dates. You were moving too fast, and I want to erase the memory of my ever having dated you."

"Hold on!" I scream to the Sky-Screen. The people around me stare, then they begin to laugh.

"Goodbye, Gardener Fletcher 211. Goodbye, citizens."

Wait...

I approach the university registrar to enroll for the next semester's classes. I'm contemplating a major in horticulture. A cute guy is standing in line in front of me and I decide to take a chance. Isn't that what being nineteen is all about?

"Hi," I say. "I'm Kelly Fletcher."

"Hi," he says, turning around. "I'm Clayton Tang. Nano-physics major."

"Ooh, physics. I just love science."

THE SHALLOW DEPTHS OF LESTER

"One canoe, please," said Lester.

He was going to kill himself. There was no way around it. Thirty-eight years and his heart had never been broken until Maureen. He had broken up with women before and survived just fine. But when Maureen left him after eight years of marriage for Eddie, the trapeze artist—Eddie, for crying out loud!—Lester had been devastated. From that moment, a black cloud descended upon him and a pervading gloom enveloped his life. There was no choice in the matter: Lester was going to kill himself.

He had not laughed since Maureen had said goodbye in November. He'd told himself that if he could only laugh, things would get better; some measure of mirth would be a sign that his mind was on the mend. But no, he couldn't manage even a chuckle. Haunted by his despair, Lester fought through March, April, and May. Therapy was of little use. The drugs the doctors prescribed were useless. He used to feel passionate about his job, but it no longer provided solace. It was as if when Lester had been made, he had been issued into the world with a defective heart and only now needed a recall.

Lester paid for the canoe rental. He was deathly afraid of guns and sharp objects, and the notion of popping pills and potentially surviving with brain damage filled him with horror. A summer drowning, though, struck him as appealing. There seemed something sweetly tragic in dying that way. He

boarded the River Adventure bus, crowded with other cano-
ers, kayakers, and tubers, all pressed up against each other in
a sweaty soup. Some complained about the claustrophobic
conditions, but Lester, accustomed to being crammed into a
vehicle, found comfort in the proximity of fellow travelers as
they made their way upriver.

Lester had never canoed before, but the six miles of Colorado River—before coming to grips with the waterfall—
would give him ample opportunity to learn. Maureen had
wanted to go whitewater rafting the last time they toured
Colorado, but Lester had refused, insisting he was too old.
She was a knife thrower's assistant by profession and didn't
run, or spin, from risk. Apparently, he was a risk that even
she wasn't willing to see through.

The bus dropped Lester, and the other tourists and adventure seekers, off at the rental shop by the river. Lester
picked out a light blue wooden canoe of about twelve feet in
length. He insisted on renting a pair of flippers, even though
the rental guy told him flippers wouldn't be needed in the
canoe. But Lester liked the feel of the flippers on his bare
feet—they also comforted him.

As he was hauling the canoe into the water, the rental guy
brought him a life jacket and told him he had to wear it.
The irony didn't escape Lester. Obligingly, he shrugged into
his life jacket. He didn't want to draw the attention of some
overzealous college kid working a summer job. Lester hopped
into his canoe. The boat pitched sideways and he went sailing
into the shallow water where he landed face-first, his flippers
sticking straight up out of the water. Bruised and cursing
under his breath, he grabbed hold of the side of the boat,
pulled himself up, and tumbled in like yesterday's seafood
catch.

Finally, after weeks of planning, he was ready to embark
on his journey. In ancient times, one would pay the boat-
man to take them across the River Styx into Hades. This was

more of a self-service economy tour. Pulling tentatively on the oars, he slowly drifted, the canoe occasionally dragging along the shallow river bottom. While still in a relatively quiet backwater, he could hear the rush of the current in the river ahead. The sun shone brightly and the gentle summer breeze carried the sweet aroma of honeysuckle. Lester noticed none of this. As he got farther from the river banks, the water moved more rapidly. His bus-mates, in their canoes and kayaks, were almost out of sight, and the tubers bobbed along like mini-donuts in a giant cup of coffee.

The rental guy, having warmed to the idea of screaming at Lester, yelled that canoes needed two people. Lester couldn't even rent a dumb boat without Maureen, it seemed. He should have known that their relationship would sour. A year ago, he'd told her she was the cream pie to his face. His great blindness had brought him to this despair—Eddie the trapeze artist.

The water lapped greedily against the side of his canoe, as if the river itself beckoned him further toward his watery end. Leaving the quiet backwater behind him, he finally faced the rush of destiny. The deep river coursed and rolled beneath his canoe with the occasional crest of whitewater here and there. The thick vegetation of the river banks gave way to rocks and boulders. Looking ahead, Lester knew that he was literally witnessing the remaining thread of his life, and it was rapidly unraveling.

Suddenly two baseball hats bobbed up at the bow of his canoe. They were, he discovered, attached to people floating on inner tubes. "Watch out!" cried Lester, paddling frantically on the right. The canoe, however, made a sharp right and turned perpendicular to the current. Where previously there had been a wooden torpedo heading toward the tubers, now they faced an oncoming wall. *Bluthump*. A scraping noise sounded along the bottom of the canoe.

"Sorry!" Lester called as the tubers emerged in Lester's

wake, cursing and spluttering. "I have no idea what I'm doing!" he offered to the hit-and-float victims. At that moment, a wave snatched one of Lester's oars from his hand and helplessly he watched it drift away. He moved to the rear of the canoe and tried paddling with his flippers but it was no use. The canoe simply couldn't be successfully steered by one person, let alone one person with one oar. Increasing his kicking efforts, he managed to propel the canoe in an awkward zigzag manner for a time, much like two uncommunicative people in a horse costume. After a short while, however, he was exhausted and cursed his lack of athletic ability.

Lester tried to take his mind off his predicament. He wondered if factories still made nets, and, if so, if there might be a fellow making safety nets who was distraught because his wife just left him. Perhaps he's not paying attention to his work, and, as a result, there's a faulty spot in his net. The quality control inspector, in turn, misses the imperfection because his own heart is broken as a result of the fling he'd had with the net-manufacturer's wife. This would all become gruesomely relevant, Lester mused, the day Eddie the trapeze artist fell right through the safety net. How he would laugh, Lester thought, to see the underlying karma in the progressions of the universe.

Lester was a good half-hour into his journey but only one hundred and fifty feet from where he had started. He decided to give up paddling altogether and allow the currents to take him to his final destination. The currents, however, seemed inexplicably to flow in different directions and his canoe, caught in this improbable riptide, made a U-turn. His craft had successfully launched itself upriver, away from the waterfall. Lester seized his remaining oar and paddled furiously in this attempt to turn his canoe. The oar slipped from his grasp and floated away from the canoe at an alarming rate, perhaps recognizing a chance at escape when it saw one.

The canoe spun around like an empty bottle at a teenager's late-night party. Lester was caught in a swirl of water. What was the word for it? he wondered. It was on the tip of his tongue; the word for the circling-the-drain phenomenon that he now found himself caught in. Why was he focusing on meaningless vocabulary and not steering his ship?

Eddie. It was that damned trapeze artist again ruining his plan.

Lester managed to right the vessel, only to find it floating again upstream. Caught in the river's vicious circle, he fought the vortex valiantly, using his flippers as oars until, exhausted, his arms told him to give up. After all that effort, he was positioned exactly where he'd started. Maybe he should just fling himself overboard, he reasoned. Maybe a thoughtful canoer might run him over, or he could retrieve a heavy rock from the riverbed, bring it to the surface, and tie it to his ankle. But if he could carry it up from the bottom of the river, it wouldn't be heavy enough to drown with, would it? Suddenly, he wished he had brought his calculator along so that he could figure out this physics problem.

What if he took a deep breath, dove beneath the surface, and tied himself to a rock on the riverbed? He'd be stuck there and that would be that. But could he hold his breath long enough to secure the knot? If not, he'd pop right back up to the surface again. He had to determine the depth of the river. His life depended on it. It was time for action. He leapt out of the boat with a mighty scream and landed in one foot of water.

The river's surface bubbled and churned but there was very little in the way of volume beneath. All this time he had spent valiantly attempting to navigate the river, and he had been in one foot of water. This discovery made him giggle slightly. The giggles deepened into chuckles, then into full-fledged guffaws. Next, standing in the middle of the river, he doubled over into tear-inducing, life-affirming laughter. The river seemed to shift currents around him as an enormous weight was lifted. Suddenly, he couldn't wait to return his canoe and tell the other clowns at work about this.

ATONE DEAF

Not content to spend yet another Saturday night alone, Jerry decides to take action. No more playing the part of the poor dateless sap. He's forty-three years old, and he will not stand for this solitary existence any longer. It is time to dock his ship into some friendly harbor, ideally for a long duration. In the ten years since his divorce—since his family stopped talking to him, since he'd boxed up his house and found a new place to live—he's had not a single romantic female contact. Without children, he longs for a family. He does, however, have a job, he's relatively young, he's in generally good health, and he doesn't drool—all good qualities that make his stock very hot on the market, according to a men's magazine he read in his therapist's waiting room.

Jerry musters his courage and develops a plan that is simplicity itself. Instead of dinner with his parents, which will invariably result in a cloud of muted disappointment hovering over Chinese takeout, Jerry decides to call Brenda. Jerry and Brenda, having known each other since they were kids, dated briefly in high school but nothing came of it. Their parents used to talk about the two kids getting married when they grew up, but Jerry had always resisted the idea; for him, it smacked distastefully of an arranged marriage. Regardless of their parental schemes, Jerry found himself strongly attracted to Brenda in their sophomore year. They broke up amicably, however, and went their separate ways. Their families broke up as well, for reasons Jerry couldn't recall. It has been almost twenty-five years since he had spoken to Brenda, yet she is the first woman who comes to mind.

The phone rings, and a flash of heat encircles Jerry's head. Isn't he too old to feel this nervous? he worries.

"Hello?" says Brenda.

"Hi, it's Jerry." An earth-shattering pause. "Remember? Jerry Susnik?"

"Jerry! My God! How are you? I can't believe it's you."

This is promising, he reflects, reassured. After various life updates, he gets around to the purpose of his call. His whole life boils down to this stew—he wants to ask her out on a date. For tonight. He fears that if he puts it off any longer, he'll chicken out, resorting to his usual craven ways. No, better to be bold, he tells himself. It's only noon; she will have plenty of time to rearrange things and get ready. It's dinner tonight, or never!

"So, anyway, Brenda, I was wondering if you'd like to catch up sometime in person, maybe for coffee?"

Shit. Shit. Shit. Schmuck. Fuck. Twattle. Shit.

"I'd love to. The next few weeks are pretty crazy, though. Maybe after that?"

"That would be great. Well, I'll call you soon. Bye, Brenda."

Freaking loser.

Jerry thinks about the empty day ahead, followed by dinner with his parents—an entrée of guilt and a side order of sesame noodles from Golden Szechuan—then to his friend's house where he's occupying a room plastered with Barney the dinosaur wallpaper. No, this can still be salvaged. The new watchcry for his administration says to be bold. Be bold, he reminds himself. Boldness wins the day! "Hi, Brenda? It's me again."

"Well, that was a fast few weeks," she says in a playful tone that Jerry has never forgotten.

"I know," says Jerry. "The thing is I would love it if you would go out to dinner with me. Tonight. I don't have any plans, and I hope you don't either. So, it would be, you know, a date. Tonight. With me. Unless you're going out with a boyfriend or something. Otherwise, it would be with me. Tonight."

"Right. Tonight. Got it." Another earth-shattering pause. "Well, Jerry, I would love to but..."

"But...?"

"I have plans tonight. You understand."

"Of course." He decides to put all his chips on the table. "Did I happen to mention that you're the first woman I thought of to call on a date?"

"Actually, you didn't mention that."

"It's just that I'm divorced now. Well, not *just* divorced. It's been, like, ten years. And I haven't dated anyone in that whole time and then I called you and..."

"Yup, I get it," says Brenda. "Look, that's very sweet. Let's talk in a few days, okay?"

Well, Jerry thinks to himself, at least I know I gave it my all. I can hold my head high. *Schmuck.*

His phone rings. "Hi, it's Brenda."

Fumbling, Jerry drops the phone, then picks it up, although it continues to slip through his hand like a freshly caught river trout. "Hi. Hi," he says, feeling like it's a good save. "That was a short few days."

"I've been thinking about what you said, Jerry. Here's the thing. My parents are coming over for dinner tonight, along with some other people. Would you like to join us? I mean, it's no big deal."

Yes! Yes! Yes! But play it cool. Cool wins the day. Steve McQueen-level cool.

"Yes! Yes! Yes! I'd love to!" says Jerry.

"Great," says Brenda. "Around six then." Jerry hangs up, then assesses the bedroom dimensions to see if there is room enough for a cartwheel. Before he's figured out the spatial physics of it, the phone rings again. "Hi, Brenda again."

"This is getting to be a habit."

"So I should probably tell you before you come over, that

my old boyfriend will also be coming tonight. We just broke up, and he has nowhere to go."

Shit. Shit. Shit. Fuck. Twattle. Shit.

"No problem," says Jerry, trying to appear magnanimous. "Sounds like I'm just one more stray."

"Thanks," she says. "I just didn't want it to be weird." She hangs up.

Old boyfriend? I can handle this. I can be that guy who shows Brenda that there are better guys than this idiot old boyfriend. The kind of guys who call up Brenda after thirty years. Guys with names like Jerry.

The phone rings. "Yes, Brenda?"

"Sorry," she says, "One more thing you should know. Elan, my old boyfriend... Well, his niece will also be at dinner. Is that okay?"

"Elan?"

"Don't even get me started."

"Um, as long as the niece isn't some psycho-killing child, I'm sure it'll be fine. Plus, I mean, I'm just a guest, so invite who you want. I'm there to see you." Jerry congratulates himself for his final statement—a clear gesture of romantic intention and far better than anything Elan could have come up with.

"Are you sure you still want to come?" she says.

"You're making all this up because you're having second thoughts about inviting me. Is that it?"

"Absolutely not. It's just a wild bunch here, and I wanted to make sure you were prepared."

"I really want to see you," says Jerry. "Can I bring anything?"

"Whatever you want. Oh, wait, nothing with garlic. Allergies," she says.

She hangs up, and it starts to dawn on Jerry that this is not going to be a typical first reunion date.

Elan? He wonders if the hospital secretary might have been tempted to include a typo on baby Elan's birth certificate so he would have to go through the rest of his life being called Flan.

Jerry looks at the phone and it actually rings again. "Seriously?" he says.

"Sorry," Brenda says. "Can you be sure to make it here before sunset?"

"What the hell is going on over there? Did your family turn into vampires?"

"Nice Jewish boy. It's Yom Kippur."

"Well, fuck me."

"Not on the menu, pal," says Brenda. "Looking forward to seeing you."

Brenda lives in a large apartment building right outside of the city. After parking four blocks away, Jerry enters the lobby to find all elevators out of order. He walks the one flight up and swallows hard as he arrives at her doorstep. The doorbell doesn't seem to be working, so Jerry knocks. Then he knocks louder.

Brenda's door is opened by a vampire. He is tall, emaciated, and pale, and he has a shock of long, thinning white hair. He is wearing black pants and a long, flowing black robe, all of which accentuates his dead, gaunt whiteness. He is in either his forties or four hundreds. "You must be Elan," says Jerry, unsure if he should cross the threshold. "You're the one allergic to garlic, I assume."

"And you must be Jerry," says Elan, his voice husky and distant. "Come in. Brenda's in the kitchen." Jerry takes a deep breath and wipes his feet on the welcome mat. Elan sticks out his hand, his palm feels cool to the touch, his skin as dry as paper. *He should be holding a lit candelabra to finish the whole Nosferatu look.*

"Cell phone, dude," says Elan, as if he were a second-grade teacher telling the troublemaker to spit out the gum.

"What?" says Jerry.

"It's Yom Kippur. I maintain an orthodox view of it. No electricity. No cell phones. Like in the old country."

"They celebrate Yom Kippur in Transylvania?" Jerry hands over his cell phone to a complete stranger, a vampire from the Shtetl.

Elan then lights a candelabra. Within the apartment, thick curtains are drawn, and Jerry can make out shadows in the other room. *It's rather festive, in an apocalyptic zombie sort of way.*

"I've turned off the apartment's circuit breakers," says Elan, trying to assert his alpha male position. "That breaker panel is locked and loaded," he says, waving a key.

Before Jerry can respond, Brenda appears and embraces Jerry. She looks great, shorter than he remembers, and her hair is curlier, but she's just as beautiful as ever. She smells of flowery perfume and onions cooked in butter. Jerry doesn't want to ever let her go.

Brenda steps back and takes a good look at Jerry. She doesn't throw him out, which further encourages Jerry to stay. Elan has conveniently receded into the shadows somewhere. "Can we talk in private?" she asks.

"Isn't that what we're doing? By the way, you look gorgeous." He hadn't planned on saying that; it just slipped out.

Brenda leads him to the small, candlelit bathroom. "Please forgive me," she says. "I panicked and didn't know what to tell my folks and my Aunt Sadie. They've known you since you were a baby and have always loved you. I didn't want to disappoint them."

"What are you talking about?"

"They're old-fashioned and wouldn't understand why I invited a divorcee to Yom Kippur. So I told them you're single."

"Brenda, won't my parents have told them that I've been married and divorced?"

"They haven't talked since that thing with Aunt Sadie and your mom. So remember, you're single and you just happen to be in town for business. I'm so sorry." Brenda adjusts his shirt collar. "It's really good to see you," she says, smiling.

"Fine." Jerry smiles back and wishes he could kiss her.

Brenda opens the bathroom door to find a six-year-old girl in a little green dress waiting for them. "Hello," she says.

Brenda pulls Jerry back into the bathroom and slams the bathroom door shut.

"Did you have a daughter at some point?" Jerry asks. "Please tell me Flan isn't the father."

"Listen," says Brenda earnestly. "That's Janie, Elan's niece. Eggshells around her, okay? Her parents are going through a nasty divorce, and Janie has major separation anxiety issues."

"Wait, so your folks would shun me for being divorced, but they're okay with the parents of Count Chocula's niece getting divorced? I'm confused."

Brenda holds Jerry's hands. "They just want the best for me."

"Then they probably shouldn't have let you date a ghoul."

"Just be careful about what you say around Janie, promise?"

"Fine."

As soon as Jerry and Brenda leave the bathroom, Janie darts in. As Jerry's eyes are adjusting to the dark living room, he feels six arms grab him. He lets out a little shriek, which probably does little to endear him to Brenda's family. But Brenda's parents, Morris and Deborah, tell him how long it has been and how good he looks. Aunt Sadie pulls him in for a tight hug and cries a little. "Jerry, I'm so sorry," says Aunt Sadie.

Well, my divorce secret didn't last long.

"My heart mourns for you," Aunt Sadie laments with a sniff. "Such a sweet boy. Poor thing. How you've suffered." She comes in for an encore hug. *Why is she reacting this way? We weren't that close.* Aunt Sadie's body vibrates with intensity as she openly sobs on Jerry's shoulder. *Boy, this family really doesn't like divorce.*

"Yo, Jerry," says Elan from across the room. His voice breaks Aunt Sadie's spell, and she recedes back into the darkness.

"Where are you?" says Jerry, squinting.

"I'm right here," Elan replies, helpfully.

Jerry is not in the mood for this Yiddish version of Marco Polo. He skins his ankle on the corner of the coffee table. "Jesus," Jerry mutters.

"Wrong holiday, man," says Elan.

Jerry hobbles along in the dark and is ultimately led back into the bathroom by the sound of Elan's voice calling for another impromptu meeting. "Want to get high?" says Elan, offering Jerry a fat joint.

"This is why you asked me here?"

"Yeah," says Elan, earnestly.

"Oh, pot is okay, but you have a problem with cell phones?"

"Cell phones aren't natural. God made this," says Elan.

"God's a good roller," says Jerry. "But no thanks."

"Suit yourself," says Elan and lights up.

"So let me ask you something," says Jerry. "Is Brenda cool with this?"

"Man, you have no idea. With my connections and deals, we would get the best stuff. Sometimes I think Brenda stuck around so long because of my weed." He laughs and Jerry wants to throat-punch him, but that would leave a mark on his undead alabaster skin. *Where's a wooden stake and a polo mallet when you need one?* Jerry turns to leave. "Oh, man, by the way, there's something you should know."

"What," says Jerry, "you put cocaine in the kugel? Heroin in the herring?"

"I heard you didn't want people to know about your divorce, which is cool. It's nobody's business. So I told Aunt Sadie that your mom just died."

"What?"

"Yeah, I figured that made sense. Like, that's why you're

here," Elan says sincerely. *His clouded brain cells were gathered at a convention, and this was the best plan they managed to come up with?*

"Aunt Sadie and my mother were best friends thirty years ago! No wonder she's mortified," says Jerry.

"That's what I mean," says Elan. "It's been thirty years, so it's cool. You sure you don't want a hit?"

Why didn't Elan coordinate with Brenda? And why does Elan think that it makes sense for Jerry to come over to Brenda's when his mother just died? Jerry doesn't ask these questions. You don't ask a stoner-vampire to explain his logic in the middle of a bathroom blunt. Instead, he walks stealthily past the living room and finds Brenda in the kitchen, stuffing the roasted chicken. Jerry knows how the chicken feels. "What the hell is going on?" he says. "I was just talking to Elan...."

"Elan and I are over. He wants a second chance. No way. I'm kicking him out tonight. He doesn't know yet. But he suspects. Now what did you want to ask me?"

Yes! Yes! Yes!

"Do I smell glazed carrots to go with that delicious chicken?" says Jerry.

Dinner is ready and everyone sits down at the candlelit table. For the first time, Jerry—sitting between Janie and Brenda and across from Brenda's parents and Aunt Sadie—can see everyone in the room. Elan occupies the head of the table, which makes sense to Jerry. The table is coffin-shaped, so this seems a natural location for him. No sooner has the soup been ladled than Elan goes to the bathroom. Brenda rises abruptly to scold him, and Elan returns looking contrite. Brenda's father gets up to check on her. Brenda returns, but then her mother leaves to check on Morris. Morris returns, and Aunt Sadie departs to check on Deborah. *If there were Klezmer music playing, this would be Yiddish musical chairs.*

Jerry looks at Janie, who seems to be freaking out every time somebody leaves the room. Her separation anxiety is hardly alleviated by the steady disappearance of all the adults. Jerry smiles at her in a comforting way. As soon as Brenda's parents and Aunt Sadie sit down, Jerry gets up, desperately trying to avoid talking about his "dead" mother. The musical chairs continue through the soup course. Elan gets higher with each bathroom trip, Brenda's family gets increasingly upset, and Janie finally bursts into tears. At one point, Brenda and Jerry run into each other in the kitchen.

"I am so glad you came tonight," she says. "I've been thinking of you."

"Is there any way we can get out of here and talk?" he says.

"I can't now." She looks at the clock. "It's a half-hour until sunset." She picks up a large platter and serves the chicken. They all sit at the table, each avoiding certain subjects so as to avoid upsetting certain parties, which leads, naturally enough, to a stony silence.

"How long have you been in mourning?" says Aunt Sadie. "I mean to say, how is the mourning process going?"

Elan laughs uncontrollably and Janie is visibly upset. "What's mourning?" she says to all the adults.

They all stare at the chicken until Elan says, "It's when someone dies."

"Who died?" Janie asks.

"The chicken," says Brenda.

"Janie," Jerry interjects. "Aunt Sadie was only asking how early I have to get up in the morning to go to work tomorrow. I have a big meeting tomorrow."

The rest of the meal entails Jerry deflecting all incoming questions as if he were defending his Wimbledon title. He survives until the dessert course when a phone rings. "Who's got their phone?" demands Elan, the Grand Inquisitor. They all look at one another, shaking their heads.

"It's you!" says Aunt Sadie, pointing an accusing finger at Elan. "You have the phone. Dracula has the phone. Answer it, maybe it's Frankenstein calling."

"Sadie," reprimands Deborah, but she's holding in her own laughter.

Elan checks his back pocket and pulls out a ringing phone. He offers no apology, just stares at it.

"Well, answer it," says Morris. "It could be an emergency."

Elan rises from the table and talks quietly into the phone, pacing the length of the room as he does so. It becomes evident that the call is from Elan's sister. She and Janie's dad are in full battle mode and she wants Elan to look after Janie until the storm blows over. Elan resumes his place at the head of the table, and everyone stares into their kugel.

Aunt Sadie picks up Janie, who is quietly sobbing, and places her on her lap. "My recommendation is that this little one sleeps here tonight," she says, shooting daggers at Elan. "Or with Uncle Twilight. No offense meant."

"Fine with me," says Elan. Jerry suspects that this is a good way for Elan to keep his life intertwined with Brenda's.

"Would that be okay with you, Janie?" says Brenda, clearing their plates.

Janie nods. Brenda carries a stack of dirty dishes into the kitchen and Jerry follows behind with another. "You have such a big heart," he tells her.

"And, suddenly, a lot on my plate."

"Do you want me to go?" says Jerry reluctantly.

"No, stay. How about we talk after I put Janie to bed?"

"What about Elan?"

"I'm still kicking him out tonight."

Aunt Sadie, Morris, and Deborah leave after the babka and coffee. They kiss Jerry goodbye and tell him they hope to see him again. They give Elan the stink-eye on their way out. Elan slams the door behind them.

Brenda exhales. She finds herself left with a recent ex-boyfriend, a really old (but hopefully next) boyfriend, and the recent ex-boyfriend's niece. She asks Elan to the bedroom, intending to give him the heave-ho speech. Jerry sits on the floor and plays dolls with Janie but can't help glancing repeatedly toward the bedroom. Either Elan is not getting the message, or he is making some convincing counterarguments to stay. Jerry's money is on the former. Elan is, after all, excessively stoned and probably cannot comprehend simple social cues. On the other hand, Elan laid down strict Yom Kippur rules and clearly relishes the idea of being in charge. Maybe he's making a very convincing argument to stay.

Shit. Shit. Shit. Schmuck. Fuck. Twattle. Shit.

Elan emerges barefoot from the bedroom with his hastily packed duffel bag, its contents half spilling out. Maybe he bet that Brenda wouldn't throw out the barefoot undead? Now he's leaving and too high to realize he'll need shoes outside.

"You better not be here when I get back," Elan growls in Jerry's direction as he tries to open the apartment door. The door appears stuck; he tries again but to no avail. "Would you mind?" he finally asks Jerry.

Taking mercy on the stoned, jilted Flan, Jerry crosses to the door to help, but he cannot open it either. Jerry seizes the doorknob with both hands and pulls with all his weight. Nothing.

"What's going on?" Brenda asks, emerging from the bedroom. She cannot get the door to budge either, and so she carries Janie into the bedroom to put her to bed. Meanwhile, Elan stands by the apartment door, glowering at Jerry. *Well, this is a tad awkward.* The lights from the candles flicker, and periodically Elan glares at the door, as if it might take mercy on him and open.

Brenda returns to the living room, followed by Janie, who declares she can't sleep. Brenda hugs Janie, and Jerry smiles at the two of them. This seems to be about as much family time as Elan can take. He makes a mad dash at the door and yanks the doorknob hard, screaming until the veins in his throat bulge. The doorknob snaps off with a metallic clang, which sends Elan flying across the room. He crashes over a folding chair and lands on the couch. A small metal bolt protrudes from the door where the doorknob used to be.

"Why don't we call the super?" Jerry suggests.

"We can't," says Elan, his white hair in mangled disarray. *It's as if a deranged bird tried to build its first nest on his head.* "It's Yom Kippur. No phones."

"But it's an emergency!" says Brenda.

"Brenda," says Jerry, "this is your place. Why are we listening to this guy?"

"This is *not* an emergency," says Elan, smoothing down his hair and regaining his composure. "Moses at the Red Sea was an emergency. The Holocaust was an emergency. This is nothing." Jerry glances at Brenda and she takes his hand. *This idiot is actually bringing them closer.* "I've got an idea," says Elan, heading to the closet.

"What's going on?" says Janie.

"Nothing," says Brenda. "Your uncle is making us play a game."

"A game no one wants to play," adds Jerry.

Elan emerges triumphantly with a screwdriver. "God gaveth man tools," he says, in as biblical a tone as he can muster. "And the tools were good."

"How did I ever date this imbecile?" Brenda mutters under her breath.

Elan gets down to business, using God's Phillips-head screwdriver. He tries to wedge the door open with the screwdriver, putting his entire body weight behind it. No luck. He wipes his brow and tries again. The screwdriver slips out of Elan's hand and lands business-end first in his foot. Blood spurts across the floor. What little blood was inside him is quickly abandoning ship.

Janie screams in terror and Brenda shuffles her away to the bedroom. Elan hops around in agony, clutching his punctured foot. The living room, which had been a somber, sacred Yom Kippur dining room just moments ago, is now a serial killer's crime scene.

"*Now* is it an emergency?" asks Jerry, calmly.

"Not yet," says Elan through his muffled pain. Most of the candles in the living room have been extinguished, and he bangs into the wall, falling down. *At least he's not hopping around like a demented fountain of blood any longer.* Brenda tosses a towel at him as Janie cries in the other room.

"Elan!" screams Brenda. "Turn on the stupid circuit breakers so we can see!"

"I can't," he whimpers.

"Come on, man," says Jerry. "No one's impressed with…."

"I lost the keys to the breaker panel," says Elan.

"Where did you put our cell phones?" asks Jerry.

"I forget," says Elan. "They couldn't have gotten far."

"And no landlines, right?" says Jerry.

"Who uses landlines?" says Brenda.

A knock sounds at the door and they all breathe a sigh of relief—they are saved.

"Dude," a male voice calls on the other side of the door.

"Oh, hey," says Elan, "what's up, Butch?"

"Butch?" says Jerry.

"Elan's pot dealer," says Brenda, shaking her head in disappointment as she goes to check on Janie.

Elan limps to the door and murmurs into the metal, so close that he is practically kissing it. He explains their situation in a story so filled with unnecessary details and unexpected detours that it has little bearing on their present situation. In this retelling Elan is, of course, the epic hero. Finally, he gets to the point. "Butch, open the door."

A period of silence follows in which Jerry and Elan assume Butch is devising a master plan calculated to break into his personal Entebbe to rescue them.

"So, you buying tonight?" asks Butch.

Elan wraps the towel tighter around his foot. The bleeding has finally stopped. "Dude," says Elan again, "we're locked in here. You need to rescue us."

Butch tries to open the door but it is locked. He jiggles it again. "Hey, open the door, man," says Butch.

"Butch," says Elan, "you're going to have to push hard against the door while I try to pull it open. Ready?"

They hear Butch's footsteps as he takes a running start, followed by a heavy thud against the door—which shudders with the impact but remains obstinately closed—followed by a louder thud as a body drops to the hallway floor.

"Butch?" Elan calls.

"He ran into the door and knocked himself out, Einstein," says Jerry irritably, wondering if his date with Brenda will ever start in earnest. Elan drags his foot into the bathroom with a defeated gait.

Brenda appears from the bedroom and sits on the floor next to Jerry. "What was that noise?" she asks.

"Nothing you need to worry about," says Jerry. "First time we're alone tonight. It's a good date, isn't it?" He gets bold and takes her hand.

"The best."

Yes! Yes! Yes!

"Hey, what is that smell?" says Jerry.

"What smell?" says Brenda and then she smells it, too—something burning. They find Elan sitting on the bathroom floor, burning Hallmark cards, thick smoke billowing around him.

"What are you doing, you idiot?" asks Brenda.

"Burning all the cards I ever gave you, so that you never remember me," says Elan, overcome by marijuana and self-pity.

Brenda slaps Elan on the side of his head which makes him cease and desist his impromptu card burning. However, by this stage, a small fire ensues in the middle of the bathroom, the smoke curling up toward the ceiling and out into the hallway. Jerry, turning on the sink faucet and the shower, attempts to splash the fire out. He succeeds in dampening the flames, but the smoke is unbearable. Brenda grabs Janie from the bedroom. The living room windows will open only eight inches—in case of fire, the building owner doesn't want his tenants jumping out the windows—and resist all attempts to wrench them open any further.

"We have to get word to the outside," says Jerry.

"How are we going to do that," asks Brenda, then glances again at the windows. "Janie, honey, how would you like to be the hero of the night?"

"Yes!" says Janie, enthusiastically.

Brenda retrieves a fashionable belt and a coil of rope from her closet. The fire has been quenched, but smoke still fills the apartment. Brenda ties the rope to the belt, which she cinches tightly around Janie's waist. Jerry writes a note explaining their situation in twenty words or less. He picks up Janie and helps her through the window opening. They lower the rope until Janie gets to the ground. She runs off to the neighboring building, the rope trailing behind her like a wild tail. Waving the note, she yells for help. Elan snores on the couch as the building's smoke alarm finally goes off. Apparently, smoke alarms are considered kosher.

The fire department breaks down the door seven minutes later. Emergency responders carry Butch, Elan, and Elan's duffel bag down the stairs to the waiting ambulance.

"I am definitely filing a restraining order tomorrow," Brenda remarks to no one in particular.

"For me?" asks Jerry.

"For everyone but you."

Downstairs, Janie is hanging out with the cops. "I'm the hero!" she yells over and over again.

After some time at the fire department and the police

station, Brenda gets the all-clear to return to her apartment. Jerry accompanies her, carrying a sleeping Janie. A makeshift plywood door has replaced the metal one. The apartment smells of smoke, but the place is warm and the lights are back on.

"Well," says Jerry, "it's been a most delightful evening. I should be going. Maybe...."

A knock on the plywood door announces Aunt Sadie and Jerry's mother. Jerry smiles at them both, just as his mother reaches out and smacks him across his right cheek. Aunt Sadie smacks him across his left, and Jerry begins to feel like the loser in a Rock 'Em Sock 'Em Robots match. Then Aunt Sadie turns around, smiles at Brenda and Jerry, and takes Janie in her arms. "Pick her up tomorrow," she says.

"Hi, Brenda," says Jerry's mother. She points at her son. "Bring him with you for dinner next week." With a wave, the two women and sleeping child depart.

"Would this be an awkward time to ask you for a second date?" Jerry asks Brenda.

"Are we done with the first date?"

"I don't want to be the rebound guy," he replies.

"Are you sure about that?" asks Brenda with a wicked smile as she steps closer to him. "Rebound guy is practically guaranteed sex on the first date."

After careful consideration, Jerry responds, "I...I could be rebound guy. I'm warming to the idea. Yes, I am definitely amenable. I mean, Michael Jordan was known for his rebound stats. I could be your Michael Jordan."

"Glad we're on the same page. Now let's go do something to atone for."

Yes! Yes! Yes!

ACKNOWLEDGEMENTS

To my friend Paul for being a great, round-house-kicking writer and encouraging me to become a writer. Long live Scorpion.

To my extraordinary son Chris for showing me what a real writer looks like and for keeping the comedy torch ablaze.

To the Ambler Writers Group for making my writing like the pints of Guinness we shared: dark, smooth, easy to swallow, and a little gassy afterwards.

To every publisher who said yes to one of my short stories, you were the lush, tropical island in the endless sea.

To every publisher who said no to one of my short stories, you were the sea.

To my editor, Pam Van Dyk, for bringing brilliant clarity to my muddled fuzziness.

To Jaynie Royal, for being Queen among publishers.

To every bad date I ever had for not requiring me to sign a Non-Disclosure Agreement.

And, of course, to my wife for the inspiration, support, and perspective. You're the Best. Date. Ever. Sorry about the whole kissing booth thing.